THE RULES of DATING

A Younger Man

VI KEELAND
PENELOPE WARD

THE RULES OF DATING A YOUNGER MAN
Cover Designer: Sommer Stein, Perfect Pear Creative
Editing: Jessica Royer Ocken
Formatting and Proofreading: Elaine York, Allusion Publishing
www.allusionpublishing.com
Proofreading: Julia Griffis
Cover Photographer: Ren Saliba
Cover Model: Shaun Collins

THE RULES of DATING

A Younger Man

CHAPTER 1

Brayden

I looked down at my cell and shook my head.

"Why the long face?" My buddy Colby walked back into the kitchen and tossed me the keys to his car. "I didn't think single guys with no kids and fat bank accounts had anything to stress over."

I caught the keys. "Bite me."

He chuckled. "No, really. Is everything alright? You were grumbling at your phone the other day when I walked into the elevator, too."

"Yeah, everything's fine. Except one of the volunteers on the renovations team for the new Ryan's House project is driving me nuts. You know how we pick two team leaders to help coordinate things on each job?"

Colby nodded. "One for the mechanics—electrical, plumbing, heating, and stuff, and one for interior design—paint, flooring, fixtures, and appliances, right?"

"Exactly. This dude Alex is the design team leader. He's driving me nuts with his *suggestions*. He questions every fixture, appliance, and molding I've picked out. Today he wants to change the living room paint color by a shade—*a freaking shade*. I couldn't even see the difference between the two paint samples online. Now he just asked if we could meet for dinner tonight to go over a few last-minute changes he'd like to make." I shook my head. "No way am I doing that. It's a good thing you clowns are coming up this weekend to help out, because I have a feeling this guy's going to test my limits."

Colby made a pouty face. "Awww... Brayden has trouble working with others."

I shook my head, but smiled. "I don't know why I tell you shit."

"Probably because no one else wants to listen to you."

"Ouch."

He laughed. "What time you getting on the road today?"

"Probably about two. I need to stop by the office and pick up a project I've been working on for a kid. He's in the hospital upstate again, so I'm going to drop by to visit over the weekend and surprise him with it."

"What did you make this time?"

I grinned. "You know I don't give hints about my master-pieces before the unveiling. I told his family I'd come by Sunday. If you knuckleheads are still around, you should join me."

"Sounds good."

I held up Colby's car keys. "Thanks again for the car swap. Mine is too small to fit baseboard heating covers."

"Anytime you want to swap my ten-year-old, beat-up SUV for your hot little six-month-old Porsche, I'm in." He grinned. "I'm going to have a good-ass time driving that thing upstate Saturday morning."

I opened the door. "Don't get arrested for going a hundred and twenty."

Later that night, I checked into the hotel up in Seneca Falls and de-cided to go down to the lobby bar for a drink. It was empty, except for a woman sitting alone. She had a drink in front of her, and a full glass of wine sat at the empty stool beside her, so I assumed she must be here with someone. I took a seat along the short side of the bar to give them some privacy.

But damn... Sitting here gave me an even better view of the woman, and she was a total knockout—sandy blond hair, big blue eyes, and high cheekbones that led down to a full set of lips. She might've been a few years older than me, but that didn't stop a rush of adrenaline from giving my body a good jolt.

The bartender walked over and dropped a napkin in front of me. "What can I get you?"

"I'll take a whiskey sour. Any chance you have Russell's Reserve Ten-Year bourbon to make it with?"

The bartender's brows pulled together, and he thumbed to the woman sitting alone. "You with her?"

"No, why?"

He shrugged. "She just ordered the same drink. That brand of bourbon and all."

"Really?"

"Yep."

I glanced over again and lowered my voice. "She alone?"

"Is now. Some guy sidled up to her when she came in a few minutes ago, but he left pretty quickly with his tail between his legs."

Alrighty then. "Any chance you guys serve food here?"

"Sure do. I'll grab you a menu."

Even though I now knew she was alone, I wasn't too enthused about striking up a conversation with the pretty blonde. Not after she'd just chased another guy away. But when the bartender brought my drink and she looked over, I raised my glass.

"Apparently we ordered the same drink."

"Whiskey sour?" she asked.

"With Russell's Reserve Ten-Year."

She smiled and held up her glass. "To good taste."

I tipped my glass to her. A minute later, my phone buzzed with a call from Colby. I swiped to answer. "I hope you're not calling to tell me you dented my car already."

"No, but how the hell do you put the top back up?"

"You know the button you pushed to drop it?"

"Yeah."

"It's the same button to put it back up. You just need to hold it for ten seconds."

"Crap. Okay, thanks."

"Where the hell are you that you have the top down?"

"I got a sitter and took my wife for a drive. The wind in our hair is making us feel young and free, instead of like the parents of two little kids we are, usually in bed by eight."

I chuckled. "Well, enjoy it."

"I plan to. Why do you think I need the top up? I just pulled into a quiet rest stop, and I need a little privacy, if you know what I mean."

"Ugh. Don't tell me that, dude. I don't want your bare ass all over my seat."

"No promises, my friend."

I shook my head. "God, I hate you. Goodbye."

After I hung up, the knockout looked over. "I'm not usually rude, but I couldn't help but overhear your conversation," she began. "I once bought a new car. When I picked it up, I found an empty condom wrapper on the floor of the front seat. I made them give me another car."

I smiled. "My buddy and I swapped vehicles for the weekend. I'm considering keeping his crappy ten-year-old hunk of junk and letting him keep my nice, new one after his ass cheeks have rubbed all over the leather."

"I think that's a good idea. Unless…"

"What?"

"What if your friend has a penchant for car sex? I'm afraid that would mean he's already done it in the one you're driving."

I pointed. "Good observation. I'll just get mine detailed."

The beautiful woman smiled again, and I found myself wondering if she had lipstick on or if her lips were naturally that color. They were just a little more pink than the fleshy red I'd expect for someone with her skin tone. Or maybe she wore some sort of gloss, because they were also perfectly shiny.

After a much-too-long analysis, I realized I probably looked like a creeper staring at her mouth and diverted my eyes to the menu the bartender had dropped off. Though I still couldn't stop myself from stealing glances in between reading about the appetizers. There was something compelling about her. It might've been that her face wasn't painted to fake-perfection like most women these days.

A few minutes later, I looked over and noticed her glass was empty. So I took a chance. "Can I buy us another round?"

She bit her bottom lip. "Ummm..."

I held my hands up. "It's just a drink. I won't invite myself over to the empty seat next to you."

She smiled. "Sure. Why not? Thank you."

I held two fingers up to the bartender. "Another round for both of us. On me, please. And when you get a chance, I'll take an order of the Mexican street corn chicken tacos."

"Oh, gosh," the woman said. "I love Mexican street corn. That sounds delicious."

"Oh, so now you want me to buy you drinks *and* dinner?"

She waved her hands. "Oh, no, I wasn't suggesting—"

I smiled. "I'm teasing." I looked back at the bartender. "Make that two orders of the tacos, please."

"You got it."

"Well, now that you're buying me food *and* a drink, I feel obligated to offer you the vacant seat next to me."

"Oh, no. There's no obligation, really."

She grinned. "I'm teasing, too."

I laughed, but I also got up and walked over to her. "Is this seat taken?"

"It's not. But I can't promise no bare butts have been on it."

"I'll risk it." I sat and held out my hand. "Brayden."

"Alexandria. Nice to meet you, Brayden."

"You, too. Are you a guest at this hotel, or just came in to flirt with a guy and get him to buy you dinner and drinks?"

She smiled. I liked that she could take a joke. "I'm staying here. You?"

"Same. What are you in town for?"

"I'm volunteering for a charity that renovates houses near hospitals for patients who can't afford a hotel while they're getting cancer treatment."

My jaw fell open. "Are you serious? You're volunteering for Ryan's House?"

"You know it?"

"I'm the founder. But once a year, I also volunteer to swing a hammer. This is my once."

"Really?"

"Let me get this straight. We drink the same drink, both love street-corn tacos, both dislike ass imprints on our car seats, *and* we're volunteering for the same project? Do I just propose now? Or should I wait and see if you love candy corn as much as I do?"

Her eyes sparkled. "I love candy corn."

I covered my heart with my hand. "Alexandria Foster. It even has a nice ring to it, doesn't it?"

The bartender interrupted our love fest to deliver our drinks. When he walked away, we were both still smiling.

"So you really founded Ryan's House?" Alexandria asked. "How did that come about?"

"Almost a decade ago, I lost one of my best friends to leukemia. Ryan and I were both engineering students in college when he started treatments. He spent a lot of time in the hospital and became interested in designing prosthetics with more flexibility. We started working on ideas together to pass the time during my visits. After he passed away, I continued with some of the concepts we'd come up with. Long story short, a couple of years later, I got a patent on a new type of prosthetic joint simulator. It's licensed to most major artificial-limb manufacturers now. I tried to split the profit with Ryan's parents, but they wouldn't take anything. So his half goes toward buying the houses we renovate each year for Ryan's House."

"That's incredible."

I sipped my drink. "How about you? Are you just volunteering, or is there a story behind why you picked Ryan's House to donate your time?"

Alexandria smiled sadly. "I lost my husband a few years ago to leukemia."

"I'm sorry."

"Thank you. He was older than me, but still way too young."

"Is this your first time volunteering, or did you work on another of the houses?"

"It's my first time. To be honest, I'm kind of nervous about it."

"What's there to be nervous about?" I asked.

"I don't have too much construction experience."

"I'll tell you what, I'll make sure you're on the good team then."

"I didn't realize there was a good team and a bad team."

"Usually there isn't. But we split the volunteers into two crews, each with a team leader who coordinates who does what and makes sure we have the supplies and stuff. One of the team leaders is a real pain in the ass, a know it all. He wants to change everything that's been planned before we even start. He's definitely going to micromanage his crew."

"Oh, wow. Okay. Thank you."

"We usually just count off the volunteers who show up to give each team an equal number. But I'll make sure you're in Jason's group and not Alex's."

"Oh. So Alex is the pain in the ass?"

"*Giant* pain in the ass."

The bartender walked over with our food. It looked as delicious as it had sounded on the menu. Conversation slowed as we dug in, but I enjoyed the quiet with the company sitting next to me. After we finished eating, I turned to ask Alexandria something, but I lost track of what I was saying three words in. Her eyes were that mesmerizing.

"What?" She wiped at her cheek. "Do I have sauce on my face?"

I shook my head. "Sorry, no. I hope you don't mind me saying so, but you are absolutely beautiful. I'm relieved I got to sit next to you because I couldn't stop myself from staring when I was sitting over there."

Her cheeks pinked. "Thank you."

Both our drinks were almost empty again, so I motioned to the glasses. "You want another one?"

"I think I'm going to call it a night."

Disappointment flooded through me. I hoped I hadn't upset her with my compliment.

Alexandria motioned to the bartender. "Could I close out my tab, please?"

"Sure thing."

He walked away and came back a minute later. I was still trying to decide if I should apologize. Maybe I'd been too forward?

She signed the check and hopped down from the stool.

"Listen, Alexandria. I didn't mean to upset you by saying how beautiful I think you are. I apologize if that came off creepy."

"No, that wasn't what insulted me."

"*That* wasn't? So something else I said insulted you?"

She looked at me a moment. "Such a shame. Because I find you attractive, too."

"I'm confused. Why is that a shame?"

She shook her head. "Goodnight, Brayden. I'll see you in the morning. Oh, and you don't have to worry about which team I'm on. I'm happy on Alexandria's team."

"Alexandria's team?"

"Oh. Did I say Alexandria's team? I meant *Alex's* team. I go by both names. Alexandria is my given name, after my grandmother. *Alex* for short."

CHAPTER 2

Alex

"Hey. Could I talk to you a minute?"

The next afternoon, Brayden came into the upstairs bedroom as I was finishing taking measurements. I pressed the button to retract the measuring tape, plucked the pencil out from behind my ear, and lifted my notepad off the floor.

"Sure," I told him. "I'm almost finished. Just let me write this number down so I don't forget it."

It was the first time the two of us had been alone together since I'd left the bar last night. When I'd arrived at the house this morning, the other team leader was already here. The three of us had talked for a while, and then Brayden had run out to pick up a long list of supplies. Twenty volunteers were scheduled to arrive at eight AM tomorrow morning, so each of us had a lot to do to prepare.

It was no surprise that Brayden had mistaken me for a man in our email exchanges, and I'd managed to avoid any conversation about last night until now. I wasn't really upset with him for calling me a pain in the ass, especially not after I'd gone back to my room and looked through our messages back and forth. I *had* suggested a lot of changes, but it was only because I wanted the house to come out perfect. Plus, I'd been called *particular* and *extremely detail-oriented* by people before, including my business partner, which was just the polite way of saying *pain in the ass*. So it wasn't news to me that I was picky. I was more upset with myself than Brayden—for allowing myself to feel tingly over a man. I hadn't done that since my husband died three years ago, and guilt weighed on me, even though I knew I had nothing to be guilty about. Besides, Brayden was too young for me anyway.

I finished scribbling in my notepad and flipped it closed. "What's up?"

Brayden raked a hand through his hair. "I want to apologize for last night."

"It's fine." I shrugged. "I realize I can be difficult. But it's because I want to do a good job."

"I should never have spoken poorly about anyone who volunteers. You're doing a good thing, and I was being a jackass. I really am sorry."

"It's okay."

He extended a hand. "Friends?"

I nodded and shook. "Sure."

I hated that the tingly feeling I'd had last night came rushing back as soon as I put my hand in his. I also couldn't help but notice how big his hand was, and how warm it felt wrapped around mine. I pulled away as quickly as possible, a fraction of a second longer than coming off as hasty.

Brayden tilted his head toward the front door. "Do you want to take a ride to Home Depot with me? You can help me pick out the moldings."

"Do you *want* my opinion, or are you asking because you realize I obviously like to give it?"

Brayden smiled. "I'm going to go with honest here. Both."

I rolled my eyes. "Fine. But I'm joining you because I saw the vanity you picked out when it was delivered this morning."

"What's wrong with the vanity?"

"Nothing. If you live in a dorm room."

"It's simple. I like simple."

"It was the first one that came up on the website, wasn't it?"

His lip quirked. "No."

I pointed to the grin he was trying to contain. "You're full of crap, Foster."

I followed him downstairs and outside, and Brayden was quiet for the first few blocks of the drive.

"So what's the Rejuvenation Center?" he asked out of the blue.

"How do you know that name?"

"It's the website at the bottom of all your emails. TheRejuvenationCenter.com."

"Oh, that's right. It's my business. I own a medi-spa. Well, half a medi-spa. I'm partners with my best friend, Wells."

"A spa? Like massages and stuff?"

I shook my head. "A medi-spa is different than a relaxation spa. It's short for medical spa. We do non-invasive cosmetic treatments like laser hair removal, Botox, lip filler, chemical peels, teeth whitening…that sort of thing."

"Interesting. How did you get into that?"

"I'm an RN. Years ago, I worked for a plastic surgeon. A ton of people came in for consults, and then wound up not having the surgery they were considering because of cost, or after they found out how many hours they had to be under anesthesia. They'd often ask for referrals for alternative treatments that were less invasive. I figured, why refer them to someone when I could offer those treatments myself?"

"So you left to open your own business, and the doctor started referring people to you?"

I smiled. "He didn't have a choice if he wanted dinner. The plastic surgeon was my husband."

At the next light, we stopped. Through my peripheral vision, I could see Brayden checking out my face. I spoke looking straight ahead. "Are you trying to figure out if I've had work done because I was married to a plastic surgeon?"

"No," he answered *way* too fast.

"Yes you are."

"I was actually looking at your lips."

"Because you think I have filler?"

"No, because they're pink. But it doesn't look like you have lipstick on. I noticed it last night too."

"Do you always scrutinize people that closely when you first meet them?"

"Only the ones I can't keep my eyes off of."

I chuckled. "Smooth."

"It's not a line. It's the truth. I barely slept last night because I was so pissed at myself for the dumb stuff I said. I think you're beautiful, and I really enjoyed talking to you."

I'd slept crappy last night, too. I couldn't stop thinking about a certain guy with a sexy, dimpled smile. But I wasn't about to share that tidbit and encourage him.

Home Depot was a block ahead on the right. I pointed. "You have to pass the store. There's a parking lot around back."

"Do you live in the area?"

I shook my head. "No, I live in Connecticut. But I came here yesterday afternoon to look at other vanities. I was going to suggest a different one. That is, *before* I found out what you think of my suggestions."

Brayden hung his head. "I'm never going to live down being a jerk, am I?"

"Probably not."

Inside Home Depot, Brayden let me pick out the moldings. After that, we stopped by the paint department, and I showed him the difference between his shade of blue-gray and the slightly different one I'd picked out. Under a light box, it was easy to see that his had a green base and mine didn't.

"There's a lot of light in the living room," I told him. "So your color is going to look more green than it appears on the little paint sample square, even though mine is only a shade different. The adjoining kitchen is going to have blue tile, so I thought the one I picked would coordinate better, yet still keep to the color palette you'd selected."

"I can see that now."

I squinted. "Can you? Or are you still kissing ass to make up for what you said last night?"

Brayden smiled. "No, I actually do notice the difference now. But I couldn't on the paint website, so I thought you were just being difficult."

"You see?" I plucked the sample square from his hands. "There's a method to my madness after all."

When we returned to the project house, Brayden pulled to the curb. "Do you have to go back inside, or are you done for the day?"

"I'm all done and ready for my volunteers tomorrow."

"Would you want to get something to eat?"

I nibbled on my lip. "Are you asking as colleagues or as a date?"

"What if I say a date?"

"Considering you're young enough to be my son, I'd have to decline."

Brayden's face scrunched up. "There's no way in hell you're old enough to be my mother. Not unless you've got the fountain of youth at that medi-spa of yours."

"Maybe not physically, but I have a stepdaughter who is probably close to your age. And my guess is I have ten years on you, at least."

"How old is she?"

14

"Thirty. My husband was seventeen years older than me."

He shrugged. "So you didn't care about an age gap when you married him. Why do you care now?"

I smiled. "It's not a good idea, Brayden."

"Alright, so we'll have dinner as colleagues."

I wanted to. *Really, really* wanted to. Which is why I knew I needed to say no. I sighed. "Thank you for the invite. But I think I'm going to have a quiet dinner alone."

He frowned. "Fine. Where did you park? I'll drop you at your car."

I pointed to the car directly in front of his. "I'm right there. Have a good night, Brayden."

He sulked. "You, too."

I got out of the car and walked to mine. Just as I opened the door, Brayden rolled down his window.

"Hey, Alex?"

"Yes?"

"You might be a stepmom, but I don't know any moms who look like you."

❤CHAPTER 3

Alex

That night, I decided to have dinner at the hotel restaurant. In retrospect, that was probably a stupid idea if I was trying to avoid Brayden. I realized my mistake the moment he waltzed in, looking so freaking good I wanted to scream.

He wore a navy polo and dark jeans, the thick watch around his wrist the perfect complement to his sexy hands. When he noticed me sitting in the corner, the way his eyes creased as he pretended to be surprised was so freaking adorable.

He headed straight for my table. "Fancy meeting you here."

"Yeah, totally crazy, right? Considering we're both staying here." I laughed.

He held out his palms. "I'm not stalking you, I swear. I'm just hungry, and there aren't a lot of options in the immediate vicinity."

As his eyes lingered on mine, all I could think was: *You're hungry, alright. Just not for food.* And quite frankly, I wouldn't have minded taking a bite of him right about now.

He flashed a mischievous grin as he pointed to the chair across from me. "Is this seat taken?"

"In fact, it's not."

He batted his sinfully long lashes. "Would it be okay to join you, then?"

I felt my cheeks flush. "That would be fine."

Brayden sat down and drummed lightly on the table. "Have you ordered yet?"

"No." I faced the menu toward him. "I was just looking when you got here, but I can't decide what I want." *Well, for food.* Based on the way my body was reacting right now, it definitely knew what *it* wanted. Except *Brayden* wasn't on the menu. He never would be.

A waft of his incredible scent blew in my direction. My nipples hardened, a sign that my body and my common sense were on a break, completely disassociated from each other.

He perused the choices. "How hungry are you?"

"Pretty hungry." I cleared my throat.

He looked up at me. "Would you want to share a pizza and try the eggplant parmesan, too? I feel like both but can't decide between them." He closed the menu. "Maybe we could split them in half?"

Or you could split me *in half. What the hell is wrong with me?*

"That sounds great. I'd been eyeing both of those things," I said. *Along with your lips. Your hands. Your strong forearms.*

"Not surprising, considering how similar our tastes have been thus far." He winked.

"On *certain* things…not necessarily home décor." I winked back.

He set down the menu and looked straight at me. I felt like there was a spotlight overhead. His eyes were piercing. This man gave you every ounce of his attention, and it was a bit overwhelming.

A waiter came by and took our order, giving me a moment's reprieve. But once he left, Brayden's attention yet again focused intently on me.

"So…you mentioned a stepdaughter," he said. "Do you have other kids?"

"No." I stared down into my water glass. "My husband didn't want any more kids, so we didn't have children of our own."

"What about what *you* wanted? Did you want kids?"

His question caught me off guard. The truth was, while I'd been neutral at the time, now I sometimes wished Richard and I had at least one child together. Caitlin would've had a sibling. I shook myself out of my thoughts, dodging the question. "It just wasn't meant to be." I tilted my head. "I assume you don't have children?"

"Why would you assume that?"

"Because you have so much energy, I suppose." I chuckled. "Kids are exhausting."

"You'd be correct. I don't have kids yet."

Yet. "So you definitely want them..."

"Someday, yeah," he said.

Another reason I shouldn't be playing with fire. "I also figured you had no kids because if you had a child, it might be difficult to take off on weekends to come upstate like this."

"Well, that's true. And it's why my buddies can't be here most weekends, although they're coming up tomorrow. All of my close friends have kids now."

"Tell me about your friends," I said, shuffling the ice in my water glass.

"Ryan was the fifth in our crew. We all grew up together in Pennsylvania. Colby, Holden, Owen, and me. Ryan left us a large amount of money after he passed away, and we used it to buy the building we all live in. We rent out the other units."

"So you're a landlord."

"I am."

"Impressive."

"Not really. I'm much prouder of my work in prosthetics and with Ryan's House."

"Of course, but I mean, it's impressive that you all came together and put that money to good use rather than wasting it. Investing it in real estate was a smart idea." I smiled. "And I assume it's pretty cool living in the same building as your friends."

"And then we all go down to Central Perk for coffee," he quipped.

I snapped my fingers. "Oh, right. Like the show. I thought you were too young to remember *Friends*."

"Ouch." He laughed. "Admittedly, I used to watch that show in my Superman pajamas. So perhaps you're not totally off-base."

"Those must have looked adorable on you."

He sighed. "Actually, it *is* fun living in the same building as my friends, but the drawback is that we're always up in each others' business." He cocked his head. "Are you seeing anyone?"

"That was an abrupt change in topic."

"That's how I roll when I'm curious about something…or someone."

"No. I'm not, at the moment."

"So you've dated here and there since your husband passed away…"

"Yeah. Lots of bad apples, for the most part. No one serious." *Certainly no one I have chemistry with like you.*

"Well, someone like you can afford to be picky."

"Thank you, but that's assuming there are lots of great choices." I chomped on some ice. "Most of the men in my age bracket are divorced, with complicated baggage. And if they're not… Let's just say there's often a good reason they never got married."

"See?" Brayden wriggled his brows. "This is exactly why you should go younger."

"Let me guess, you know *just* the person for me."

"He even likes the same bourbon as you."

I chuckled.

After our food arrived, the easy conversation continued to flow nicely. Once we'd devoured our pizza and eggplant, I decided to just ask already. "How old are you anyway?" I'd joked earlier that he was young enough to be my son, but I knew that was an exaggeration.

"Thirty-one. I'll be thirty-two this year." He shrugged. "See? I have nothing to hide." He grinned. "What was your guess?"

"Anywhere from twenty-five to thirty."

His eyes widened. "Damn. Twenty-five?"

"That was a worst-case scenario," I admitted.

He sighed.

After a few moments of silence, I prodded, "You're not gonna ask my age?"

"Nope." He shook his head as his eyes seared into mine.

"Why?"

"Because I don't give a shit how old you are. You can tell me, if you want. But it's not gonna change anything."

I crossed my arms and leaned back in my chair. "You're not even gonna try to guess?"

"You don't look any older than thirty-five. That's the only opinion I have on the matter."

"What if you found out I was twenty years older than you?"

He crossed his arms. "You're clearly not."

"You're right. But that wouldn't matter?"

"It wouldn't," he answered without hesitation.

"Well, it should."

Brayden narrowed his eyes. "Why?"

"Because there's a huge difference in life experiences with that much of a gap."

"From what you just told me, the *experiences* you've been having with men your age haven't gone so well." He arched a brow. "Have you ever dated a younger man?"

"No."

"So you have no experience by which to judge us. I volunteer as tribute to show you what it's like. I think you need to try it before you knock it."

"*You* won't be knocking anything," I taunted.

He laughed. "You're lucky I get right up when someone shoots me down. Most of the time, I'm even more motivated."

I shook my head. "What am I gonna do with you?" He'd opened his mouth when I added, "Get your dirty mind out of the gutter."

"Alright, I'll be serious." He played with his napkin. "You said your stepdaughter is around my age. And your husband was seventeen years older. That must have been an interesting dynamic between you and her when you first came on the scene."

I stared off, thinking about those early days with Caitlin. "It wasn't easy at first. Her mother had passed away when she was ten. I came into her life when she was a young teenager."

"She's lucky to have you, especially since both of her parents have passed now."

"Our relationship was a little tumultuous at first. But I understood why it was tough for her. A younger woman moving in? No child is gonna have an easy time with that. But she gradually began to get along with me—and to trust me. Over time, I took on more of a motherly role. Now we're super close, and I'm extremely grateful." I smiled. "She's pretty much my best friend."

He rested his chin in his hand and grinned. "That's awesome."

"Anyway…" I took a sip of my wine. "Have you ever dated an older woman?"

"Nope." He scratched his chin. "Well, not that I know of."

"What does that mean?"

"It means I might have slept with a few women in my life whose age I didn't know."

My stomach sank. "Oh."

"Does that bother you?" He frowned. "I'm just being honest. But if it makes you feel better, I'm long over the one-night-stand thing. I'm tired of it and really would like to find the one."

It's not going to be me. I exhaled. "Well, not knowing someone's age doesn't count. You're one to talk, telling me to date someone a lot younger than me when you've never *knowingly* dated anyone older."

"It's another reason *this* is perfect." He gestured between us. "We have a lot to learn from each other."

"You know what you can teach me?"

Brayden leaned in. "What?"

"How to use a nail gun." I laughed. "I'm starting to worry I've gotten a bit in over my head with the hands-on aspect of this project. I don't have any real experience outside design."

His teeth gleamed. "I got your back. You need help with anything, I'll be right there."

That was part of my worry. This project would mean spending quite a bit of time with him. It would be really helpful if he weren't so damn irresistible. Speaking of which, it would be smart for me to get back to my room before this dinner turned into a nightcap.

After Brayden paid the bill, refusing to let me contribute, I reached for my purse and said, "We've got an early day tomorrow. I think I'm gonna head upstairs."

Disappointment crossed his face. "Are you sure? I feel like it's too early to say goodnight."

"It's nearly ten."

"Like I said, *early*."

"We'll have to agree to disagree on that."

"Among other things." His eyes sparkled. "Come on," he urged. "Have one drink with me at the bar."

My body tightened as I hung on to my resolve. "I can't. My shower and bed await."

"That sounds like fun, too."

I rolled my eyes.

"Can I at least walk you to your room?" he asked.

I wasn't about to turn that sentence into famous last words. "No, thank you. I'm gonna stop by the concession stand and grab some Advil on my way."

"Did I give you a headache?" he asked.

Um, no. It's just an excuse since I can't trust myself with you. I started walking away before he could say anything else to sway me. "Goodnight, Brayden."

"'Night, Alex. Don't let the bedbugs bite," he called.

I turned to face him one last time, walking backward. "We're in a hotel. Don't say bedbugs."

Brayden blew me a kiss, and I nearly knocked into someone before vowing not to look back at him again for fear I'd change my mind about going back to my room like a good girl. Nonetheless, a perma-smile seemed plastered across my face as I headed upstairs.

When I got back to my room, I looked at myself in the bathroom mirror. My cheeks were rosy from either excitement, arousal, embarrassment, or a combination of everything. I slapped myself on the face. "Snap out of it!" Then I laughed at how stupid I was acting. For someone who thought she was too old for this guy, I sure was acting like a silly schoolgirl.

My phone rang, snapping me out of my stupor. I answered the FaceTime call, and my stepdaughter, Caitlin, popped up on the screen.

"What's going on?"

I blew out a long, shaky breath. "Not much."

"You look like something's got you frazzled."

Biting my lip, I placed some hair behind my ear. "I do?"

"Yeah. Like I caught you with your Lilly Pulitzer pants down or something." She giggled. "Someone there with you?"

"No. Why would you think that?"

"I don't know. You look guilty. Like you're not alone, maybe?"

"I'm most certainly alone." I turned the phone so she could see my empty hotel room. "See?"

"Everything going okay over there?"

"Yeah." I paused. *God, I want to tell her.*

What did I have to hide? For years I'd told Caitlin everything.

What was different about this? "There's a guy here who's…interesting," I blurted.

She pointed at me. "I knew it!" She kicked her feet in victory. "Do I freaking know you or what?"

I immediately began to downplay things. "It's not like that. I mean, nothing is actually happening and nothing will happen, but gosh, I'd nearly forgotten what it was like to flirt with someone. There's nothing like it."

"Wait." She narrowed her eyes. "Why *can't* anything happen?"

I gnawed at my lip. "I think he's too young for me."

"How young are we talking?"

"Your age."

My heart raced as Caitlin seemed to process that. "Okay. Well, how is this any different than me dating Greg, who was a decade older than me?"

Greg was a man she'd dated for about six months. It didn't last. *Probably the age difference.*

"It's not different. It just…" I didn't have a good comeback for that. "I don't know."

"Alex, you look amazing. You blow most women my age and less out of the water. Who cares if he's younger?"

"I guess *I* care. I'm at a point where I need to enjoy my life and not worry about some guy who might want kids someday. Stuff like that."

"You're getting way ahead of yourself here. Why not have some fun with this guy while you're on the project? You don't even live in the same place, right? Who says you need to worry about any of that serious stuff at all?"

I didn't have an answer for her, except that deep down, I knew there was something special about the connection I felt to Brayden. I could see myself falling for him. And that was precisely why I needed to be *very* careful. It didn't feel like *just* physical attraction.

Despite constantly warning myself, though, a part of me didn't want to hear it. I couldn't help being excited to see him again tomorrow. *Giddy* was a better word to describe it.

"There it is," she said, snapping me out of my thoughts.

"What?"

"That look again." Caitlin covered her mouth in laughter. "You should see yourself."

Believe me, I already did—in the mirror. *Maybe I need to smack myself harder.*

CHAPTER 4

Brayden

"**W**hat did you do, require photos and pick the volunteers by how hot they are?" Holden raised his hands, showing me his palms. "Not that I have an interest in any of them. My wife is my queen. Still, I can't help but notice that there are quite a few attractive women here. I've volunteered for other projects, and the crews certainly didn't look like this."

My buddies—Owen, Holden, and Colby—had driven up this morning to support the start of renovations on the twenty-third Ryan's House. We all volunteered for Ryan's House when we could. Most renovations lasted three to four months, so it was a hefty weekend commitment. But when one of us managed a project, the others all tried to pitch in for at least a weekend or two. It always felt good when we came together like this in Ryan's honor.

I looked over at Kyra, a super-sexy twenty-something. She caught my eye and flashed a flirty smile. I shook my head. "I have no idea how it happened. But last year when I managed a renovation, I had seventeen dudes, a lesbian couple, and a sixty-year-old woman who reminded me of my aunt and chain smoked. She spent more time outside puffing on butts than she did working inside."

Holden laughed. "That Kyra has been giving you *the look* since we walked in an hour ago."

Normally a woman like Kyra would be right up my alley, but I seemed to have a one-track mind lately. Just then, the object of those singular thoughts entered the room, walking with Chad, a decent-looking volunteer in his mid-forties. They were both smiling.

"Excuse me a minute," I said to Holden. "I'm going to kick things off. I think an hour for coffee, a tour, and introductions is more than enough."

Holden put a hand on my shoulder. "Go be the man of the hour, buddy."

I tossed my empty Dunkin' cup into the trash and walked into the center of the room. "Can I have everyone's attention again, please?"

The group of twenty-two gathered around.

"We're going to get started. As I mentioned when we did introductions earlier, we have two project leaders—Jason and Alex. Jason is going to lead half of you to work on electrical, plumbing, heating, and other mechanics. You'll see different contractors coming by at various times during the weekends to do the work that requires a license or a special skill. But the teams will do the legwork to support the contractor. For example, an electrician will be coming in to rewire the house. He'll deal with anything to do with live wires, but you guys might do things like running the Romex cable through the walls before everything is hooked up. The other team will be led by Alex, and they'll focus on interior-design elements like paint, flooring, fixtures, and appliances. We have a contractor coming in this morning to give lessons on installing the Pergo flooring, and we'll work alongside him to keep the costs down. Anyone have any questions so far?"

Everyone shook their heads.

I picked up a clipboard from the table. "Alright. Great. When you filled out the volunteer application, we asked if you had any construction experience. A few of you do, so we're going to split you guys up so both groups have a mix of experienced and inexperienced workers. Everyone else we assigned randomly to one group or another."

I looked down at the list of teams I'd put together last night and made a last-minute swap. Dave and Holden were the two with the most construction experience, so I'd assigned Holden to Jason's group and Dave to Alex's. Subconsciously, I'd probably separated my buddy, whom the ladies always loved, from the woman I had an interest in. But Holden was happily married, and *Dave* looked a little too excited to spend time with Alex for my liking. So I was definitely swapping the teams those two were on.

I was just about to read the list of team members when Kyra raised her hand. "I have a question."

"Sure. What's up?"

She grinned and swayed back and forth. "Can I be assigned to *your* team?"

From the corner of my eye, I caught Alex frowning. *Maybe there's hope after all.* "Sorry. I'm not on any team. I float. But if you need anything, I'll always be around."

I read the list of names for each team, silently smirking at the disappointment on Dave's face when I put him with Jason. After, I gave instructions on where each group would start and sent everyone on their merry way.

To keep the teams from bumping into each other, one group started on the first floor while the other would work on the second. Alex started up the stairs with her folks, but I grabbed Holden's elbow before he could follow.

"Got a second?"

"For you, I have a lifetime, my friend."

"Just to let you know, I made a connection with Alex."

Holden grinned. "Oh yeah?"

"I'm not telling you to ward you off. I know you only have eyes for Lala. But maybe you can talk me up, if the opportunity arises."

"If talk you up means tell her about the time you pissed your pants in first grade and tried to say one of the fish in Mrs. Reardon's fish tank jumped out and splashed you, absolutely. I'll fill her in."

I shut my eyes. "Why the fuck did I even tell you I was into her?"

Holden chuckled. "Hell if I know. It was pretty dumb." He lifted his hand. "Yo, Owen. Come here for a second."

Owen walked over. "What's up?"

"Our buddy here has the hots for Alex, the design-team leader."

"Oh yeah? Does she know about when he was four and got angry at me because I accidentally hit him with the ball when we were practicing pitching in the yard, so he held his breath until he passed out and landed in a pile of dog shit?"

I groaned. "I hate you guys."

Owen cupped his hands around his mouth. "Hey, Colby! Come here for a minute."

The last member of our squad joined us. "What's going on?"

Holden lifted his chin to me. "Brayden here has the hots for one of the ladies."

"I'm guessing Kyra?"

"Nope. Alex."

Colby looked surprised. "Really?"

"Yep." Holden grinned. "So if you happen to spend time with her, make sure you put in a good word for our buddy."

"Of course. I'll tell her all about your volunteering."

"Finally," I said. "One friend who's not a total douchebag."

Colby smirked. "Like that time you volunteered at church when we were in eighth grade and snuck into the confessional to jerk off."

My eyes widened. "I did *not* jerk off in a confessional. I went in there to wipe off the freaking Bengay on my dick because stupid-ass Owen told me it was hand cream, and then I went to take a piss and touched my dick. The minute I came out of the church bathroom, he jumped right in so I couldn't get in there when it started burning. What the hell was I supposed to do? Whip my pants down on the altar?"

Owen patted my shoulder. "Still sticking with that Bengay story, huh?"

I dropped my head, shaking it. "You guys *suck*."

The electrical contractor I'd hired arrived a minute later, so everyone went to work. One thing after another seemed to pop up, and before I knew it, it was mid-afternoon and I hadn't even gone upstairs to check on Alex yet. I'd been looking forward to giving her the nail-gun lesson we'd talked about last night. So I grabbed the carrying case and headed to the second floor.

Alex, Holden, and a volunteer I thought might be named Joe were in the room at the top of the stairs. I heard them laughing as I approached. When I walked in, they looked at me and laughed harder.

"Crap," I murmured. "This isn't good."

Alex tried to say something, but when she opened her mouth, she fell into a fit of hysterics. Tears rolled down her cheeks as she spoke. "Did you really stand up on your first day of preschool and announce, '*I'm not allowed to play with myself in the tub anymore while my mom washes my hair. I have to wait until we're done and I'm in my room all alone.*'"

I shut my eyes. "I was *three*, and they made each of us get up and tell something about ourselves. It was the only thing that came to mind. My mother hadn't told me it was something to keep private."

Holden rolled on the floor—*literally rolled on the floor*—he was laughing so hard.

I shook my head. "Thanks a lot, buddy."

Alex climbed to her feet. She put her hand on my chest, which took the sting out of my buddy's betrayal ever so slightly. "Don't worry. He also told us some really great things about you."

I frowned. "Yeah, I bet."

"How was your day?" she asked. "I came downstairs to grab a box of screws earlier, and you looked busy."

"Yeah. But it's been good. We have a lot started already." I lifted the case in my hand. "I came up to give you a nail-gun lesson, like we talked about last night. Do you have a few minutes?"

"I do. Two of the guys just went to get boxes of the flooring we're putting down. But if you're busy, I can ask Holden to show me how to use it."

Holden stood and smacked dust from his hands. "Actually, I'm handy. But Brayden is your go-to power-tool guy. He taught me everything I know."

Of course he was completely full of shit, but I appreciated the bow out. Holden winked from behind Alex.

I nodded toward the door. "Why don't we go down the hall to the primary bedroom? The beams are all exposed, and no one is working in there today. That way you can practice."

"Okay!"

In the bedroom, I unpacked the cordless nail gun and gave her a quick tour.

"This is the safety tip. It won't retract until you press down on whatever you're going to nail."

"Oh, alright. Great. That makes me feel better about using it."

I showed her the jam-release latch, magazine, magazine-release button, and the trigger switch. It wasn't really very difficult, but considering it was powerful and you could easily shoot a nail through your own hand, I understood her hesitation.

"You ready to try it out?"

"As ready as I'll ever be."

I handed her the gun and stood behind her. There wasn't any certain position you needed to be in, so I took a little advantage of the situation. "Put one foot in front of the other for the best balance," I said.

"Okay."

"Now just place the nail gun where you want it." I reached around her and pointed to eye level. "Let's tack one in right here. I'll hold the gun while you pull the trigger the first time so you get the feel."

My arm wrapped around Alex, enveloping her petite frame in a hug from behind. I liked the feel of it, so I wasn't going to nudge her to hurry.

"Should I do it?" she asked after a moment.

"If you're ready."

She pressed the trigger, and the loud sound of a nail tunneling into the beam echoed around the room. Alex whipped around with an excited smile. "That was easy!"

A piece of hair fell across her cheek. I couldn't help myself. I reached out and brushed it back from her face. With just the two of us in the room standing so close, the moment grew intimate.

"You're really beautiful, Alex."

She nibbled on her bottom lip. "Thank you."

My eyes fell to her mouth, and her breathing picked up.

"You feel it, too, don't you?" I whispered.

She swallowed and leaned in. "What?"

"It's hard to put into words, but it feels like there's a magnetic force between us. Anytime I go near you, something pulls me closer."

I heard footsteps pounding down the hall, but I was too lost in the moment for it to really register. At least until Dave ran into the room.

"Pipe busted! Where's the main shut off?"

Fuck. "I gotta go."

Alex blinked. "Yeah. Of course. Thank you for showing me the, umm…thing."

I bolted down the stairs with the smile still on my face. But it wilted when I got to the kitchen. Water sprayed from a pipe in the ceiling. The main shut-off valve was in the basement, so I took the steps two at a time and twisted the knob.

"Water stop?" I yelled up the stairs.

"Not yet!"

"Give it a minute. Whatever's in the lines is going to piss out before it's done."

After another thirty seconds, someone yelled down that the water was slowing, so I went back upstairs. "What the hell happened?"

"It's my fault," Jason said. "We were doing wall and ceiling prep work. I had a couple of people pulling all the old nails out. But I didn't specify to remove only nails in the beams. Apparently there was an old, rusty nail lodged in a pipe. Drywaller must've hit it when they were sheetrocking decades ago. Guess it was acting like a plug, until one of the ladies removed it."

Kyra pouted. "It was me. I'm sorry. I got carried away and wasn't thinking."

I held up a hand. "It's okay. There shouldn't have been one there to begin with."

Holden came into the room. "What happened?"

"Hole in a pipe. I'm going to run to the plumbing-supply store. Hopefully they're still open, or we're not going to have water. They close early on Saturday."

"I'll take the ride with you."

"We'll get everything cleaned up while you're gone," Jason said.

Since it was two thirty already, I hit the gas as soon as we got on the highway, just in case they closed at three.

"That was the only bad story I told her, you know," Holden said. "I'd been talking you up all morning and thought my spiel would sound more genuine if I added something that didn't make you seem like a priest."

"Uh-huh."

"No, really. But tell me what's going on with you and the MILF?"

"Don't call her that."

"Why not? It's just a term. I don't actually mean I want to fuck her."

My jaw tensed.

"Holy shit." Holden pointed to my face. "You really like her, don't you?"

"Yeah, I do." I shrugged. "We're obviously not an ideal match since she lives in Connecticut and has a stepkid my age. But I don't know… There's something about her."

"Dude, my wife is a researcher with a PhD. I'm a dumb drummer who doubles as a handyman. Who we're attracted to doesn't always make sense."

"Have you ever gone out with an older woman?"

"Hell yeah. Best sex of my life, aside from my beloved wife, of course. They know what they want and aren't afraid to take it."

I sighed. "Not sure I'll get to find out. Alex wants nothing to do with me."

"I wouldn't be so sure. I noticed the way she frowned when that Kyra woman was flirting with you this morning. You don't get jealous over things you don't want."

"You caught that, too, huh?"

"Yep. But you've never dated someone older before, have you?"

"Never."

Holden scratched his chin. "I guess it kind of makes sense you'd be into an older woman, if you think about it."

"Why is that?"

"Because you have mommy issues, dude."

"What the hell are you talking about? I do not."

"Your mother took off when you were nine and left your dad to raise you and your brother. The four or five times she came around to visit each year, she had some random young guy with her that she wanted you to call Uncle whatever. You probably have an underlying need to be coddled or some shit."

I glanced over at Holden and back to the road. "I think you should leave the research and analysis to your wife."

He shrugged. "Whatever. But it makes sense."

Hours later, we'd fixed the busted pipe and most of the volunteers had left for the day. My buddies, the two team leaders, and Kyra were the only ones left.

"What do you say we all go out for a drink?" Colby asked. "We deserve it after all the work we got done today. There's a sports bar not too far from the hotel. They'll probably have the Rangers game on."

I looked over at Alex. "You in?"

"Umm…"

"Come on. At least for one drink?"

I sensed she was about to say yes, but then Kyra looped her arm through mine. "I'm in!"

Alex's face fell. "I think I'm going to pass. It's been a long day. But you young people should go enjoy yourselves."

Young people.

She pretty much ran out of the house after that.

My mood was somber the rest of the night. I always had a good time with my friends, but after two beers, I was ready to go to my room and get some sleep. Kyra, on the other hand, had a little *too much* fun in a very short time. She could barely walk when we got back to the hotel. Owen, Colby, and Holden had rooms on the first floor. Lucky me had a room on the same floor as Kyra, so I got the honor of making sure the drunk girl got back to her room safely.

I pushed the button for the elevator and guided her inside when it arrived. As the doors slid closed, she threw her arms around my neck.

"I think you're schmexy," she cooed.

I peeled her arms off. "And I think you're a little drunk."

She leaned in, pushing her big tits against my chest, and traced my mouth with her fingernail. "I thought you were sexy before I had anything to drink."

I reached over and pushed the button for the fifth floor, even though it was already illuminated and we were moving. The damn car felt like it was crawling.

I put my hands on Kyra's shoulders and gently nudged her a few steps back. "What's your room number, Kyra?"

She batted her eyelashes. "Have you ever had elevator head?"

Before I could respond, she sank to her knees and reached for my belt.

Which was exactly the position she was in when the elevator doors slid open on the fifth floor…

And *Alex* was standing on the other side.

My eyes flared wide. "*Fuck*. This isn't what it looks like."

CHAPTER 5

Brayden

Alex disappeared into another elevator instead of sticking around to let me explain. The doors closed, and she was gone.

Great.

Just fucking great.

I couldn't even blame her. That had looked bad. I was going to have a hell of a lot of explaining to do.

"I have to go," I said to Kyra, leaving her to go back alone to whatever room she was in on this floor.

I returned to the elevator and pressed the button for the lobby as quickly as possible. Of course, as luck would have it, the elevator stopped on the very next floor. My forehead started to perspire as an old man with a walker entered at a snail's pace.

The doors finally closed, and we began descending again.

Come on.

Come on.

Come on.

Once on the ground level, I ran out of the elevator and surveyed the lobby. Alex was nowhere to be found. I went straight to the bar. A flash of blond hair met my eyes, but I soon realized it was someone else. She wasn't in here either.

Next, I headed for the front desk. The attendant was chatting with her co-worker, so immersed in her conversation, she didn't notice me standing there. I cleared my throat to interrupt. There was no room for politeness at a time like this. She flashed me a dirty look.

"Excuse me," I said. "I have an urgent matter and need to find someone who's staying here. Can you tell me what room Alex Jones is in? Or maybe her room is under Alexandria."

She didn't look like an Alexandria to me. She looked like an Alex.

"I'm sorry." The woman at the desk shook her head. "It's against hotel policy to give out that information."

"What if I leave my ID with you for collateral or something so you know I'm not an axe murderer? I really need—"

"I'm sorry. It's not something I can divulge."

What the hell do I do now? Running my hand through my hair, I let out a deep sigh. I smacked my hand against the counter in frustration before taking off.

I wandered around once again in search of the beautiful blonde who'd had me under a spell from almost the moment we met. Alex was probably wishing she'd never met me at all. It messed me up to think she might believe I could jump so quickly from my interest in her to a girl like Kyra. If Alex only knew that I'd thought of nothing but her all night, hating the fact that she'd intentionally separated herself from the rest of us "*young people*." That comment irked me to no end.

I considered going upstairs to the fifth floor and randomly knocking on each door, but I thought better of that, considering how late it was. It would've crossed the line into desperation, although I wasn't far off at this point. My best bet, I supposed, was staying put in the hopes she was still down here. I camped out in a seat that overlooked the elevators so I wouldn't miss her.

How the hell do I not have Alex's number?

That needed to be rectified as soon as I found a way to redeem myself.

As the minutes passed, I knew I should go to bed since we had to be up early tomorrow to work on the house. Then Alex and I both had to drive home in the afternoon. But if I couldn't talk to her tonight, I wouldn't get a lick of sleep.

Had I ever lost sleep over a woman? I couldn't recall a time I had. Or maybe it was that I hadn't met a woman worth losing sleep over. I wasn't sure why the eight hours or so between now and the time I'd see her in the morning mattered so damn much, but they did. I hated the idea of her going to bed tonight thinking I was a scumbag. I somehow *felt* like a scumbag, even though I hadn't done anything wrong.

"What's got you looking so down, son?" a man waiting for the elevator asked.

I decided to just let it out to this stranger. "I disappointed a good woman tonight because of a misunderstanding. And now I can't find her to apologize properly for the thing she thinks I did, which I didn't even do."

He blinked. "I'm too tired to decipher that. But I hope you find some peace."

"Me, too, man." I placed my palms together in thanks. "Have a good night."

After he disappeared into the elevator, I hung my head.

After a full hour downstairs, I came to the conclusion that I wasn't going to get to explain myself tonight. Feeling defeated, I took the elevator back up.

I wandered the halls of the fifth floor a bit, but there was no sign of her. After returning to my room, I retreated to the bathroom and took the piss I'd been holding for way too long before tossing off my clothes and jumping in the shower.

As the hot water rained down on me, I tried to calm my mind, but remained focused on the fact that Alex was somewhere in this hotel hating on me right now. The look of disappointment on her face when she saw Kyra on her knees was etched in my mind.

You know how I knew I was upset? I couldn't even jerk myself off as I normally might've in the shower. I was too preoccupied to get it up at the moment.

After I got out, I felt no better, not a bit refreshed. I still felt like the asshole Alex surely thought I was tonight.

I threw on a T-shirt and some gray sweatpants before lying down. The springs of the mattress on the uncomfortable bed pressed against my back. It was eerily quiet in my room, aside from the noise in my head. I contemplated turning on the TV, but what was the point? I wouldn't be able to focus on anything anyway. So I just lay there, staring at my own pathetic reflection in the glass of the TV screen.

A few minutes later, a knock at the door caused me to sit up.

Without checking the peephole, I opened it. A long breath escaped me as I took her in—the beautiful blonde I'd been searching for all night. Alex looked neither happy nor sad. I couldn't read her expression. "Thank God," I muttered. "I've been looking everywhere for you."

She stepped into the room, and the door clicked behind her. She fiddled with her hands, but didn't say anything.

"Remind me to get your phone number after we talk. Tonight would've been a lot easier if I'd had it earlier," I told her. "Not that you would've answered me after what you *thought* happened." I sighed. "How did you know which room was mine?"

"I asked the woman at the front desk."

"Hold up." I scratched my chin. "She said it was against hotel policy to give out room numbers."

"She mentioned there was a man who was also looking for me. Since we were clearly in search of each other, she agreed to give me your room number after I gave her your name."

"I'm so sorry about what you saw earlier. But it was absolutely *not* what it looked like."

Alex nodded. "I know that now."

My eyes widened. "You do? How?"

"Right after I saw you with Kyra, I went downstairs. But I didn't stay. When I came back up to our floor, you weren't here, but she was still out in the hall. She'd lost her room key. She was also slurring her words, and I realized she was pretty drunk. She started rambling on about how you blew her off when all she was trying to do was *blow* you."

A breath of relief escaped me. *Well, thank God Kyra is good for something.* Who would've imagined she would be the one to save my ass?

"I've been worried you thought I was a horrible person."

She tilted her head. "Getting a blowjob wouldn't have made you a horrible person."

Now I *knew* I was more relaxed, because the word *blowjob* coming out of her mouth caused my dick to twitch. Any sexual arousal I'd lost in the shower was back in full force. This bombshell of a woman—a real woman—had me aroused in a way I'd never felt before.

"You know what I mean, Alex. There was no way I would've been messing around with her." I took a few steps closer. "There's something happening between us, whether you want to admit it or not. I sensed the way your body reacted to me when we were up close and personal earlier…" My eyes fell to her neck, which was turning pink. "It's the same way you're reacting to me now."

She shook her head. "I don't know what you're talking about."

Despite her attempt at denying things, her breathing became heavier. When she ran her tongue across her bottom lip, I wished I could reach out and bite it. There was so much I wished I could do right now.

I wanted to fuck this woman in the worst way. But it was more than that. I would've been fine just staying up all night and talking to her, too. Anything she wanted to give me, I'd take. I wondered what would happen if I kissed her right now? But instead of attempting that, I stepped back. "Why did you say what you did earlier about *young people*?"

She narrowed her eyes. "What did I say exactly?"

"When you bowed out of coming out with us, you said us *young people* should go enjoy ourselves, as if there's a world of difference between you and me just because of our ages. You know damn well there's not."

"I didn't mean anything by it."

"Well, it pissed me off."

She arched a brow. "But it's the truth, isn't it? You and your friends *are* younger than me."

"It felt like you were trying to tell me I should stick to women my own age, when I'm not interested in anyone else right now but you. I don't give a shit what it looked like earlier with Kyra hanging all over me. I didn't ask for it. And absolutely *nothing* happened with that girl."

"Okay…" She looked down at her shoes. "I *was* caught off guard to see Kyra hanging all over you earlier. I'll admit that."

"Finally, she's being honest with me." My mouth curved into a grin. "You were jealous?"

"I didn't say that."

"Not in so many words, no." I moved in slowly. "Let me make something clear. Me being interested in her is laughable, considering I've thought of little besides you this weekend. It's not easy chasing someone who runs from me, you know. There's a chance I could end up never catching you. But it's a risk I'm willing to take if it means I've got a shot. It's even a little invigorating. Women don't play hard to get with me all that often. But I don't give up easily on things I want."

She said nothing as I continued to stare into her eyes.

"Why did you come to my room tonight, Alex?"

She crossed her arms. "Get your mind out of the gutter. I didn't come here for any reason but to talk."

"I know that. What I mean is, you could've just left well enough alone, if you were hoping I'd move on to someone younger. You could've let me think you were mad. You didn't need to come see me. We could've cleared things up in the morning." I licked my lips. "But...you like me."

She swallowed. "I need to go."

Despite her words, she didn't move.

"Go, then. No one's stopping you."

Her chest rose and fell. That was all I needed to see. Because her body's reaction still didn't match the words coming out of her mouth. She didn't *want* to go at all. She didn't want to want me—but she did. I could feel it in every fiber of my being. She was holding herself back, though. *How the hell do I get her to stop doing that?*

"Goodnight," she finally said, turning around and heading back down the hall, leaving me wanting more. But I was surer than ever that she'd caught feelings, too.

Damn. I never got her number.

The following morning, a hint of sun peeked through the dark curtains in my hotel room.

As I blinked my eyes open, I looked over at the alarm clock, and my stomach dropped.

Nine AM!

I was supposed to have been at the worksite by seven.

How the fuck could I have let this happen? Apparently, I'd been so distracted last night that I'd forgotten to set my alarm. Whipping the covers off, I jumped out of bed and started throwing on clothes. I grabbed all of my stuff, tossing everything into the suitcase. I needed to check out since I'd be heading straight home from the worksite.

My head pounded because I needed coffee so badly, but I refused to stop to get some before heading to the project. By the time

I arrived at the house, everyone was already busy at work. I was the only asshole moseying in late.

I spotted Alex in a corner of the bedroom off the first floor. She was immersed in conversation with a couple of male volunteers. She laughed as they painted together, and it seemed like she didn't have a care in the world. She looked amazing in black leggings that accentuated her long legs and a white T-shirt tied in a knot at her waist. Her hair was up in a messy bun. It pissed me off that I'd missed a good chunk of the morning with her.

As I continued admiring her from afar, someone crept up behind me.

"I can see why you like her," Holden said.

I turned to find him with a smirk on his face. I'd forgotten that while the other guys had already headed back to the City, he was sticking around to help again this morning.

Irked by his comment, I raised a brow. "Why do you say that?"

"I chatted with her earlier. Where were you anyway?"

"I forgot to set my alarm last night." My eyes drifted over to her again. "You and everyone *else* around here seems to like her."

"Maybe you should set your alarm next time, if you don't want to miss the fun." He punched me lightly on the arm. "Anyway, what the hell happened last night? The way that chick was hanging all over you, I didn't know how the evening was going to play out."

"Kyra was drunk as a skunk, and I wanted nothing to do with her."

Ironically, Kyra was nowhere to be found this morning. Probably nursing a hangover.

I filled Holden in on everything else that had happened last night—from what Kyra pulled in the elevator to Alex coming to my room.

He shook his head. "You got lucky that Kyra told her the truth. Not sure I would've believed you either, if I were Alex."

"Keep it down," I whispered. "I don't want her to know I'm talking about it."

He lowered his voice. "Anyway, I think you should keep going for it."

"I've been trying, but she's hard to get."

"Some of the best things in life are." He patted me on the back. "Anyway, hate to drag you away as soon as you got here, Romeo, but I need you to come with me to the store. I'm gonna need your help unloading a couple of appliances."

I looked back over at her. "Shit. Okay. Let me just go say hi first."

He nodded. "Don't take too long. I gotta get back to the City soon."

I entered the bedroom where Alex was still chatting with those guys.

"Hey." I forced a smile.

She turned and blew a hair up into her forehead. "Hey."

"I'm sorry I'm late," I said.

"I didn't think you were gonna show," she said, walking over to where I stood.

"Yeah, well, I stupidly forgot to set my alarm last night."

Alex raised her eyebrows. "I didn't take you to be so irresponsible."

"I'm generally not. *Distracted* is a better word."

"What has you distracted?"

"A certain woman who's wrong about being too old for me, but probably not wrong about being too good for me." I exhaled. "Anyway, I'm pissed at myself for missing half the morning."

She looked around to make sure no one had heard me. "I got news for you…" She chuckled.

"What?"

"I forgot to set my alarm, too."

"You were late?"

She shook her head. "I just got lucky because I couldn't sleep and was up by five AM anyway."

"Sounds like we're both pretty distracted."

"Hey, Ashton Kutcher!" Holden shouted. "Don't mean to interrupt, but we need to get going."

I'm gonna kill him.

"You'd better go." Alex blushed as she turned toward the wall she was painting.

"I'll see you when I get back."

"Yeah, okay," she said without turning around again.

After Holden and I went to the home improvement store, I'd never moved so fast as we loaded and unloaded those appliances. But one catastrophe after another ensued once we tried to hook everything up. All I wanted was to convince Alex to get coffee with me before we both had to leave. But it was late afternoon before I had a chance to go talk to her again.

When I returned to the room she'd been working on, though, I realized any luck I might've had left with Alex this weekend had officially run out.

She was gone—without saying goodbye.

CHAPTER 6

Alex

"You have no idea how many faces are going to light up when they see these, Mrs. Jones."

"Please, call me Alex."

After I left the renovation site on Sunday, rather than heading straight home, I'd stopped over at Memorial Cancer Center, the hospital the latest Ryan's House would support, to drop off a few of the newest electronic gaming consoles and some games. I'd read an article in the Seneca Falls paper that said donations were down due to the economy. It had mentioned that the pediatric wards had outdated gaming systems, so I'd decided to do something about it.

"If you have time," Liz, the social worker, said, "you're welcome to come with me up to the floor to deliver these. The kids are usually gathered in the rec room before dinner. Donors should get to see the impact they make when they can."

"I'd love that."

"You'll just have to wear a mask and not touch anything. Many of our patients have weakened immune systems from treatment."

"Oh, of course."

I followed Liz up to the fourth-floor pediatric oncology unit. We stopped at the nurses' station to let them know we'd come bearing gifts, and then headed down to the patient recreation room.

After my husband was diagnosed, I'd spent a lot of time around cancer patients, but nothing could've prepared me for the heartache I felt walking into a room full of sick children. Many had bald heads and sallow skin, and the majority were hooked up to IV poles with multiple bags hanging. The room started to sway back and forth, and my chest felt like an elephant had parked his ass on it. "God," I mumbled.

"I know." Liz patted me on the back as we stood just inside the doorway. "But hang in there. I promise you're going to feel better in a few minutes. These kids aren't just what we see. They're resilient and inspiring. Watch." Liz walked to the center of the room and smiled. "Hello, everyone! Who remembers my name?"

A boy who was probably about eight raised a hand. "You're Lizzle the Schizzle."

Liz chuckled. "That's Little Ray. He gives everyone a rapper name."

The kid looked over at me. "What's your name?"

"Alex."

He gave me a thumbs up. "A-dog."

I smiled. "I like it."

"He calls Dr. Artemis, our chief who never smiles, MC Remission. I crack up every time."

The heaviness in my chest seemed to float away over the next half hour. Liz had said the new gaming consoles would light up faces, but they did more than that. They made my spirit soar. The kids ripped open the boxes and hooked up the equipment in less than five minutes. After, we watched them try out all the new games. By the time Liz said she needed to get back downstairs, I'd decided I'd be making the same delivery to my local hospital when I got home.

We said goodbye to everyone and started down the hall side by side. Halfway to the elevator, I heard a familiar voice. At first,

I'd thought I'd imagined it. But when I heard it a second time, I stopped and looked around. Inside a small visiting room to my left, a little boy in a gown sat on a couch between his parents. A man dressed in paper scrubs, a surgical cap, and a mask stood in front of them, holding a large box. The only thing I could see were his green eyes, but that's all it took to know it was Brayden.

Liz pointed to the man behind the glass window. "That's Brayden from Ryan's House."

"I know. We've…met."

"That's right. I forgot you said you're working on one of their projects."

"Why is he dressed like that?"

"It's required when a patient is under protective isolation. Unfortunately, it's necessary when someone is severely immuno-suppressed. Only parents and members of the treatment team are permitted to visit, and they have to take every precaution."

"But…" I was about to ask how Brayden fit into that category when the reason became clear. Brayden set down the box in his hands and took the top off. When he reached inside and pulled something out, the little boy's eyes flared wide. He jumped out of his seat with a giant smile. I hadn't noticed the boy was missing an arm—not until I saw the prosthetic one. And it wasn't just any prosthetic. This one was something out of a Marvel comic book. The entire muscular arm was painted glossy red, and black web lines ran up the forearm. A 3D spider embellished the top of the hand, and the knuckles of the fingers were bright blue. I wasn't into superheroes, but even I could appreciate how awesome this Spider-Man arm was. My heart melted as I looked through the glass.

Liz interrupted my staring. "Do you mind if we get going? I have to meet a family downstairs in a few minutes."

"Oh. Yes, I'm sorry. Of course." I stole one last look before walking the rest of the way to the elevator. Brayden might've been out of sight, but it was going to take a long time to put what I'd just seen out of my mind.

Back in Connecticut the following Monday morning, Wells, my best friend and partner, walked into a treatment room while I was looking at myself in the mirror.

"Morning, Kitten," he said.

I pulled the skin on my face taut on both sides of my eyes. "Should I get Botox? Or maybe filler?"

He came up behind me and looked at my reflection. "Yes."

My face fell. "Thanks."

"What? Don't ask my opinion if you don't want it. You're gorgeous, but you can't stop Mother Nature without a syringe, sweetheart."

I sighed. "Getting old sucks."

Wells took a seat on the stool we used during treatments and spun around. "Talk to me. What's going on?"

"Nothing. What do you mean?"

"You've never once considered injections. You're one of the few women I know who actually likes her appearance as is and has natural confidence. So there's something going on if you're suddenly considering joining the frozen-face fan club, like me." He pointed to a cabinet and started taking off his shirt. "We have a half hour before either of us has a patient. Can you do a touch up under my pits? I'm starting to sweat again."

Unlike me, Wells used every service we had, including injections for hyperhidrosis—excessive underarm sweating.

I shook my head, yet reached for a vial of Botox and gloves. "You know sweating is natural."

"You say *natural* like it's some prize. You know what's natural? A banana. You know what happens when it sits around too long? It rots and shrivels up. You know what doesn't shrivel? *Plastic.* It sticks around for a thousand years. I want to be plastic."

I chuckled. "Lift your arm, crazy man."

Wells and I caught up while I injected poison into his underarms. He told me about a horrible date he'd had this weekend, and I told him about my time at Ryan's House.

"Are there a lot of hot, sweaty construction workers at this place? Maybe I should come with you next time."

My mind went to one man I knew I'd like to see sweaty. "Can I ask you something and you won't interrogate me about why I'm asking?"

"Sure, honey, let's pretend that's possible."

"Am I too old to go out with a thirty-one-year-old?"

"Absolutely not. I went out with a twenty-four-year-old last weekend."

"You did?"

Wells nodded. "His name was Cash. He had washboard abs and told me his life goal was to meet Scott Disick."

"Who?"

"Oh Jesus. You might be too old to date someone in their fifties, Grandma."

"Great."

"Seriously, though, who's the guy? Because I don't like him already if he's making you feel this insecure."

I sighed. "It's not Brayden making me feel this way. That's all on me."

"Brayden, huh? Cute name. Tell me more."

I finished the last injection and dropped the needle into the red box hanging on the wall. "He's the guy who founded the charity I'm working at."

Wells wiggled his brows. "I like givers."

I laughed. "He's a super nice guy. Not to mention, he's gorgeous, and we seem to have a lot in common."

"So the only problem is that he's younger than you?"

"He's a lot younger than me."

"You said thirty-one. That's not even a decade."

"I know. But he's almost the same age as Caitlin. And he's never been married and will want a family someday. So it's more than an age difference. It's where we are in life."

Wells sat up and tugged his shirt back on. "I thought you said you weren't even sure if you would ever want to get married again. Since when are you shopping for another husband?"

"I'm not, but…"

"But what? You do know you can *just* have a good time with someone, right? You don't need to map out a ten-year plan."

"I know."

"Why does an age gap bother you now, anyway? You weren't concerned that Richard was seventeen years older than you."

"That's different."

"Why?"

"Because…I…"

Wells grinned. "Good answer."

"Shut up."

He smiled. "Seriously, Alex, thirty-one is not too young for you. Especially if the guy has his shit together and runs a charity. Even if you think he doesn't have long-term potential because he wants to have kids and you don't, there's no reason you can't enjoy him short term. Where does this guy live?"

"Manhattan."

"How long does this renovation project you're doing take?"

"About three months."

"Then you have an expiration date anyway." He shrugged. "Sounds like a fling made in heaven, if you ask me."

"I guess…"

"Stop overthinking it and just have fun for a change."

"You say that like it's simple."

Wells stood and kissed my forehead. "It is, pumpkin. Just raise your arms and enjoy the roller coaster of life."

A little while later, I finished my first appointment and went to catch up on some paperwork and mail in my office. When I was done, I somehow wound up on the Ryan's House website. I clicked around for a bit, looking at photos from all the projects they'd done, and then went to the *About Us* tab. A photo of five young guys standing with their arms around each other's shoulders popped up. I recognized Brayden first, before realizing I'd met most of the other guys, too. They were his friends Holden, Colby, and Owen. I assumed the one who didn't look familiar was Ryan. They were probably only late teens or early twenties, all of them different from each other, yet each very handsome. I imagined that crew of five had made a lot of heads turn when they went out together. Underneath was a story about Ryan, and then a bio of each of the guys, who were apparently all on the Ryan's House Board of Directors. I read through everything once, but went back for a second read of Brayden's bio.

Brayden Foster is the founder and chief executive officer of Ryan's House. He holds both a Bachelor's and Master's degree in mechanical engineering from the University of Pennsylvania. At just twenty-three, he received his first patent for a revolutionary artificial limb joint, which is currently licensed to the world's biggest prosthetic companies. Brayden founded Ryan's House to honor his childhood best friend, Ryan Ellison, who passed away from leukemia. Brayden's passions include developing artificial limbs that look like action heroes', skiing, kick boxing, traveling, ant farming, and knitting.

I chuckled to myself at those last two hobbies. Ant farming was odd, but it didn't give me the visual the other did—Brayden sitting on a rocker with a giant ball of yarn and knitting needles. Maybe he wasn't too young for me after all. Underneath was a giant red donate button. My eyes shifted to the check sitting to the right of my keyboard—my husband's old partners sent him a small percentage of the practice's profits each quarter. The payments were part of their partnership agreement and would continue for ten full years after his death. I'd been mailing them to Caitlin whenever they came in, but last quarter she'd told me not to send them anymore. Instead, she wanted me to donate the money since she was doing well enough on her own. My eyes shifted back to the donate button on the screen. The foundation did support cancer patients, and I was certain Ryan's House was a charity my husband would have really liked. So I figured *why not?* and typed in the exact amount of the check. The screen then prompted me to enter information for a tax receipt, including name, telephone number, and email. I did so, and after another ten minutes, I finally forced myself away from the photo of Brayden and shut my laptop. As I did, my phone buzzed with an incoming text, though it wasn't from a number I knew. I swiped to open the message:

> **Unknown: $11,842.88? I can't wait almost a week to ask. Do you have an aversion to round numbers?**

A second text came in before I finished reading the first.

> **Unknown: This is Brayden, by the way. Stole your number from the donor information that came in.**

I smiled so wide, it felt like my face might crack.

> **Alex: Hi! I donated the exact amount of a check I received. Not sure why I didn't round up or down. I can see why that seemed strange.**

I hit send and then sent a second text:

> **Alex: Though not as strange as your hobbies...**

I chewed on my fingernail as I waited for him to respond. It took only a few minutes.

> **Unknown: Crap. It took me a minute to figure out what you meant. I had to go check my bio. That's Owen. He maintains the website for me. Anytime he goes in to do an update, he adds a new ridiculous hobby to the end of my bio. Apparently two this time.**

I laughed out loud.

Alex: Damn. I was going to put in a request for a red merino wool cap and scarf. I lost mine.

Unknown: Sorry to disappoint. But I might consider taking a knitting class if you don't run out on me next weekend...

I didn't really *run out*, though I did leave without saying goodbye.

Alex: I actually saw you at Memorial Hospital. I donated some gaming consoles and happened to pass by as you were giving a little boy a Spider-Man prosthetic. It was really cool, by the way.

Unknown: That was Landon. Why didn't you tell me you were there?

Alex: I didn't want to interrupt. Plus, I needed to get home.

I started to type that I needed to get home before it got dark, because I didn't see so great driving at night anymore. But that would only make me sound even older than I was. So I hit send and waited. This time, the dots started to bounce around, then stopped for a minute or two before resuming jumping, and then again stopping once more. Nothing happened for a full five minutes, so I started to think maybe our chat had come to an end. Then my phone vibrated.

Unknown: This might be inappropriate, but I haven't been able to stop thinking of you since yesterday. Actually, since we first met...

Reading that made me way more excited than it should've. But I wasn't sure how to respond. Did I admit that I thought about him all the time, too? I could...but I didn't want to lead him on. I could lie... Or change the subject without an answer? While I was still mulling over my choices, another text arrived.

Unknown: I know you're sitting there carefully considering how to respond, so I'll let you off the hook and change the subject. Think you can get back upstate on Thursday again this week? I could use help picking out tile and appliances. And before you say no, you might want to think about the poor patients with cancer who are going to be looking at gray walls, gray tile, gray paint, and gray appliances if you don't help a guy out...

I really, really wanted to. But my gut said it wasn't a good idea. I didn't trust myself to spend time with him alone. Wells might be able to compartmentalize his experiences into simple flings vs. relationships, but I wasn't so sure I had it in me. I wanted to give it some more thought, though, so I kept my options open.

Alex: I'm pretty busy at work this week. I probably won't be able to, but I'll try.

I heard the disappointment in Brayden's voice, even via text.

Unknown: I won't bug you any more since you're busy. Thank you for the donation. It was very generous of you. Have a good week.

I typed back *thank you* and tried to get back to work. But when I opened my laptop, the screen illuminated right to Brayden's face again. Guess I hadn't closed the website. *Damn. He's so handsome.*

Wells strolled into my office. He came around my desk and looked at my screen. "Lord, have mercy. Who is that beautiful creature? *Please* tell me you're on a gay dating website."

"It's Brayden. The guy I was telling you about earlier."

"You said he was good looking, not an Adonis."

I exhaled. "It doesn't matter what he looks like. Nothing's going to happen, Wells."

"Why not?"

I shrugged. "I don't know. Flings are not for me."

"When do you see him again?"

"Friday. He actually just asked me to come up a night early to help pick out some things for the house. But I said I didn't think I could."

Wells pointed to Brayden's face on the screen. "Oh, you're going early. Even if I have to tie you up and drive you there myself."

CHAPTER 7

Alex

I'd arrived upstate even earlier than expected the next weekend and decided to stop by Memorial Cancer Center. Since my last visit here, I'd spoken to the hospital social worker over the phone, and she'd suggested I become a volunteer. They'd run a background check on me, and I'd sent in some paperwork. Now I just had to sign in as a volunteer before each visit.

There was no better way to make use of my time today than to visit a special young girl, who seemed in desperate need of company. Ashlyn was twelve and currently undergoing treatment for non-Hodgkin's lymphoma. Her big, beautiful eyes stood out against her perfectly smooth bald head.

We spent the better part of an hour talking about reality TV and music until a nurse interrupted to check her vitals. I took out my phone and scanned messages to give them as much privacy as I could while being in the room. But I felt Ashlyn eyeing me the whole time.

"You're really beautiful," she said after the nurse walked out.

"Why, thank you."

"I hope I have hair like yours when it grows back."

"What did your hair look like before?"

"It was curly, but I'm hoping it grows back straight."

I wasn't going to burst her bubble and tell her I'd actually heard that the opposite happened sometimes after chemo—previously straight hair grew back curly. Maybe she'd get lucky. She certainly deserved it.

Ashlyn adjusted her blanket. "Are you doing anything fun tonight?"

A vision of Brayden popped into my head. "I'm not sure, actually. I might be meeting a friend for dinner."

"Is it a girl?"

"Actually, no. It's a…boy." I chuckled. Brayden *was* technically a boy in my mind, I supposed.

"Make sure you wear a pretty dress."

I looked down at my black pants and white cowl-neck sweater. "You don't like my outfit?"

"It's okay, but if I were going out tonight, I'd put on a pretty dress."

"Well, I'll tell you what, I'll put on a pretty dress for you."

"Pink," she clarified.

"Pink?" My eyes widened. "I don't generally wear—"

"Pink! It has to be pink." She laughed. "Wear a pink dress for me. Because I'm stuck here and can't."

When she put it that way, how could I not? I nodded. "A pink dress it is. You got it."

She pointed her finger at me. "Pictures or it didn't happen."

"Okay."

"You need pretty shoes, too."

This little angel wanted to live vicariously through me. I took a deep breath. "What might these shoes look like?"

"They have to be glass, like Cinderella shoes."

"Pretty sure glass slippers don't really exist, but maybe I can find something that looks clear. Would that work?"

She nodded. "That would be acceptable."

"Okay, good." I sighed. "Well, you've left me with a lot to do this afternoon. Find a pink dress and glass-like shoes. So I'd better be on my way." I stood.

"Text me a photo later?" she asked.

"Do you have a phone?"

"Duh!" She reached over to her side table and waved a cell in a pink silicone case.

"Okay. Sorry for doubting that." I handed her my phone. "Enter your number here, and I'll text you later."

She took my phone, pressed some buttons, and handed it back. "Thanks, Alex."

"I'll be in touch," I said before exiting her room.

As I walked down the hall, a new appreciation for life nearly overwhelmed me. Last week I'd been lamenting my wrinkles, and this poor girl just wanted to be able to leave this building and get back to her life. *It's a blessing to be healthy and to get older*, I reminded myself—something many of these kids might not get to experience. I would pray every day for Ashlyn's recovery.

My chest felt heavy as I continued walking. I stopped in my tracks when I spotted Brayden inside one of the rooms. He was talking to a boy and had on a volunteer badge like mine. I guess he and I both had the same idea today. He didn't seem to have noticed me standing just outside the door, so I listened to what he was saying.

"I got this for you." Brayden presented the kid with a box.

"What's this?"

"It's a bunch of books I took from my old room. I got them the last time I was home visiting my dad in Pennsylvania."

The boy read the title. "The Chronicles of Narnia?"

"Yup. It's this really cool adventure series. When I was younger and going through a tough time, I escaped into this world and never looked back."

"You think I'll like it?"

"I hope so. They made movies from the books, too."

"What is it about?"

"Well…" Brayden scratched his chin. "There are these kids. They were evacuated to the countryside of England during World War Two. They find themselves in an imaginary kingdom known as Narnia. There's this talking lion and an evil witch. You'll have to read it, but I'll be curious to know what you think."

"Thanks!" The kid ran his hand along the books. "I'll start tonight so I can get them back to you."

"These books are really special to me. But so are you, so I'm gifting them to you."

"You don't want them back?"

"Nah." Brayden held his hand up. "You keep them. Gift them to a friend when you're done." He suddenly turned to find me standing at the doorway. His eyes lit up. "Hey, you."

"Hi." I stepped inside. "I guess we both had the same idea."

"You were hanging out with a friend, too?" Brayden smiled.

"Yup. I just left Ashlyn."

"Cool." He turned to the boy. "Have you met Will?"

"I haven't." I held my hand up in a wave. "Nice to meet you, Will."

"You, too."

"I was just about to get going," Brayden told me as he stood. "Were you headed out?"

"I was."

He turned to Will. "I'll be back soon, okay?"

"Thanks again for the books."

"Next time I come, we'll talk about them. I wanna know what you think. You might need to refresh my memory on some stuff."

He high-fived the boy before heading out with me.

"That was so sweet of you," I told him.

"I really think he'll like those books. At least I hope so. He'd told me he likes to read. These kids… They need an escape so freaking badly, you know?"

"Oh yeah. My friend down the hall is sending me on a clothing assignment this afternoon."

He laughed. "To buy her clothes?"

"No. She wants me to dress a certain way tonight and send her a photo. It's interesting."

"You're her very own paper doll?"

"Basically." I cleared my throat. "What was the tough time you mentioned to Will?"

"Hmm?"

"You said you got into reading that series when you were going through a tough time as a kid."

"Oh." His expression darkened. "It was my mother. She, uh, sort of walked out on us when I was nine."

"Gosh. I'm sorry." I slowed my pace. "You never saw her again?"

"Only very sporadically through the years."

That hurt my heart. "I'm sorry. That must be hard."

He looked down as we walked. "I'm over it."

"Does anyone ever really get over that?" I asked.

"No choice." He turned to me. "You know?"

I nodded. And then I tried to stop where my brain was going. I'd like to think Brayden's interest in me had nothing to do with potential mommy issues. I intentionally changed the subject. "Where did you say we were going today?"

"Wherever you want."

"Wait, you said you needed my help picking out appliances, right?"

"I guess we should get that over with, yeah."

When Brayden and I pulled up at the home improvement store, we parked in two adjacent spaces.

The smell of plywood hit me the moment we entered, and Brayden's eyes gleamed under the bright fluorescent lights. "It's kind of nice being here with a guy," I said. "Normally I get hit on in these places."

"I don't blame those guys one bit." Brayden bumped into me playfully. "Although technically, you *are* getting hit on in here to-day—just by me."

"Damn." I snapped my fingers. "I thought I was gonna get a break."

We headed toward the appliances. "I loved listening to you talking to Will earlier. You seem to have a good rapport with kids."

"I love kids."

I swallowed. "You mentioned you want them someday…"

"I'm in no rush."

Yeah. That was exactly it. He had all the time in the world. Yet another reason we were not right for each other. I shook my head, vowing to forget the heavy stuff for now and just enjoy this time with him.

We picked out a stove fairly quickly, since only one model was available for pickup this weekend and that's when Brayden wanted to install it.

"What else are we getting here?" I asked.

"Fuck if I know. This whole thing was just a ploy to get you to come out here early."

"You didn't really need my help…"

He leaned in and spoke softly over my face. "I needed your company. But we do need to pick out bathroom tile, come to think of it."

We ventured to the tile section, where I chose a herringbone pattern that Brayden also seemed to like.

We checked out after that, and on the way back, I followed Brayden to the house to drop off the supplies.

"Is there a shopping mall near here?" I asked when we were done and walking back to our cars.

"We can probably find one. What do you have in mind?" He took out his phone.

"The girl I told you about, Ashlyn. I promised her I'd buy a couple of specific items to wear tonight."

"Ah. That's right. Going anywhere special?" He flashed a wicked grin.

"I told her I was going out with my friend…who's a boy."

He shook his head. "Ouch. Last I checked, I was a man. But you haven't given me a chance to prove that to you." He placed his hand on the small of my back, and a shiver ran down my spine. "Anyway, hop in my car. Let's go shopping."

Turned out there was a mall not too far from the project house. Once we got there, I dragged Brayden to the largest department store they had.

He looked around. "What are we looking for exactly?"

"I'm supposed to buy a pink dress to wear and send her a photo of me."

"You don't seem like a frilly, pink-dress person to me."

"I'm generally not. But I'm not opposed to stepping out of my comfort zone."

"Make sure you remember that later." He winked.

I rolled my eyes and laughed.

As we browsed the women's dress section, Brayden pulled a hanger off the rack. "What about this one?"

It was the color of Pepto Bismol, lace on the top with a frilly skirt.

"That might be a little much, don't you think?"

"I bet you'd look gorgeous in it."

"There really aren't a ton of pink dresses." I took it from him. "I'll try this one on."

I went to the dressing room while he waited outside. After I slipped on the frock, I realized why Brayden might have selected it. It had a steep neckline. But it was otherwise pretty perfect. It was fitted at the waist with the skirt flaring out in a whimsical way I knew Ashlyn would be pleased with.

After changing back into my clothes, I took the dress out with me. "I think we have a winner."

He sulked. "I was expecting you to come out and show me, you know."

"You'll get to see it tonight."

"Oh, I forgot. You have a date with a boy, don't you?" He chuckled. "We should go back to the hotel and get changed. I made us a reservation."

"Whereabouts?"

"It's a surprise, but you'll be good to go in that dress."

"We can't leave yet, though. I told her I would buy glass slippers, too."

"Say what?"

"Shoes that look clear, like Cinderella's."

"Ah…" He scratched his chin. "That's going to be a tougher challenge."

After we found the shoe department, I perused the selection as fast as I could.

There were no shoes at all that looked clear.

"I think I'm out of luck," I announced as I found Brayden in the clearance section. He had a box tucked under his arm.

He opened it. "What about these?"

Inside were a pair of marabou heels with pink fur covering the toe bed. They were made of clear plastic, though. And my size! *Bingo.* "I think these are the best I'm gonna get. Thanks for finding them."

He laughed. "I can't tell if they're sexy or something you'd find at the Bunny Ranch in Vegas."

"I'm thinking the latter."

Brayden had texted to say he was ready whenever I was, and I'd opted to meet him down in the lobby.

My marabou heels clicked against the marble floor as I approached.

Brayden looked fantastic in a fitted, collared shirt and black pants. His hands were in his pockets as he leaned against a pillar near the entryway. When he noticed me, he rushed over.

"Damn. You always look hot, but tonight?" He shook his head slowly. "Incredible. Talk about pretty in pink."

"That movie was before your time," I teased.

"I've seen it, wiseass."

I held out my phone. "Would you mind taking a photo of me? Before I start to look worn as the night goes on."

"Anything in particular you're planning to do to let your hair down and get all…worn?"

"Let me guess, you have some ideas?" I laughed.

"I didn't say that. You did." He held up the phone. "Say cheese."

I flashed a huge smile as he took a few photos and handed the phone back to me.

"Ready?" He held out his hand.

"Where are we going?" I asked, putting my hand in his.

"I booked us a dinner reservation at a local winery. We'll taste a selection of their offerings."

"Sounds great. You just did that today?"

"No, I called them a few days ago, since I've heard they get booked up, even on weeknights."

"So you were sure I was going to come out early?"

"I was pretty confident."

"That you are, Mr. Foster."

Brayden ordered a car that brought us to the Seneca Falls Winery.

When we arrived, a waitress led us to a beautifully decorated, candlelit table.

"Have you been wine tasting before?" he asked.

"Would you believe I haven't?"

"Nice." He pulled out a chair for me. "You'll love it."

"Thank you. I'm a little concerned about my inhibitions around you, though." I laughed.

"You don't trust yourself?"

Basically.

The waitress brought out sample after sample. I normally didn't mix red and white wines, but when in Rome…

Brayden and I also ordered two ribeye steaks. Indeed, my inhibitions were dwindling by the minute.

"You know what sucks?" he said.

I knocked back the last of my cabernet. "What?"

"Getting you tipsy was the dumbest freaking idea ever, because now I know I won't be able to touch you."

Well, that's a bit disappointing. "Why not?"

"Because I'd never know if you were only playing along because you're drunk."

I rubbed my leg along his under the table. "Well, since you won't be trying anything, I suppose it's safe for me to admit that you look good enough to eat tonight, Brayden, and it's a damn shame you won't be trying anything because I *very much* would've played along."

His eyes rolled back as he muttered, "Do you have any idea how much I want to fuck you?"

"I think I have a tiny inkling."

"I hope you give me the chance. Because I promise, you won't regret it."

"If you didn't have morals, I'd give you a chance tonight."

He waved his pointer finger at me. "That's the alcohol speaking, but believe me, I'll take what I can get, even if it's naughty talk."

I giggled, feeling happier and more carefree than I had in a long while. I also respected him so much for not taking advantage of my obvious desire for him.

On the car ride home, I might've had a full belly, but I was otherwise starving. I licked my lips. "Not even a kiss, huh?"

"Nope. Because that's how it starts. And believe me, once I start...you're not gonna want me to stop."

Yes, I was tipsy, but I was still aware. I very much knew what I was doing, what I wanted. And I wanted Brayden Foster. *Badly.*

After we got back to the hotel, I assumed Brayden would get into the elevator with me, but instead he held the door open to say goodnight while I got in.

"Aren't you coming up?"

"Nope."

"Why not?"

"Because there's a tiny piece of me that doesn't trust myself. Also, my room is on the other side of the hotel. So I'm gonna take the other set of elevators down the hall."

"Okay, well..." I tucked my hair behind my ear. "Today was really fun."

"I agree. Thank you for coming out here early, beautiful."

I'd definitely be *coming early* tonight—I planned to take care of this fire between my legs as soon as possible, in fact.

A few minutes after I got to my room, my phone rang. *Brayden.* I picked up. "Miss me already?"

"I do. Despite running away from you just now, I wasn't ready for the night to end."

"Me neither," I admitted.

"You know what else? I'm totally regretting not kissing you."

Shutting my eyes, I smiled. "There might be other chances."

"I hope so, Alex. I hope you don't come to your senses once the wine wears off." He chuckled. "Hey, did Ashlyn ever reply to the photo you sent her?"

"You know, I've been so distracted, I didn't check. Hang on."
I clicked on the text icon.

Ashlyn: This is the best! Now, show me Prince Charming.

"She loved it, but she wanted a pic of Prince Charming."

"Aw, man. I totally would've posed for her." He sighed. "I'd come over there now for a quick pic, but you know, I'm in my boxer briefs."

I sighed. "I think you should go say hello to Ashlyn personally next time you're at Memorial."

"That sounds like a plan. If I say I'm Prince Charming, she'll know who I am."

As Brayden and I continued chatting, I slipped off my shoes and slid the hotel room curtain to the side to see what kind of view I had. It faced another part of the hotel, another series of rooms. Then I noticed a man in a hotel room across the way, leaning against the window. He was wearing boxer briefs and looked like… an Adonis. He was also on the phone with *me* at the moment.

"Are your boxers black, by any chance?"

"Yeah. Why?"

"Do you always stand in front of hotel room windows half-naked, putting on a show?"

His head whipped up, and he looked across the courtyard between us. I waved.

"Holy shit. You've been watching me all this time?"

"No. I only just opened the curtain and saw you."

"What are the chances?"

"Nice abs, by the way."

"You weren't supposed to see me like this yet. Now my grand presentation is ruined."

I cackled. "Sorry."

"It's only fair if I get a little show, too," he said. "You know, I feel violated being the only one showing some skin."

"Oh, poor baby. Seeing me half-naked would make you feel better, huh?"

"Yeah. I think that's the only thing that will help."

Feeling frisky, I pondered giving him the show he was angling for.

Should I?

CHAPTER 8

Brayden

"**H**oly fuck," I muttered to myself. I'd completely forgotten I was still on the phone.

Alex's breathy voice reminded me. "I'll take that to mean you appreciate the view?"

Considering I was salivating, *appreciate* didn't feel like a strong-enough word. Alex stood at the window, pink dress gone, clad only in a nude, lacy bra and underwear. Fucking phenomenal was more like it. Where the hell was a set of binoculars when you needed one? What I wouldn't give to see that close up, run my fingers over the lace and feel her gorgeous curves beneath. "You're exquisite, Alex." I swallowed. "Would you turn around for me?"

The line was quiet, except for the sound of our heavy breathing. I stared across the way, feeling my heart hammer inside my chest. After a few seconds, she turned.

Thank you, Lord.

A thong.

A fucking thong.

I groaned. "What I would do to that ass if I were there…"

"Are you an ass man, Brayden?"

"I'm an *Alex* man. There's not one thing about you that doesn't turn me on. I'm not exaggerating either. Today when we were buying the stove, you asked the guy checking us out if he had any coupons lying around, and it made me want to wrap your hair around my fist and yank your mouth to mine."

"*Mmm...* That sounds really good."

I closed my eyes. "It's taking everything in me to stay where I am and not come to your room right now."

"Maybe that's what I want—your mouth on me, my hair pulled."

"Say that again tomorrow, sweetheart, and try to stop me—all that and more." I blew out a shaky breath. "Now turn around again so I can take one last look. As much as I'm loving every second of this, I don't want anyone else seeing you this way."

Alex turned. My eyes raked slowly up and down her incredible body, searing it into my memory. "Thank you."

"Sweet dreams, Brayden. I know I'll be having them."

"Goodnight, babe. Don't forget to pull the curtains."

"Okay."

After the line went dead, Alex wiggled her fingers in a wave before closing the drapes. With the peep show over, I turned and looked around my room. There wasn't much more to it than a bed, dresser, TV, and lamp. And I was way too wired to go to sleep now, even after all the wine we'd had tonight. I thought about going to the hotel gym, or maybe even out for a run. Although neither of those would be too comfortable with the erection currently bulging from my underwear. So I settled for a quick shower, figuring I'd take care of myself while conjuring up fresh images of Alex in her sexy underwear.

In the bathroom, I turned on the water and waited for it to warm up before peeling off my boxer briefs. I didn't even have to close my eyes to remember every detail—her striking blue eyes, naturally pink lips, her creamy, long neck. Her body was perfect, curvy—not rail thin like too many women aspire to be—hips that begged to have fingers dig into them, and a handful of tits I was almost positive were natural. Alex was all woman—so much so that she made every woman who'd come before her seem like a girl in comparison.

Yet at the same time, something about her felt oddly innocent—untouched or pure. Which, of course, was ridiculous considering she'd been happily married for a decade. Maybe I was just adding to the fantasy to get my rocks off—not that I needed more than looking at her. Closing my eyes, I let the warm water sluice over my shoulders and reached for my cock. But as I stroked up and down, a feeling I wasn't used to came over me.

Guilt.

It felt wrong to jerk off to Alex.

Why? I had no fucking idea. It had never been a problem before. Hell, I'd spent most of my freshman year of college jerking off to my married English professor, and she was married to a *woman*. Every Tuesday and Thursday I'd said good morning with a big-ass, guilt-free smile.

This is ridiculous.

I needed a release after seeing Alex practically naked. In fact, she probably *wanted* me to do it. I'd even wager that she was currently in her own room, writhing on the bed with her fingers inside her wet pussy, getting herself off.

Visualizing *that* took my already steely erection up a notch. So I reached for the conditioner, squirted a healthy amount into the palm of my hand, and went back at it. It felt good, but no matter how hard I tried, I couldn't seem to relax like I needed to in order to reach the finish line. It was frustrating as hell. Eventually, I gave up and got out of the shower. Hours later, I was still staring at the ceiling in the dark, wondering how I was gonna function with constant blue balls if I didn't get to touch Alex soon.

I was late getting to Ryan's House on Friday morning. Luckily most volunteers only came for Saturday and Sunday, so it was only the team leaders and two other volunteers who'd gotten into town early.

Alex smirked when I walked into the kitchen. "Good morning, sleepyhead."

I raked a hand through my hair. "What's so good about it?"

She bit her lip, trying to hide her amusement. "Did you not sleep so well?"

"No, I didn't."

"Gosh, I slept like a baby."

I grabbed a paper cup and pulled the lever on the Dunkin' Box O' Joe on the table. A few drops trickled out.

"Sorry," Alex said. "We finished the last of it. But I was just about to go pick up some waters. I can grab you a coffee."

"Whatever." I pouted.

Then Chad, another volunteer I hadn't realized was here, walked into the room. I wasn't a big fan of his, mostly because he was good looking, closer to Alex's age than me, and followed her around like a puppy.

"I'm going for a Dunkin' run," Alex said. "You want anything, Chad?"

"No, but I'll take the ride with you."

Great. As if I weren't already in a piss-poor mood. But whatever. I had shit to do. So I went about starting my day while the two of them disappeared. I was on my second trip hauling in boxes of tile from my car when a man walked up. He was dressed in tattered clothes, had silver duct tape wrapped around the front of one sneaker, and had a large green duffle bag slung over his shoulder. He looked vaguely familiar.

"Is this the Ryan's House project?"

I nodded. "It is. How can I help you?"

The man extended his hand. "Charlie Nolan. I'm volunteering."

I set down the box of tile and shook. "Good to meet you, Charlie."

He gestured to the tile and then my car, which was parked out front. "You got more of those in there?"

"About a dozen."

Charlie nodded. "Let me put my bag down, and I'll give you a hand."

"Thanks."

The new volunteer and I carried in the rest of the tile. When we were done, I smacked dirt from my hands. "You look familiar. Have we met before?"

"Were you at the last project?" he asked. "The one in Jersey?"

"I wasn't. Did you volunteer for that one, too?"

Charlie nodded. "I live in New Brunswick. Well, I used to anyway."

"Do you live here now? Upstate New York?"

He shook his head. "Not really. I'm sort of floating these days. A couple days here, a couple days there…"

It hit me where I'd seen Charlie before. Yesterday when I'd arrived, I'd parked my Porsche in a remote area of the parking lot—so it wouldn't get dinged by a big truck opening its doors. There had been a homeless guy setting up a cardboard shanty in the grassy area right behind me. I'd waved, but kept going.

"Well, we're glad to have you here. Do you mind if I ask what brought you to volunteer at Ryan's House?" It was a question I asked everyone. Some people just looked for a project to help out with, but the majority of our volunteers had a story—a reason they donated their time to a cancer-related charity. And those people liked to share what had brought them.

"My wife had cancer. Bone," he said. "She passed a year ago. While she was sick, we spent a lot of time in Texas, at the MD

Anderson Cancer Center, so Arlene could get some experimental treatments. Traveling, living expenses, and the cost of the uncovered medical bills wiped us out. I had to sell our little house in Jersey to keep up. Lost my job as an accountant after my family leave time was over. Not long after my Arlene died, I read an article about Ryan's House. I don't have a single regret about going through our savings and losing our house and my job. I'd do it all over again to have that time with her. But…if someone else doesn't have to go through what I did? That's a cause I can get behind."

"Wow. I'm very sorry for your loss. It sounds like you've been through a lot."

Charlie nodded. "It was a rough few years, but things are starting to look up. And I owe a lot of that to Ryan's House. For a while after my wife died, I'd sort of given up. No wife, no home, no job…it's easier to succumb to self-pity than to fight your way through the losses. Building the last project made me feel useful again. Made me remember, I might be sixty-one, but I've got a lot to offer still. Even have a job interview lined up for next week."

"Good for you."

Our conversation was interrupted when Alex and Chad came back in. I introduced everyone and told Charlie to stick with Alex. Something told me she'd be good for him. Then the appliance delivery came, and before I knew it, most of the morning was gone. I wasn't sure if it was Charlie's positive attitude that had brightened my day or the coffee, but I felt like less of a curmudgeon by the time I found Alex alone in the hall bathroom taking measurements.

She scribbled a number on her notepad and stuck the pencil behind her ear with a smile. "Hey. Feeling better than this morning?"

"I am now." I closed the bathroom door behind me. The room grew smaller.

"You look tired." She tilted her head. "Did you really not sleep well?"

"Nope. Slept like shit. You said you slept like a baby though, huh?"

Alex's cheeks heated. "I did."

I took a step closer. "Oh yeah? Anything you did before you fell asleep that helped?"

"Nope," she answered, *waay* too quickly.

I leaned so we were nose to nose. "*Liar.*"

Her pink cheeks bloomed into a full face of crimson.

"Tell me what you did, Alexandria."

She bit her lip. "You *know* what I did."

"Maybe. But I want to hear you say it anyway."

"Because you're an egomaniac?"

"Because I had to go to bed alone after you got me all worked up. Give me at least this little satisfaction."

"Fine. I touched myself. Are you happy?"

I smiled from ear to ear. "Ecstatic."

A knock at the door behind me interrupted our conversation. I opened it to find Chad. He tried to look around me to talk to Alex, but I wouldn't move. Except to broaden my shoulders. Too bad I wasn't a peacock, because I could've blocked his view entirely with my feathers.

"I finished up in the living room," he said. "Figured I'd see if Alex needed any help."

"She doesn't."

"Oh… Okay."

"But I could use someone to clean out the gutters, if you're free." *Nothing like cleaning muck and bird shit with your hands instead of hanging out in a tight little bathroom with Alex.*

Chad's face fell. "Sure."

"Thanks."

Alex scolded me once I shut the door again. "You aren't very nice to him."

"Maybe he should spend more time focused on what he came here to do instead of the woman he wants to do…"

She rolled her eyes. "Chad's a nice guy. He's not interested in me in that way."

"Uh-huh."

"He's not."

I folded my arms across my chest. "Care to put your money where your mouth is?"

"What do you mean?"

"I'll bet you that Chad asks you out before this project is over."

"What are we betting?"

I grinned. "Oral sex."

Alex's eyes widened. "That's crazy."

I lifted a brow. "Doesn't matter what you bet if you're sure you have a winning hand, right?"

"Fine. But he's not going to ask me out, so you won't be getting a blowjob."

"You're right. I won't be. Because when I said oral sex was the prize, I meant *giving it*." I whispered in her ear. "You have no idea how badly I want to taste you, sweetheart."

"Hey, Charlie?"

He stopped setting up his makeshift house at the far end of the parking lot and turned around. "What's up, Brayden?"

I extended a hotel room keycard. "Room two-eighteen."

His bushy brows dipped. "You need help carrying stuff?"

"Nope. It's your room. I prepaid it for a week."

"Why would you do that?"

"You have a job interview next week. Figured you could use some good sleep, and you need to be able to shave and stuff before your appointment."

"That's very nice of you. But I can't accept it. It's a few hundred dollars a night for a room here."

"You told me why you give to Ryan's House. But I didn't get to tell you my story. My buddy Ryan had leukemia. He had a lot of time on his hands during treatments and hospitalizations. We were both engineering students. I kept him company, and during that time we developed a technology that sold for a lot of money after he died. His half of the profit goes to build houses to help cancer patients. So I'm not giving my money to a charity. I'm giving his away to honor him." I extended the key in my hand again. "You're honoring your wife by donating your time. Let me honor my buddy this way. Please."

Charlie's eyes welled up. He nodded and accepted the key-card. "Thanks, man."

"I also made you an appointment at a suit store a few blocks from the project house. Tomorrow at ten AM. Whatever you pick out is prepaid, and the tailor said he can get the alterations done in twenty-four hours. I'll go with you."

"I don't know what to say, how to thank you."

"No thanks necessary. Just tell your Arlene to keep an eye on my Ryan."

He smiled. "You got it."

I helped Charlie pack his stuff, and we walked into the hotel together. Alex was at the desk, so I told Charlie to have a good night and went over to see what she was up to.

"You're not checking out, are you?"

She shook her head. "No, my key isn't working. My wallet has a magnetic closure, and it keeps deactivating the swipe card. I need to remember to keep it in my pocket."

I nodded.

She lifted her chin to Charlie, now waiting for the elevator. "He seems like a really nice guy. I talked to him a bit today. I guess he's staying here, too?"

"Yep."

"Good. I was a little worried he might be sleeping in his car or something."

"Nope. All good."

The woman behind the desk gave Alex a new keycard, and we walked to the elevator together. I pressed the button, and the doors slid open. "You up for some dinner?"

The look on Alex's face told me the answer before she spoke. "I don't think that's a good idea. Last night was…a mistake. I had too much to drink and…" She shook her head. "It just shouldn't have happened."

My heart sank. I wasn't sure if it was the lack of sleep or being rejected one time too many, but I didn't have the heart to argue with her. I forced a smile. "Okay."

"I'm sorry."

I raised a hand. "It's fine. Nothing to be sorry about."

An hour later, I was still feeling glum when room service knocked on my door. I'd ordered a bunch of shit I normally wouldn't allow myself to eat—macaroni and cheese, a BLT, and a side order of tater tots from the kids' menu. Just as I sat down to munch away my sadness, my phone buzzed. Alex's name flashed on the screen. I was tempted not to pick it up, but I couldn't help myself.

Alex: Is it too late to take you up on your offer for dinner?

I started to type back, but decided it would be quicker to call. She answered on the first ring. "Hey, Brayden."

"I'd love to have dinner with you. But what made you change your mind?"

"Charlie."

"Charlie the volunteer?"

"Yeah. I went to get a water from the vending machine on my floor, and he was there getting ice."

"Okay…"

"He told me what you did for him. The hotel room, the suit… It made me realize my attraction to you is more than just physical. I'm attracted to the man you are, Brayden. I don't know

80

where this can go or what it means, but I know I would love to have dinner with you."

"How does ten minutes in the lobby sound?"

"It sounds perfect."

I did a quick cleanup—swiping on deodorant and brushing my teeth—then wheeled the food cart out of the room with me, and down the elevator. At the second floor, I stepped off, walked down to room two eighteen, and knocked.

Charlie opened the door and looked at the cart. "What's all this?"

"Dinner."

"Wow. Thanks, Brayden."

"Don't thank me. Thank Ryan. Actually…" I smiled. "I think Ryan did me a solid tonight, too. So we both can thank him."

CHAPTER 9

Alex

Dinner with Brayden tonight had not helped my predicament in the least. I was even more hot for him than I'd been earlier in the day. Our conversation had flowed so easily. After I'd asked him to tell me more about his job, Brayden had explained some of the ideas he had for future prosthetic designs. He really impressed me. And for a guy who could be cocky when he wanted to, Brayden was quite humble. He hadn't bragged about helping Charlie. He could've used that to his benefit, but he didn't.

After we came back from the restaurant, we stepped into an empty elevator and headed upstairs to our respective rooms.

"I don't want this evening to end," he said. Brayden stared hungrily at my mouth but stopped short of doing anything.

I desperately wanted him to kiss me. Suddenly his lips were only inches from mine. But he still didn't budge. *Is he waiting for permission?* I couldn't wait another second to taste this man, and in a flash, I decided to go for it. Leaning in, I pressed my lips to his, appreciating the low groan of satisfaction that emanated from his throat.

"Fuck, yeah," he muttered over my lips. Brayden pulled my body close, his rock-hard erection growing against my abdomen.

Opening wider, I let his tongue in, appreciating the hint of beer. Our kiss grew deeper as I raked my fingernails through his hair.

Oh, God. This is—

Then the doors slid open.

We pulled back, but not before a few of the volunteers from Ryan's House who'd been waiting for the elevator caught us.

I looked down as Brayden and I walked past them, without acknowledging anything. Once we were a few feet down the hall, I got a glimpse of the massive bulge in his pants.

He caught me looking. "What do you expect? I'm like a fucking animal in heat for you, Alex."

Panting, I knew with absolute certainty that if one of us stepped into the other's room tonight, we'd be having sex. And as much as my body wanted it, I wasn't ready to cross that line. Because then what? "Goodnight," I announced before walking away without looking back.

I wasn't surprised when a text from Brayden came in shortly after I'd escaped into my room.

Brayden: How am I supposed to make it through two more days with you?

Alex: That's exactly why I left. The less time alone the better. Look what happens when we're alone.

Brayden: I liked how you took what you wanted.

Alex: It can't be more than that kiss.

Brayden: You're killing me. But I know this isn't about you playing hard to get. You're not ready. I need you to be a hundred percent comfortable. Because I want you to give every bit of yourself to me with nothing holding you back. I can be patient.

Alex: There's pretty much just a tiny string holding me back at this point.

Brayden: Remind me to bring my scissors tomorrow. ;-)

The following morning, I slept in before heading to the worksite. I needed the sleep after being wired with uneasy excitement the past couple of days. When I finally showed up around eleven, Brayden was nowhere to be found.

After last night's blue balls repeat, had he decided he couldn't stand to be around me? My mind ran wild as to why he was a no-show. He had questioned how he was going to get through two full days with me. Maybe he'd finally agreed that the less time we spent together the better?

One of the women I knew had seen Brayden and me kissing in the elevator last night came over as I was about to get started peeling some wallpaper.

"Hi," I said. She looked as though she wanted to say something.

"I don't believe we've formally met, even though you and I have been working alongside each other." She held out her hand, which had some paint splatter on it. "I'm Cora."

"Alex. So nice to meet you."

Cora was tall with short brown hair. She was wearing denim overalls.

"Can I be nosy?" she asked.

"Sure."

"You and that hottie Brayden... A few of us saw you kissing in the elevator last night, as you probably know."

"I do." I cleared my throat. "Sorry for the spectacle."

"Oh, please." She waved her hand. "It was hot as fuck."

"Well, happy you think so. It wasn't meant to be a show, though."

"You guys were so into it, you barely noticed the elevator doors opening."

"We got a little carried away."

"I think that's amazing." She tilted her head. "So when's the wedding?"

I turned to the wall and began scraping. "There's no wedding. We're not even dating."

"Really? Well, you had me fooled."

"We're mainly…flirting."

Scrape.

Scrape.

Scrape.

"Damn. That's some flirting, then."

"He's too young for me."

Scrape.

Scrape.

Scrape.

The longer Brayden and I hung out together, the more my excuses seemed flimsy. If I didn't believe what I was trying to sell, how could anyone else?

"Then I suppose you wouldn't mind if I made a play for him?" Cora asked. "Dude's smoking hot."

A rush of heat rose from the base of my neck to my head as I abruptly stopped scraping.

"Oh my God. You should see how red you just got. I was totally joking. Also, I'm totally gay. I have more interest in you than him. You don't swing both ways, do you?"

"I don't."

She laughed. "Okay, then why are you denying what's obviously an amazing connection? Age is just a number anyway."

"Even aside from the age difference, Brayden and I…are in two different places in our lives."

"It looked like you were in exactly the same place last night." She looked over my shoulder. "Speak of the devil…"

I turned to find Brayden walking in with Charlie. Immediately, I felt like an idiot for wondering where he was. *That's right.*

Brayden had told me yesterday that he was taking Charlie this morning to get fitted for a suit.

Brayden headed straight toward me, carrying two coffees.

He held one out. "I figured you could use this."

I took it. "Thanks. I had a coffee at the hotel, but could really use another."

"Long night?" Brayden arched a brow.

I felt my face heat as I peeled back the plastic lid.

"Were you up late doing anything in particular?" He flashed me a mischievous grin.

"Why is that any of your business?"

He lowered his voice. "Because we started it, and I want to know how it finished without me."

"It finished great."

"Damn, what I wouldn't have given to be a fly on the wall for that. Or better, a bedbug with a front-row seat."

I couldn't help but laugh.

He winked. "I forgot… I'm not supposed to say bedbugs around you."

Taking a sip of my coffee, I couldn't believe it. *Is that cinnamon? A hint of caramel?* It was precisely the way I liked it. Glancing down at the details printed on the side of the cup, I noticed he'd indeed figured out my usual order.

"How did you know how I take my coffee? I never told you."

Brayden tapped the side of his head. "I'm just smart like that."

"No way. Oat milk with two sugars, one pump of caramel, and a dash of cinnamon? That's way too specific for you to have gotten lucky."

"You brought a coffee with you to the house one time. I memorized what was on the sticker on the side, so I'd know what you like."

Wow.

For some reason, my thoughts went to my husband, God rest his soul. Richard was always too busy with work to bother with

86

such minute details. He couldn't have told you how I took my coffee if his life depended on it. I never faulted him for that. I understood. It just wasn't in him. Now, though, it felt foreign to have such attention placed on me.

"That's not the only thing I know about you," Brayden went on to say.

"Oh really?" I blinked. "Do tell."

"Blue is your favorite color. You've worn it approximately four times. That's how I know."

He's right.

"One of your eyes is slightly darker than the other. It's subtle, but I notice it because I'm constantly staring into them."

It's getting hotter in here.

He continued, "You write with your left hand but eat with your right. You lick the corner of your lips when you're nervous." He smiled. "Should I go on?"

Please don't, because I don't know how to stop liking you.

After work that afternoon, Brayden accompanied me back to the hotel. We somehow found ourselves in an empty elevator again. Before I could even contemplate whether we'd end up in the same predicament as last time, Brayden had backed me up against the wall.

"You kissed me first last night. So…an eye for an eye," he muttered over my lips before taking my mouth with his.

Ohhhhhhh. My legs felt weak as I melted into him. He wrapped his hands around my face and kissed me harder than I'd ever been kissed. So commanding. So freaking perfect. When the doors opened, he pushed back immediately. Thankfully, this time there was no one standing there who knew us.

We started down the hall, and I knew that kiss had been way too short. My mouth burned with unsatisfied desire. I needed more. My nipples were hard, and my body was in flames as I walked along with jelly legs.

He brushed against me. "Come to my room so I can finish what I started."

I wanted to. Or at least every inch of my body did. But I *knew* what would happen.

"I can't," I said.

"This isn't just about sex, Alex." His hair was sticking up a little. "I want to date you. Why can't you take my interest in you seriously?"

"Are you dating anyone else?" I blurted.

He stopped in the middle of the hallway. "No."

My chest rose and fell. "You're not seeing someone back in New York?"

"What part of no don't you understand? Now, what time are we going to dinner tonight?" When I hesitated, he said, "I'll meet you downstairs at eight."

Then he walked back the other direction, toward the elevators, and disappeared.

I caught myself licking the corner of my lips. He was right. I did do that when I was nervous.

That evening, Brayden took me to an Indian restaurant he'd wanted to try. The food was spicier than I normally liked—too hot to handle, like pretty much everything else about this day.

At one point he left his phone on the table while he went to the bathroom. It lit up with a call, and a woman's face appeared on the screen. She had long black hair and dark red lipstick. She was beautiful, and I panicked inside.

Jealousy tore through me. *I'm too old for this shit.* He said he wasn't dating anyone. I *wanted* to believe him. But who was this gorgeous woman?

Brayden returned to the table, and his smile faded as he got a look at my face. I guess I wasn't very good at hiding my emotions.

"What's wrong, Alex?"

I slid his phone toward him. "You missed a call."

He narrowed his eyes and looked down. "Yeah. Okay. It was Billie…"

"Who's Billie?" My heart pounded.

"My buddy Colby's wife." His eyes widened. "Wait, did you think…" He exhaled. "I get why you might've assumed that."

"Who bothers to upload a photo of his friend's wife to his caller ID? I would never have imagined that's who she was."

Brayden rolled his eyes. "*I* didn't upload it. She did. Billie grabbed my phone one day and did it to bust my balls. Did you not notice she's giving me the middle finger in that pic?"

I hadn't. I'd been too busy noticing how beautiful she was.

"She said I never answer my damn phone, and that's why she did it." He sighed, and then a lightbulb seemed to go on. He snapped his fingers. "You know what? You and Billie need to talk." He scrolled on his phone.

"What? What are you doing?" I asked.

Brayden waited for her to pick up. "Hey, Billie. What's up? I saw you called…" He scratched his chin. "Oh, yeah. Tell Colby I got them down to two thousand. I meant to fill him in on that." He paused. "Listen, I need a favor. I'm on a date right now. Her name is Alex. I need you to talk to her and tell her she can trust me." Without further warning, he handed the phone to me.

I cleared my throat. "Um…hello?"

"I can't believe that jackass just handed you the phone." She laughed.

"It's because I saw your photo on the screen when you called and thought you were more than a friend after he'd told me he wasn't dating anyone." I sighed. "You're very beautiful, by the way."

"Aw, well, I like you already and don't even know you."

"I'm sorry. This is terribly awkward. Not sure what I'm supposed to say right now…" I looked over at Brayden, who stared at me intently.

"I don't know you or what's going on between you and Brayden," she said. "But I can tell you a couple of things even so."

"Okay…" I licked the corner of my mouth.

"Brayden never talks about the women he dates. He's generally the most secretive of the bunch. So, the fact that he wanted me to speak to you says a lot. And one thing he's not is dishonest. None of the guys in their circle are. If you ask them a question, you can bet their answers are the truth, even if you don't wanna hear it."

"Thank you." I nodded, letting out a relieved breath. "Anything else?"

"Not that I can think of. Just if you're ever in the city and need a tattoo, I'll get you in without an appointment. Any friend of Brayden's is a friend of mine."

"Well, that's very generous of you. It would be my first tattoo, if that ever happened."

"Then we definitely need to rectify that."

"It was nice talking to you, Billie."

"Same, Alex. Bye."

I handed him back the phone.

"Thanks, Billie." After he hung up, he crossed his arms. "Did she have anything interesting to say?"

"She deems you trustworthy."

"See?" He winked. "Don't get me wrong, Alex. I like that you might've been a little jealous."

"It wasn't only jealousy. It was also…fear."

"Why are you so afraid of me?" he asked. "I swear, I'm not out to hurt you."

"I know you're not looking to hurt me, Brayden."

"But you're still looking for reasons this can't work."

"I'm not gonna lie…sometimes you seem too good to be true. I do believe you're a genuinely good person. The way you've been helping Charlie, your work with kids—both with the prosthetics and volunteering. You never brag about anything or try to use it to your advantage. All of that stuff makes you even hotter than the way you look."

"If that kind of stuff makes you more hot for me, I should let you know I helped a little old lady across the parking lot today."

I cackled. "You're funny, too. That's another thing in your corner." I paused, trying to collect my thoughts. "My fear, though, relates to whether I am the right woman for you."

His expression turned serious as his tone grew softer. "Let's talk about it, then."

"I think sometimes in life you have to look beyond the present moment. There's not a single reason why you and I don't work *right now*. But there are things that will come up in the future and cause us to end badly. For example, you want kids. You said it yourself. That's not something I would likely be able to give you. So, essentially, isn't that a deal breaker?"

"Of course not," he said.

My eyes went wide. "How can you say that?"

"There are ways to have kids besides biologically. Unless you wouldn't be open to that, either?"

"I don't know." That was the truth.

"While I understand you thinking ahead about the potential problems we could face many months or years from now, that's not how I operate, Alex. If Ryan's death taught me anything, it's that we need to live every day like it's our last. I could get hit by a truck tomorrow. And you know what? The thing I'd regret most is not getting to see where things went with you."

My heart lurched. "You're unbelievable," I mumbled.

"Come back to my room tonight, and I'll show you unbelievable."

"That's dangerous, and you know it."

"Absolutely."

"I don't think so."

"How about if I promise to be good? Not try anything. Seriously, I hate that our nights end so early because you're afraid to be alone with me. We have such limited time as it is. Why can't we be in a room alone together and not have sex?"

I was still pondering that question as we headed back to the hotel. Tonight, we didn't get lucky with an empty elevator, so I never got my kiss. After we stepped off, I still hadn't decided whether to go back to his room.

Brayden stopped me midway down the hall, wrapping his hands around my waist and backing me against a wall. A shiver ran the length of my body.

"How about this…" he said. "I swear on Ryan's soul that I will not make a move on you if you come back to my room. I won't touch you."

I nodded. "Well, now I know you're telling the truth. But I'm still going to my room."

"Why?"

"I don't trust *myself* not to make a move on *you*."

His eyes filled with mischief.

"Goodnight," I called as I once again ran off to my room alone.

"It's a good thing your favorite color is blue, because it matches my balls *perfectly*," he yelled after me.

❤CHAPTER 10

Alex

I couldn't seem to relax. Not even after a hot shower. Unlike the other night when we'd had a little window peep show, it wasn't my body that needed settling. It was my mind. Though anytime I was around Brayden, my body hummed with desire, so it wasn't like I couldn't get into a round of self-care. Yet while I was certain it might relax me a bit, I also knew I'd be staring at the ceiling in the dark after. I needed to talk out what I was feeling. Picking up my phone, I looked at the time. It was almost eleven, but Wells would definitely be up. I was the one in our friendship who went to bed early.

I scrolled down to the last name in my contacts and hit the video button to FaceTime.

Wells answered on the third ring. He said hello, but I could barely hear him over the pulse-pounding music. "Give me a second! I need to step outside!"

I watched the screen as he walked, passing dozens of men dancing. He was definitely in a club. Eventually the loud music settled into the background, and I could see he was outside. Wells lifted the screen to his face, and his buddy Kennedy jumped into the video over his shoulder.

"Hello, Kitten! Are you calling me to tell me you just knocked boots with youngblood?"

"*Oooh*. A younger man?" Kennedy cooed. "Deets, please."

I sighed. "I didn't sleep with Brayden."

Wells pointed to the screen and looked at his buddy. "Do you see the lines in her face? She either needs dick or Dysport." He turned back with a frown. "Honey, this is why old maids die alone—they have a full face of wrinkles from lack of orgasms."

I chuckled. "I hate you."

"Well you're interrupting Gays Night Out, so spill the beans. What's going on? If something wasn't on your mind, you'd be in dreamland. Tell Daddy what happened."

"Brayden and I had a great dinner, and then he kissed me in the elevator."

"I *looove* elevator kisses," Wells said. "Why are they so freaking hot?"

"I don't know much about other elevator kisses, but kissing Brayden was definitely hot. If we would've gotten stuck between floors for even a few minutes, I would've had sex with him."

"You should have hit the red button! That's what it's there for. Emergencies!"

"I once did that in the Empire State Building," Kennedy said, pulling the phone to face him. "And when we got off the elevator, security escorted us to the exit. Apparently they have cameras in some of them." He held up his pointer. "They did *not* start the car moving again until we'd finished. So I think whoever was watching us was busy busting their own nut, but *whatever*."

Wells tilted the cell back to him. "What happened after the kiss? Let me guess. You blew him off when you should've *blown* him off?"

My shoulders slumped. "I chickened out and practically ran to my room."

"What are you so afraid of?"

"I don't know. Getting hurt? What if six months down the line, he realizes he wants biological children? Or he wants a woman who can share his firsts—first marriage, first home, first child to raise. What if after a year—"

Wells cut me off. "Jesus, Alex. You're lucky I'm here and you're there because if I was standing next to you, listening to you ramble about ridiculous shit like you are, I'd Joan Crawford bitch-slap you across the face to smack some sense into you."

"But—"

Wells held up a hand. "No buts... We've been best friends since we were what, eight years old? Have I ever steered you wrong?"

"Except for the shoulder pads you told me looked great in my *prom dress*? No."

"I still think you looked fabulous. It's not my fault the girls at our school had no taste and decided to dress like hookers. But forget that. Have I ever steered you wrong in relationship advice? You had to kiss a lot of frogs to find your prince of a husband, and I always knew who was a toad and who had potential before you, didn't I?"

Wells did have an uncanny ability to see the truth in the men I went out with. In fact, he'd told me I should marry Richard after our very first date.

"No." I sighed again. "You've never steered me wrong."

Wells smiled. "I am pretty great, aren't I?"

"Let's get back to me, egomaniac."

"Fine. Let me ask you something simple. How are you going to feel when this volunteer project ends if you never see Brayden again? Do you think you'll be sad? Wonder what would've happened if you'd taken a chance?"

I didn't have to think very long. "I would wonder."

"Then here's my advice, Kitten. Stop worrying about whether you can marry this guy, and go have fun. Take it one step at a time. You only live once. You can get over trying something that doesn't work out—I promise you that. But you never get over the regret you have from the things you didn't try. Tomorrow you could get hit by a Mack truck and then what? You die without having enjoyed that hot man's dick."

The last part made me smile. But I supposed Wells was right. I mean, there were risks to any relationship, weren't there? A guy my own age could break my heart just the same as a younger one, even if the reasons were different.

I took a deep breath and nodded. "Okay."

"That's my girl. Now go jump that man and call me in the morning to thank me."

I smiled. "Thanks for letting me interrupt your night."

"This wasn't an interruption. It was a divine dick intervention."

"Enjoy the rest of your night, guys."

Wells held the phone out and curtsied. "Later, Kitten."

After I swiped to end the call, a weight lifted off my shoulders. I still wasn't sure if Brayden was *right* for me in the long term, but I was determined all over again to focus on the *right now* instead.

I thought about texting Brayden, telling him about my change of heart. But I'd been so hot and cold, and he deserved better than that. So I got dressed, swiped a little mascara on since I'd already washed off my makeup, and headed over to his room.

When I got to his door, my courage wobbled a bit. But this was exactly what I *wasn't* going to do anymore. *Overanalyze*. I liked Brayden and wanted to spend time with him. Simple as that. So I took a deep breath and knocked.

Brayden opened the door *with no shirt on*. My jaw dropped.

He smiled, clearly recognizing the effect he had on me, and grabbed the top of the door. The pose accentuated the curve of his bulging biceps, the cuts in his six-pack abs, the deep V carved into his waist. My eyes couldn't stop jumping around, unsure what to focus on first.

Brayden lifted a brow. "See something you like?"

Of course, the cocky jerk couldn't give me a free pass. I rolled my eyes. "I like you a lot better when you're humble."

"Really? 'Cause you seem to like me a whole lot half naked..."

"You know, you're making what I came here for harder."

"Trust me, you make it *hard* for me too." He chuckled. "Would you like to come in?"

I shook my head. "It's safer to stand right here. What I came to say won't take more than a minute."

"Okay…"

I took a deep breath and blew it out. "I like you, Brayden. I've been pushing you away because something about you scares me. But I don't want to do that anymore. I want to take a chance, see where things go."

"Wow. Really?"

I nodded.

"I'm freaking psyched. But can I ask what made you change your mind?"

I shrugged. "I don't want to look back and have regrets."

Brayden smiled. "Come here."

"Where?"

He crooked his finger. "Kiss me."

I took two steps forward and pushed up on my toes, pressing my lips to Brayden's. The second we connected, he took over. He wrapped a hand around my waist and turned me so my back was against the open door. Our lips fused. It was slow at first, but then he grasped the back of my neck and tilted my head, deepening the kiss. His other hand went to my ass, and he hitched me up, guiding my legs to wrap around him.

He groaned. "Fuck. I feel how hot and wet you are through our clothes."

My legs tightened around his waist. "*Stop talking. More.*"

It felt euphoric, like I'd finally given in and couldn't wait to give it all. After a few minutes of groping and grinding in the doorway, it was Brayden who pulled back. He wrestled his mouth away and leaned his forehead against mine. We were both panting.

"Gotta stop now, Alex. You came here saying you felt safer staying outside, and I'm about two seconds away from dragging you into my room and stripping you naked."

I pouted, but knew it was the right decision. Later, I'd probably appreciate that one of us had found some self-control. Though my body would need to stop throbbing by then. Brayden took my bottom lip between his teeth and gave it a firm tug.

"You said you don't want regrets. I don't want you to have them either. So I'm going to have to ask you to go back to your room."

I sighed. "You suck."

Brayden smiled and set me on my feet. He looked down, and my eyes followed to find a bulging hard-on. I licked my lips. Brayden groaned and pointed down the hall. "Go. *Run!* And lock the top lock on your door."

The next morning, there was a knock at my door at eight AM. I opened to find Brayden with a picnic basket in hand. "What are you doing here so early?" I asked.

"I know you have to leave right after the project today, and I didn't want to wait a whole week for our first official date."

Warmth spread through my chest. "That's so sweet." I stepped aside. "Come on in."

Brayden hesitated.

I laughed. "I need to finish getting ready. It'll only take five minutes. I think we can control ourselves that long."

He didn't look so confident, but nevertheless came inside. Brayden set the basket on the dresser. I couldn't help but be nosy and peek inside. "Oh my gosh. Where did you get all this?" I asked.

There had to be at least four different types of cheese, fresh strawberries, cherries, grapes, and breads. Not to mention a bottle of orange juice and a big bottle of champagne. He even had champagne glasses and an opener.

"There's a twenty-four-hour market over in Guilderland."

"Guilderland? That's like a half hour away, isn't it?"

Brayden shrugged. "I couldn't make a picnic out of Cheez Whiz from the gas station, now could I?"

"What time did you go there?"

"About six."

I shook my head. "I can't believe you did all this for me. You are the sweetest."

"I'm actually not." Brayden frowned. "I'm a pig."

"Why are you a pig?"

He slanted his eyes to a pair of underwear I'd left on the bed. "Because while you were rummaging through that basket, I was trying to figure out if I could swipe those and take them home without you noticing."

I covered my mouth and giggled. "Maybe we can't control ourselves in here. Just give me a few and I'll be ready to go."

I went into the bathroom and finished drying my hair, then brushed my teeth. I was already dressed, but before I went back out, I decided to do a quick change.

Brayden was fiddling with his phone, sitting on the edge of the bed. He stood. "You all ready?"

"I am."

He grabbed the basket. "There's a park about a mile away. I thought we could go there. I have a blanket in my car."

"Sounds good. But I have a gift for you first." I walked over and used a finger to pull out the front pocket of his jeans and stuff what I'd hidden in my fist inside.

He looked down. "What was that?"

I pushed up on my toes and pressed a kiss to his lips. "My underwear."

He glanced to the bed and back. His brows drawn tight.

"Not those," I whispered. "The ones I just took off, so they smell like me."

♥

Brayden tossed a grape into the air and caught it with his mouth. His head rested on my lap, legs spread out longer than the blanket, while I looked down and enjoyed the view.

"I have one. What did you think of me when we first met that night in the bar?"

We'd been playing a version of Truth or Dare for the last hour, except our version was Truth or Kiss. We took turns asking each other questions, and if you didn't want to answer, you had to kiss the other person wherever they pointed. So far, I'd kissed Brayden's cheek, neck, and mouth. It would've been a dangerous game if we weren't in a public park with kids twenty feet away on the swings.

"I thought you were very handsome," I said. "And funny. And clearly modest since you just dragged this compliment out of me."

Brayden smiled and held up a grape. I leaned down and took it from his hand with my mouth. "What did you think of me?"

"I thought you were the most beautiful woman I'd ever seen."

I started to laugh, assuming his corny answer was an exaggeration, but his face was dead serious.

"I'm not kidding," he said.

"So you're telling me you thought I was more beautiful than say…" I tapped my finger to my mouth as I chewed. "A supermodel? Like Gigi Hadid or Kaia Gerber?"

"Absolutely."

"I think you need glasses."

He shrugged. "Believe what you want. But I'm telling you, I've never been more attracted to a person in my life. My entire body felt it."

I rolled my eyes, but I think I was more *afraid* to believe him than anything. There were plenty more-beautiful women than me. Yet I could've sworn Brayden was being honest, and that scared the crap out of me. I reached for my second mimosa and finished the last of it. "My turn. Have you ever been arrested?"

Brayden's face fell. "Where do you want the kiss?"

"Really? You're not going to answer that one?"

"We've been doing so well, and I don't want you to think less of me."

"I'll take the kiss if you really aren't comfortable sharing, but I feel like I should know if I'm spending time with a hardened criminal."

"It was once, and they knocked it down so I just paid a fine."

"Come on. Now I'm so curious. Tell me."

Brayden sighed. "Solicitation of prostitution."

My jaw dropped. "You got caught picking up a sex worker?"

"I was at a bachelor party in Vegas for one of my buddies. One of the guys had hired a stripper, but she canceled at the last minute. I got dragged down to some sleazy strip club to see if we could find a replacement. I didn't even want a damn stripper to begin with. I just wanted to gamble and get drunk. Anyway, apparently the place we went to had been under investigation because it was a front for a prostitution ring. We had no clue. My buddy I went with started flirting with a dancer, and I just wanted to get the heck out of there, so I asked the guy working the door if any of the girls could be hired for a private party. He asked what I wanted, and I said dancing. Then he asked me if the dancer needed to do any tricks. I swear I didn't know he meant sex. A few months before, another buddy had gotten married, and the stripper shot ping pong balls from between her ass cheeks. So that's what I was thinking. I said sure and asked if that would be extra. He pointed me to a woman sitting at the bar and told me I needed to pay her. I paid whatever the guy asked. Thirty seconds later, I had cuffs slapped on me."

I covered my mouth. "Oh my God."

Brayden frowned. "Do you believe me?"

"Why wouldn't I?"

"Because it's hard to believe someone could be as much of a dumbass as I was."

"I suppose if there's any area where it's admirable to be a dumbass, it's that area."

"What about you? Ever been arrested?"

"No."

Brayden's phone chimed. He groaned and dug it from his pocket. "I set an alarm to let me know when we had five minutes left."

"Oh."

He smiled. "It makes me feel better that you don't look like you want to leave either."

"I don't."

"How about one last question?"

"Okay."

"You asked the first one, so this one's mine."

I laughed. "Why do I have a feeling you've had whatever it is in your pocket all day, waiting to ask?"

"Because you're a very smart cookie." He tapped my nose. "What's your biggest turn-on in bed? What can I do that will drive you wild?"

"Oh boy. I hate to disappoint you, but I'm going to take a kiss and not answer."

Brayden pouted. "Really? You don't want to share that with me?"

I leaned down and brushed my lips with his, keeping them there when I spoke. "It's not that I don't want you to know. It's that I think it will be more fun for you to figure it out."

His lips curved into a smile. "I can't fucking wait."

Eight hours later, it was finally just Brayden and me alone again. We'd both been busy at the house all day, and we'd barely seen each other. I had to leave tonight, so I waited until we could say goodbye in private.

Brayden swung our joined hands back and forth. "What time do you have to be at the spa?"

"Midnight. The promo is called Midnight Madness. Wells came up with it last year. We open at midnight and stay open for twenty-four hours. All our services are half off, and we serve free champagne and finger foods all day and night. The first time we did it, I thought we'd be empty at midnight. But we advertised in places like hospitals that have multiple shifts. You'd be surprised how many women came in after work and loved it."

Brayden pulled me to him. "I'd like to get a service from you."

I smiled. "I bet."

"When are you going to sleep?"

"I'll take a short nap when I get home. Then Wells and I will take turns napping whenever it's slow."

"Would it scare you if I told you I'm already dreading not seeing you all week?"

I shook my head. "It actually makes me feel better. Then I know I'm not alone in feeling that way."

"Can you come a night early next week again? On Thursday?"

"I think so. But I need to double-check the schedule at work when I get back."

"I'd like to take you out on a better date."

"A better one? I know it was short, but I really enjoyed our picnic this morning. I had a good time. It's going to be hard to top."

"I like a challenge."

I tilted my head. "Is that what I am, Brayden? A challenge?"

"No, sweetheart. You're not the challenge. You're the prize."

♥CHAPTER 11

Brayden

I t was like I lived two different lives now—my usual one in New York City, and the life I couldn't wait to get back to upstate. The latter was much more exciting.

Getting through the week was growing tougher. I was antsy for the days to pass.

On Wednesday afternoon, I decided to walk home from work to expend some of my energy. It was a clear, cool September day in the City with not a cloud in the sky. It made me wish Alex were here. How I would love to take her to dinner at my favorite Italian restaurant, then bring her back to my place and—well, there was no end to the things I'd want to do with her alone in my apartment. Knowing Alex, though, she'd make some excuse and run before we got to that point. Not to mention, bringing her back to the building would raise some eyebrows among the friends I hadn't been keeping apprised of my personal life as of late. I couldn't wait, though, to have Alex here for a visit.

Almost at my building, I passed the café around the corner and found Colby's wife, Billie, and Holden's wife, Lala, sitting by the window chatting. Billie looked up for a moment and noticed me. Smiling, I attempted to keep moving, but Billie urgently waved me in. I should've known I wasn't going to get away with nonchalantly walking by.

"Not so fast!" she mouthed through the glass. "Get over here."

Great. No doubt she wanted more information after the phone call I'd subjected her to with Alex last weekend. Probably about time I explained that. "What's up, ladies?" I asked as I entered.

"What's up with *you*, Brayden Foster?" Billie smirked.

"Not too much." I smiled guiltily.

"Not too much, huh? That's not what I heard…" Lala winked.

The smell of fresh coffee wafted in the air, the sound of grinding a welcome distraction from the inquisition.

"You know what? I could use a pick-me-up," I told them. "Be right back."

I walked over to the counter and decided to order Alex's favorite drink, see what all the fuss was about.

"I'll have a coffee with oat milk, two sugars, one pump of caramel, and a dash of cinnamon, please."

"Can you repeat that?" the barista said.

I laughed inwardly at what a dork I was as I repeated the order.

After he made it, I took my coffee back to the table where Billie and Lala were eagerly awaiting my return.

"Now spill," Billie said the moment I sat down. "This Alex must be pretty damn special for you to put her on the phone with me. You're normally so secretive."

"She *is* special."

They both *awww*ed in unison.

"Tell us about her," Lala said.

So I told them the tale of my experience thus far with Alex. They listened attentively as I recounted my growing attraction to a woman who wasn't making it easy. It felt good to let it all out, though. It made me realize how many emotions I'd kept bottled inside lately.

"How much older are we talking?" Billie finally asked.

"That's the funny thing." I chuckled. "I don't actually know."

Lala's eyes widened. "Really? How is that possible?"

"Told her it didn't matter to me, and she never specifically divulged."

"That's wild." Lala licked foam from her mouth.

Billie pursed her lips. "You must have *some* idea, though…"

I shrugged. "Ten years-ish, maybe a little less, maybe a little more. But I don't really give a damn. She's physically the hottest woman I've ever known, and there's something so special and unique about her. She's not superficial or one-dimensional. She cares about people. She just started volunteering at the hospital. And she's *lived*, you know? Lived and *lost*. Her husband was a lot older than her. He left behind a daughter—Alex's stepdaughter, who's ironically around my age. Anyway, losing a spouse like that? It has to change you, help you understand your priorities. It's why she's being so cautious. As annoying as it can be, I kind of love that she's taking her time and not just jumping into things." I sipped my drink—sweeter than I normally liked it, but still tasty. "I'm honestly loving the chase."

Lala crossed her arms. "But on some level, her taking her time means she's hesitant. Why do you think that is?"

"I *know* what her hesitation is. She thinks we want different things and are at different places in our lives. Alex knows I want kids. I think that scares her."

"She doesn't want kids of her own?" Lala asked.

"I think she feels like the opportunity for that has passed."

"She thinks she's too old?" Lala frowned.

"I'm not entirely sure," I admitted.

"If she doesn't want or can't have kids, does that matter to you?" Billie interjected.

"Not enough, honestly."

"Well, it doesn't matter to you *now*, during the infatuation period," Lala said. "But it might later."

"A lot of things might happen *later*. I could get struck by lightning *later*. I don't really care about the later in life. The time is always now. No one is guaranteed tomorrow. Your brother, Ryan, taught us all that, remember?"

Lala nodded.

Billie took a sip of her coffee. "Okay, but I can understand Alex's concern. I mean, if she knows she's not going to have kids and you want them, that's a serious consideration. It makes sense why she wouldn't want to get her heart involved with someone she thinks she'll have to let go someday."

I shook my head. "Life doesn't have to be that hard, that complicated. A lot of people can't have kids. What do they do? They figure out a way around it. They adopt. Or they find other joys in life."

"Wow." Lala leaned back in her seat. "I can't say I've ever seen you this into a woman."

"That's exactly it," I said. "She's a real *woman*. And when something feels right, you want to share it." I stared down into my cup. "Although…Holden is really the only one of the guys I've told about her. Owen's been so wrapped up in Devyn. He and I haven't caught up in a bit." I turned to Billie. "But you're welcome to fill Colby in."

"Oh, you *know* I will." She winked.

That evening, Colby, Owen, Holden, and I had our board meeting at a local bar. The meetings were to discuss building business, but we mostly got the boring stuff out of the way so we could shoot the shit and tool around for a couple of hours.

Tonight, though, I decided to duck out early, after one drink. Holden followed. "Wait up," he called, placing his hand on my shoulder. "I know why *I'm* leaving early. I have a sick baby at home. But what about you? Why'd you rush out of there?"

We stepped into the cold night air and began to walk, side by side, back to the building.

"I have a phone call to make."

"To Alex, I take it? Lala told me she and Billie were giving you the third degree earlier today."

"Yeah. I tried to walk past them at the café, but that didn't work. So I joined them instead."

"I hadn't realized how much things have escalated between you and Alex. You guys were talking about kids and shit?"

"Only in the context of Alex not wanting them," I clarified.

"Still, even just *mentioning* it. That's some serious stuff. Lala kept saying how smitten you seem."

"*Smitten* is a strong word," I said, though she was right.

"How come you didn't mention anything about Alex to the guys just now? You were totally vague the whole night."

"I'll fill them in another time. I still don't know how it's gonna pan out. As much as I like her, *she's* not there yet. So I don't have anything solid to report. I guess I don't want to jinx it and get ahead of myself, you know?" I sped up my steps. "By the way, can you walk faster? Why the hell are you so slow?"

"What's the rush?"

"Alex seems to think ten PM is late, and I want to catch her before she goes to bed."

"Yeah, you're not smitten." He chuckled as we picked up the pace.

Back at my apartment, I sent Alex a text.

Brayden: Are you down to FaceTime? Or am I too late?

A few minutes later, she sent a reply.

Alex: I'm actually out with a friend.

Hmm...

Brayden: A friend?

Alex: Wells. We're having tapas.

Relief washed over me—her gay friend and business partner.

Brayden: Ah.

Before I could text anything else, my phone rang.

It was Alex. Except when I answered the FaceTime call, it wasn't Alex's face on the screen. It was some dude wearing an earring.

"Wow. You're even more stunning in person," he said.

"Wells..."

"I love hearing you say my name," he purred. "Say it again."

I narrowed my eyes but complied. "Uh...Wells?"

"I'm sorry, Brayden!" I could hear Alex say from somewhere behind him.

Wells glanced over his shoulder. "I asked Alex who she was rudely texting while we were having dinner. She wouldn't tell me, so I grabbed her phone. When I saw it was you, loverboy, I gave her a pass. But I think it's time you and I had a chat."

"I'm here for it, Wells. And I suppose this is payback since I made Alex talk to my friend Billie the other day."

Wells scratched his chin. "So, I have some questions..."

"Shoot." I settled into my couch, feeling my pulse speed up.

"What are your intentions with my friend?"

"You don't start out light, do you?"

"Well, I was gonna ask whether you shave your pubes, but, you know, first things first."

"Ooh-kay." I chuckled. "Got it."

Alex stuck her head in. "I'm so sorry—"

"No worries, Alex. I can handle this."

He glared at me. "Well?"

Rubbing my palm on my pants, I cleared my throat. "My intentions are honest, Wells. But I can't make any promises about what the future holds for us. We're still getting to know each other. Right now, I just want to keep spending time with her. I have no intention of playing games. I'm serious about wanting to see where things go. I love her company. I love all of her little idiosyncrasies. And I count the days until she and I can be together on the weekends. I've never experienced anything like this before. And as I've told Alex, I can be as patient as she needs me to be." I exhaled.

"From what I hear, you've been *quite* patient. Might be going for *Guinness World Records* for blue balls…"

Ain't that the truth. "She's worth it."

"I agree." He took a sip of what looked like a Cosmo, then set it down. "Now, let's get to the nitty gritty…"

I raised a brow. "That wasn't the nitty gritty?"

"No. Not in the least. We're just getting started."

Damn. I was the one who needed that Cosmo. "Okay…" I sighed and licked my lips.

"Why an older woman, loverboy?"

"Why not?"

"Good answer. But you're gonna have to give me a bit more than that."

"My attraction to Alex isn't because of her age. I want *her*. Plain and simple. The age part is a non-issue, as far as I'm concerned. Therefore, I can't really answer *why an older woman*. I didn't set out to meet an older woman. I met Alex. End of story."

I'd thought that was clear enough and hoped he'd let me off the hook, but no such luck.

"But there *is* an age difference. Might there be a reason you're drawn to Mrs. Robinson?"

"Mrs. Robinson?"

"That's a term for an older woman who dates a younger man. You've never heard that before?"

"Nope."

"Well, that shows your age." He winked.

"Anyway…" I rolled my eyes. "I've never been drawn to an older woman before. So it's not a habit. It's the first time for me."

"So you're *inexperienced* with older women, then…"

I sighed. "I guess you could say that. But I don't see that as a bad thing. Alex has never dated a younger guy either. So we're even."

"Hmm…" Wells tilted his head. "Any mommy issues?"

"Wells!" Alex shouted from behind him.

"It's fine, Alex," I said, hoping she could hear me. Taking a deep breath, I admitted, "My mother did leave home when I was nine."

His expression turned serious. "Do you think that could have something to do with your attraction to an older woman now?"

Quite honestly, I found that assertion annoying. It actually made me a little angry, but I tried not to show it. I needed this guy on my side. "I don't see what my mother leaving has to do with anything. If you want to deconstruct my mother's abandonment and somehow correlate it to my attraction to Alex, go ahead. But it would be impossible to prove. Is it possible that there's some connection to my mother I'm not aware of? Maybe. *Anything* is possible. But it's not a conscious correlation for me. Why does there have to be a reason for me to want to be with Alex besides just really liking her?" I paused. "Does your family history dictate who you're attracted to, Wells?"

"Definitely not."

"Well, there you go."

"Fair enough." He nodded. "What do you like best about her?"

"How much time do you have?"

"All night, my friend." He took a sip of his drink.

"I'll say this… My absolute favorite thing about Alex is her heart. Just the circumstances of how we met tell you what a good person she is, so giving of her time. The more I get to know her, the more examples I find of that. But, honestly, man, I could never list all the things I love about her. It's just…everything." I closed my eyes momentarily. "I love everything."

When I looked again, Wells seemed lost in thought with a goofy smile on his face. "Any other questions?" I asked.

He sighed. "Yeah. When are you gonna come to Connecticut so I can size you up in person?"

"Whenever Alex invites me, I'm there." Feeling a weight lift from my chest, I winked. "You can hook me up with a spa service."

"You're too damn perfect. Not sure there's much we can do for you. I would suggest maybe teeth whitening, but yours are pretty damn spectacular as is."

"Well, you both have an open invitation to come to Manhattan. Anytime."

"That's something I can get down with."

I had a sudden thought. "Are you single, Wells?"

"Yeah. Why?"

"I know a guy. He just became single recently, too. Name's Deek. He's good shit. Lives in my building. I can hook you up."

"*Deek*. I like the sound of that."

"You like 'em big and brawny?"

His eyes sparkled. "Do I ever."

"Tatted up?"

His eyes widened. "Fuck yeah!"

I winked. "Let's talk."

He finally turned to Alex. "I like this guy." He handed her the phone.

Her beautiful cheeks were pinker than I'd ever seen them. "Can I call you later when I've kicked him to the curb?"

"Of course."

"Thanks."

She ended the call, and I laid my head back and took a few moments to decompress from that mini-interrogation. After, I busied myself around the apartment.

About a half hour later, the phone rang. It was a regular call from Alex, not FaceTime. I picked up. "Hey. Isn't it way past your bedtime?"

"I don't normally go out so late on weeknights, but Wells wanted to try that tapas place, so…"

"I'm kind of disappointed you didn't FaceTime me just now. I was counting on getting to see you."

"Well, considering I've just taken my face *off*, you're out of luck." She laughed.

"You don't wear that much makeup, though."

"I know, but I like to look my best for you. So I prefer a little help."

"Trust me, you don't need any help. And fair warning, one of these days I want to see it all—bare face and bare everything else." I paused. "Speaking of bare, Wells apparently forgot to ask about my pubes when all was said and done."

"There's always next time." She laughed and let out a long breath. "I'm sorry again about tonight."

"No apology needed. But it's funny, I feel like I've spent this entire day on the stand when it comes to us."

"What do you mean?"

"Before Wells, Billie, and Holden's wife, Lala, gave me the third degree. It was the first time I'd seen them since I put you on the phone with Billie. So naturally, they wanted to know what was up."

"And then Wells saw an opportunity tonight and took it. I hope that wasn't too painful."

"I'm happy you have friends like Wells who care enough to grill the guy you're dating."

"*Are* we dating?"

"Alex, I think about no one else and count the days until I can see you on the weekend. If that's not dating, I don't know what the hell is."

❤CHAPTER 12

Alex

"Wow…you look great."

I'd answered FaceTime to find my smiling stepdaughter. "Are you and Wells going out for your birthday?" she asked.

"Actually, I'm already in New York, upstate for the Ryan's House project."

Caitlin wiggled her brows. "Ooh. You're going to see the hottie? No wonder you look smokin'. You never wear eyeshadow anymore."

"Is it too much?"

"Hell no. It makes your eyes pop. You should wear it more often. What's going on with youngblood anyway? You haven't mentioned him in a while."

I sighed. I'd thought about talking to Caitlin about Brayden again. The two of us didn't keep many secrets, especially since her dad died. But something kept stopping me. She'd encouraged me to get back out there, but a part of me wondered if her saying it and me *doing* it were two different things. Caitlin had revered her dad, and I thought she might feel a bit territorial about me moving on when push came to shove. Or…was I just telling myself that as an excuse to not share because part of me was still ashamed to be dating a guy her age?

Ultimately, both reasons were stupid and not worth risking the open relationship I'd worked so hard to establish with her over the years.

"I'm…" I nibbled my lip. "…going on a date with him tonight."

Caitlin shrieked so loud, I couldn't help but smile. "You naughty girl! I love it! Tell me everything about him. The only thing you've spilled is that he's my age. Big whoop-di-doo. I want to know the rest."

I smiled. "Well, he's very handsome. Muscular, but lean. But what I like most about him is he's humble."

Caitlin rolled her eyes. "Humble bumble. Does he have a six pack?"

I tried not to grin, but failed. "I think it's more like an eight pack."

"So you've seen him naked already? Go, hot momma!"

I chuckled. "No, I haven't seen him naked." While I was sharing, I drew the line at mentioning Brayden's window peep show. "I went to his room to talk to him once, and he answered without a shirt."

"So what are you two kids doing tonight that has you all glammed up? Is he taking you somewhere special for your birthday?"

"I haven't actually mentioned that my birthday is this weekend. But we're going out to dinner."

"Are you nervous?"

"Very. We've gotten to know each other pretty well over the last month, so it's not like typical first-date jitters with someone I just met. I think it's more the prospect of taking our relationship to the next level. I'm not sure what his expectations might be for… after the date."

"Well, these days most people have sex *before* they know each other a full month like you guys have. So I suppose you're overdue."

My eyes widened.

Caitlin cackled. "Oh gosh. I'm sorry. You look like you might poop your pants. I didn't mean to make you even more nervous or say anything was expected of you. I just meant if you feel like it's the right time, it's not too early."

"I haven't…you know…since your dad. I've gone on a few dates, but none of them got to that point where we were intimate."

"Oh wow. It's been a while, then. Well, I can certainly understand why you're nervous. But I'm pretty sure it's like riding a bicycle, just hop on and *ride, girl, ride*." She grinned. "Pun intended."

A few minutes later we were still on the phone when there was a knock at my hotel room door. I took a deep breath. "I think he's here."

"I'll let you go."

"Alright. I'll call you tomorrow. Wish me luck!"

"Good luck. Love you, Alex."

"Love you too, sweetheart."

I lowered my phone and started to swipe off, but Caitlin yelled, "Wait!"

I lifted my cell back up. "What's the matter?"

"Nothing. I just wanted to say that Dad would want you to be happy. He wouldn't want you to be alone."

My eyes welled up. "He was a good man."

"And it's not just Dad who wants to see you that way. I do, too, Mom."

Mom. I had to wipe a rogue tear that escaped. "You're going to ruin my makeup."

"Eh. It's going to get ruined when you're all hot and sweaty in a little while anyway." She winked. "Have a great time."

After I hung up, I took a few deep breaths to compose myself before opening my hotel room door. But any attempt at controlling my emotions flew out the window when I got a look at Brayden. His normally shaggy hair was slicked back in an old-fashioned-movie-star way, and he had on a full suit and tie. He held up a black hat box, stuffed with at least two dozen white roses.

"For you."

"They're beautiful." I touched the petals of one of the flowers. "Wow, are they real?"

He nodded. "They're preserved roses. Supposed to last a year. I figured you wouldn't have a vase here, and even if the hotel gave you one, it would be a pain in the ass to take regular flowers home. Plus, if these things last as long as they say they do, you're going to be reminded of me for a long time to come."

"Thank you." I smiled and stepped aside. The man really did think of everything. "Come in. I just need a minute to slip my shoes on and apply some lipstick. I was on the phone with my stepdaughter and lost track of time."

"No rush." Brayden let the door close behind him, then caught my hand. "But before you put on that lipstick…" He gave my arm a quick tug, and I practically fell into his chest. His eyes sparkled as he cupped my cheeks. "I have been dying for this all week."

Brayden's lips crashed down on mine, and I melted into him. If it were possible, he tasted even better than I remembered. After a minute, I felt him growing hard against my stomach.

"I fucking missed you," he growled into my mouth.

If he hadn't already had me lost in his kiss, the needy sound of his voice would've done me in. It was raw and real and left no doubt that he wanted me. It also made me ache with need. I was seconds away from stripping off my clothes when there was another knock at my door.

I ignored it, but eventually Brayden wrenched his mouth away. He leaned his forehead against mine. "I hate whoever that is."

I groaned. "Me too."

Neither of us made a move to answer the door, and I might've stayed quiet hoping they'd just go away so we could get back to the kiss. Though no such luck. Whoever it was knocked again, this time louder. Brayden used his thumb to wipe under my lip and tilted his head toward the door. "You're going to have to answer. I need a minute."

I smiled. "Okay."

I assumed it was housekeeping or some other hotel employee, so imagine my surprise when I swung open the door and found *Cher*.

The woman had to be six-feet tall *without* the giant feathers sticking out of the hat on top of her head. She had a mane of black curly hair, and her mouth was overlined with bright red lipstick. "Are you Alex Jones?"

I took a hesitant step back. "Yes?"

She smiled and held her arms up. "Happy birthday from your best friend, Wells!" She pushed a button on her iPhone, started some music, and belted out a full rendition of "If I Could Turn Back Time" followed by "Happy Birthday, You Bitch." Guests came out of their rooms and joined us in the hall to watch. I couldn't stop laughing. The woman was really good. She even sang out of the side of her mouth like Cher. Brayden stood behind me, looking a little confused, but this was par for the course for Wells. After the show was over, the woman handed me a dick lollipop while Brayden dug some cash from his billfold and tipped her.

I shut the door, still laughing.

"What the hell was that?"

"Apparently Cher."

"Is it really your birthday?"

I nodded. "It's Sunday. But Wells and I celebrated this morning before I left Connecticut. His dad passed away on my birthday a few years back, so we changed our celebration to three days earlier."

"Why didn't you tell me?"

"Because unlike you, I've stopped celebrating getting another year older."

He raked a hand through his hair. "I have to leave Sunday—I have an appointment early Monday morning."

"It's fine. It's just another day."

"Is it…a big birthday?"

I raised a brow. "Are you asking me if I'm forty? Or worse yet, *fifty*?"

"I don't care how old you are. But I would've liked to have done something for you."

I grabbed his tie and pushed up to kiss him. "If you play your cards right, I might let you *do something for me* before the weekend's over."

Brayden groaned, but my little tease seemed to erase the stress wrinkles from his forehead. "Go do what you need to do," he said. "Or we're going to be late for dinner…by a couple of days."

"Would you like another bottle of wine?" The attentive waiter looked back and forth between Brayden and me.

He shrugged. "I'm game, if you are."

"Sure. Why not?"

Brayden reached across the table and laced his fingers with mine. "If I'm being honest, I don't even care about the wine. I'm just not ready for the night to end."

I smiled. "Me neither."

Before the waiter interrupted, Brayden had been talking about the new project he was working on—a superhero leg for a boy who'd lost his to bone cancer. I'd witnessed firsthand the excitement his creations brought a child, but the way Brayden's eyes lit up when he talked about the details, I was pretty sure he got just as much out of making the prosthetics as the kids did receiving them.

"You know, you've inspired me," I said.

He wiggled his brows. "To take off your clothes?"

I chuckled. "To do more for cancer survivors. I can't make artificial limbs or anything as cool as you, but I *can* offer free services to patients going through treatment to spoil them a little. Like facials and massages, and we've even started offering banana bags—IV vitamin infusion. But really, I could offer anything they were in the mood for, to give them a day to relax and be pampered."

"I think that's a great idea."

"Thank you. I sort of stole it from a handsome guy I know."

The waiter returned with our wine. He showed us the label before opening the bottle, then poured a sample for us to taste before filling our glasses.

I sipped and watched Brayden over the rim of my glass, getting lost in thought for a moment.

Not surprisingly, he noticed. "What's going on in that head of yours?"

"How do you know I'm thinking about something?"

He pointed to my face. "Your eyes glaze over and sort of go out of focus when you're trying to figure something out."

I shook my head. "Is there anything you don't notice?"

"Not about you..." He sipped his wine and set down his glass. "Talk to me. What's bugging you?"

"Nothing really..."

He gave me a look that said I was full of shit.

I sighed. "I was thinking I should probably not have another glass of wine after this."

"You're feeling it?"

"A little."

"I would never try to take advantage of you, if that's what you're worried about."

"Oh no. It's not you I'm worried about. It's me."

Brayden's brows shot up. "You're thinking about taking advantage of me?"

"It's all I can think about these days."

"And that's a problem, because…"

"I haven't…you know since my husband."

"You haven't had sex since your husband?"

I nodded.

"Wow. Okay. Well, I'm glad you told me that. Not that I was planning on pressuring you, but I'll rein it in. I want you to be sure."

I smiled sadly. "You saying that just makes me want you more."

He winked. "I can't help it if I'm irresistible."

He was joking, but I really did find the man impossible to resist.

Brayden leaned across the table and lowered his voice. "There's no rush, Alex. Okay? I want your head clear when and if it happens, and I don't want you to have regrets the next day."

"Thank you for being so understanding."

We clinked our glasses together.

A little while later, we were back at the hotel, and Brayden walked me to my room.

"Would you like to come in?" I asked.

"Yes. But I'm not going to."

I was disappointed but understood. "Okay."

He tilted my chin up and planted a sweet kiss on my lips. "I'm crazy about you, Alex."

My heart squeezed. "I'm crazy about you, too."

"Go in." He tilted his head toward my door. "I can't even trust myself to give you more than a peck. And lock the door behind you. I'll wait."

"Thank you for dinner."

"Thank you for taking a chance on me."

The next two days were busy at Ryan's House. A couple of volunteers had come down with the flu, so we were shorthanded, and everyone had to pitch in a little extra to get things finished by the time we left tonight. Brayden and I didn't get to spend much time with each other during the days, but we still had breakfast and dinner together. Something had been brewing between us since the first moment we met, but this weekend it felt like things had moved into relationship territory. And you know what? I liked it. The more time I spent with him, the more my fears subsided.

The front door at Ryan's House had barely closed behind the last volunteer when Brayden pulled me into his arms. "Get over here, birthday girl."

I giggled. "I thought those pesky do-gooders would never leave."

Brayden took my face in his hands and planted a chaste but passionate kiss on my lips. My entire body relaxed into him.

"I changed my appointment tomorrow," he said. "I'm taking you out for your birthday tonight."

"Really? You didn't have to do that."

"I want to. You're important to me, and I want to show you that."

I looked back and forth between his eyes. "You already have, Brayden. Every single time I'm near you, you make me feel special."

"It's not hard to do, because you are." He kissed my forehead. "Come on, let's get out of here."

On the drive back to the hotel, I stared out the window, thinking. I wanted this man more than I could ever remember wanting anything. A few days ago, I'd felt like holding back on a physical relationship was the right thing to do to protect my heart, but the truth was, my heart was already in pretty deep. If things went sour now, it was going to hurt. So why not enjoy myself to the fullest? Like Wells and Caitlin had advised me a *number* of times.

We walked from the parking lot to the hotel entrance. "Are you in the mood for anything in particular?" Brayden asked. "Italian, sushi, French?"

I was, but it wasn't anything found on a menu. "I want... you."

Brayden stopped in place. "Come again?"

I threw my arms around his neck. "I want *you*, Brayden."

"Are you sure?"

I smiled. "I'm positive. The only thing I want for my birthday is to spend the night with you, Brayden Foster."

"Well then..." He grabbed my hand and dragged me through the lobby. "Let's go, woman. Chop, chop."

I laughed. "How about I take a quick shower, and after I'll meet you down here? We can grab a quick bite in the hotel restaurant and maybe bring a bottle of wine back to my room when we're done?"

"That sounds like a birthday gift for *me*."

"How does an hour sound?"

"Like fifty-nine minutes too long. But okay."

My body hummed as I took a shower and got ready. Now that I'd made the decision to sleep with Brayden, it couldn't happen fast enough. I almost texted him and suggested we skip dinner, but the way I was feeling, he was going to need his energy.

Anxious, I headed down to the lobby a few minutes before we were supposed to meet. When the elevator doors slid open at ground level, I stepped off but stopped when I caught sight of a woman standing with her luggage.

My brows furrowed. "Caitlin?"

She threw her arms up. "Surprise!"

I hugged her. "Oh my God. What are you doing here?"

"We've spent every one of our birthdays together since I was a kid. I didn't want to break tradition. Besides, when we texted yesterday, you said youngblood wasn't going to be around for your birthday. So I thought I'd take you out."

"Oh." I forced a smile, not wanting to hurt her feelings and tell her Brayden had changed his plans and I'd very much been looking forward to our private night together. "Thank you."

A few seconds later, the other elevator car dinged. Brayden stepped out looking freshly showered and shaved. He smiled when he saw me and walked over.

Caitlin turned, and her eyes grew wide. "Brady?"

"Kate?"

Maybe I was in denial, but I didn't immediately understand what was going on. I stood there confused while my stepdaughter swamped Brayden in a big hug.

"It's been forever. How are you, Brady?"

I looked at Brayden, still lost. "Brady?"

Caitlin stepped back. "Alex, remember the guy I went out with for a while in college who was supposed to go skiing with us over Christmas break? You and Dad had a big fight over it because he still wanted to treat me like I was twelve and insisted that if a boy was coming on the trip, we'd have to stay in separate rooms? But then Dad wound up having to cover someone at work so we never went."

I blinked a few times. "I…I think so."

She pointed to Brayden. "Well, this is him. Brady and I went out during my junior year of college."

❤CHAPTER 13

Brayden

The room felt like it was swaying. Kate...was Alex's stepdaughter, *Caitlin*? The Kate I'd dated for a few months in college. The Kate who was so sweet I didn't know how to break her heart when I began to lose interest, so I'd just distanced myself until *she* ended things. *That Kate.* The Kate who deserved better than the immature guy I'd been back then. The Kate who was from fucking Connecticut and used to talk about her beautiful, young stepmom she looked up to. *That Kate.*

Fuck!

Caitlin.

Kate.

This can't be happening.

There was no time to figure out the best way to handle this situation. I had to move quickly. My gut instinct was to protect Alex. And the only way I knew how to do that was to pretend she had nothing to do with me.

"Nice to meet you." I smiled as I stared into Alex's eyes, silently pleading with her to forgive me. *Please forgive me.*

She swallowed, her voice barely audible as she began to play along. "Hi."

126

"What are you doing here in Seneca Falls?" Kate asked.

In a daze, I turned back toward her. "Just, uh, here on business."

She nodded. "What are you up to these days?"

I glanced over at Alex, whose face had turned practically white. Feeling outside of my own body, I said something trite to Kate about my job—I mentioned living in New York and the building. I might've asked her what was going on in her life, but I sure as hell didn't absorb the answer. My brain was on autopilot while my heart was going a mile a minute trying to make sense of this. How had this never occurred to me? Surely there were clues I'd missed.

I needed to get the hell out of here, because standing in front of them and lying through my teeth while Alex was clearly hurt wasn't something I could continue for much longer. "It was so great seeing you again after all this time, Kate. Truly. But I'm late meeting someone, and I forgot something upstairs, so I'd better go."

"Good seeing you, too," she said. "Take care."

"Enjoy your evening." I gave Alex one final apologetic look before walking away.

My heart raced as I dashed back into the elevator.

It felt like I was floating down the hall as I headed to my room in a surreal fog. How had this night, that was supposed to be epic, turned into my worst nightmare?

Once inside my room, I paced. All that mattered was getting to Alex and figuring this out. I needed to find a way to talk to her tonight, needed to make sure she was okay. But I knew that wasn't going to happen. It killed me that Alex was hurting and I couldn't comfort her. It killed me even more that *I* was the cause of her pain. Never in my life had I wished so badly that I could turn back time. But this whole thing would've come out eventually.

I needed to talk to someone. The first person I thought to call was Holden. He was the only one of the guys who knew how things had been developing with Alex. Although he wouldn't have a solution for me, I needed to let this out before I went insane.

After dialing him, I pulled on my hair as it rang.

He picked up, and I could hear his baby daughter, Hope, babbling. "Hey, man, what's—"

"I'm going out of my mind, Holden."

"What's wrong?"

"You're never gonna believe what just happened."

"Try me."

"Do you remember me mentioning a girl I dated back in college named Kate?"

"Vaguely, maybe?"

"We weren't together that long. Like a few months."

"Don't freaking tell me you have a child you didn't know about. Am I gonna have to start calling you Colby?"

I laughed bitterly. "That scenario might be easier than the one I'm currently dealing with."

"Well, fuck. What can be worse than that? Tell me what's going on."

"Alex and I were having a nice weekend. It's her birthday. Tonight was supposed to be…" I hesitated, deciding not to share what was *supposed* to happen tonight. "It was supposed to be special. But her stepdaughter just showed up here, maybe to surprise Alex for her birthday. Well, turns out Alex and I were *both* surprised."

"I'm not following."

"Her stepdaughter and my old college girlfriend, Kate, are one and the same."

"Oh. Shit. No way!"

"Yeah."

"How did you not figure this out before?"

"I'd never seen a picture of her stepdaughter. And Alex always referred to her as Caitlin. Caitlin went by Kate in college. Now that I think of it, Kate was from Connecticut. So is Alex. But that's such a minor similarity. I would've never thought to connect the two. Everyone I went to school with called me Brady, remember? That's what I told them my name was—figured it was short for Brayden. I'd had that stupid idea that I wanted to create a new identity at college, and that shortening my name to Brady would somehow help. Boy, that came back to bite me in the ass."

"Okay, so that's why her daughter didn't make the connection…"

"I guess." I shook my head. "God, this is so messed up."

"Alright." He sighed. "It is…but listen, as hard as it may be to believe right now, it's not the end of the world. What you had with Kate wasn't serious, right? And it's been a decade. Very good chance she doesn't give two shits about any of this. So who cares?"

"Pretty sure Alex does. There's no way she's gonna get over the fact that Kate and I were together at one time, no matter how many years have passed. And there's absolutely no way she'd do anything if there was a chance it would upset her daughter. I *know* her. It's family first. Alex and Kate? They're all each other has. Alex and *me*? We're done." My voice cracked. "We're fucking done, Holden."

"You need me to come there?"

"No, man. Thank you, though. I appreciate the offer."

He sighed. "I don't know what to say. This is the craziest shit that's ever happened to one of us. I'm truly sorry."

"Figures it would happen to *me*." I rolled my eyes. "I'm more worried about Alex than anything, though. She'd *finally* decided to trust me. I don't know if she's told Kate the truth by now or not. Either way, it's a shitshow."

"Wait…back up. The daughter hasn't figured it out yet?"

"Everything happened so fast. I'd just gone downstairs to meet Alex when I saw them both standing there. Kate recognized me before Alex could introduce us. Once I figured out what was happening, I didn't know what to do. I basically pretended to introduce myself to Alex, made small talk with Kate for a minute or two, and then left. I can't imagine what's going on in Alex's head right now."

"Okay. Here's what you're gonna do…" he said. "You're gonna breathe. Calm the fuck down. And don't beat yourself up about this, Brayden. You didn't do anything wrong."

"Sure as hell doesn't feel that way." I exhaled. "At the moment, I feel like the worst person on the planet."

"Sometimes things happen for a reason, even if we can't figure out why."

"I have a hard time believing that *anything* good could possibly come out of this."

"I'm putting my money on your ex not caring as much as you think she does."

"Even if it didn't bother Kate—which I highly doubt, because who wouldn't be fucked up by this situation—it's the principle of the matter. Alex is a woman of principle. She overthinks everything. Super cautious. And Alex especially values her relationship with Caitlin…Kate…more than anything. She told me it took years for them to get to where they are today. Alex would never risk hurting her."

"Well, try not to jump to conclusions. As much as you think you know how this is going to play out, you might be surprised."

"I'd give anything to be wrong, man." I let out a long breath. "I'd better let you go."

"You sure? I can stay on as long as you need to."

"Nah. I need to think about this alone for a while."

"Alright. You call me if you need me."

"I will, dude. Thank you. I appreciate you trying to calm me down."

After several minutes of bouncing my legs up and down as I sat on the bed, staring blankly at the wall, I sent Alex a text.

Brayden: Please let me know when you have a moment to talk. I'm going crazy over here.

As expected, she didn't immediately respond. I assumed she was still with Kate. I had no idea whether she'd decided to tell her the truth.

Later that evening, I was mindlessly flicking through the channels on the TV when a text came in.

Alex: I'm coming down to your room.

Thank God.

I jumped up from the bed and stood by the door. She'd barely had a chance to knock when I opened to let her in.

Alex brushed past me as she began to pace, rubbing her hands along her arms.

Her eyes were distressed when she finally turned to me. "I don't know what to do, Brayden."

I wanted to reach out and hug her, but I wasn't sure if that would make things worse. "Tell me what happened after I left, Alex."

"I chose not to tell her about you." Her eyes glistened. "I couldn't ruin her night when she'd come to surprise me like that."

"Okay." I sighed. "I wasn't sure."

"I do have to tell her, though. And it really can't wait much longer." Her voice shook. "But I don't know *how*. I've never lied to her, Brayden. I don't think I can live another day like this. I need to tell her first thing in the morning, because even these past two hours of lying felt like a lifetime. I couldn't look her in the eyes. It was such a horrible feeling."

"Where is she now?" I asked.

"She went back to her room after dinner. I'm supposed to watch a movie with her in a few. She has no idea anything is off. God knows how, because I feel like it's written all over my face. I told her I wanted to change and wash my makeup off. So I don't have too much time." She stared up at the ceiling. "This feels like a bad dream I can't wake up from. I'd give anything to go back in time and—"

I pulled her into a hug, interrupting her train of thought—I couldn't help it. Despite the turmoil of this night, it still felt so damn right to have her in my arms. "I'm sorry, Alex. I feel like this is all my fault."

She let me hold her for a few seconds before stepping out of my arms. "It's not your fault. But we do have remarkably shitty luck."

"I worried you were mad that I'd forced you into lying to her."

She reached for my hand. "You did the right thing. I wasn't ready to admit everything to her right then and there. We needed time to process first. I knew from the look on your face that you were as shocked as I was."

"I would've never knowingly put you through this. Please know that."

"I do know that, Brayden. It just doesn't make the situation any easier."

"Did she say anything about me after I left?"

Alex nodded. "She laughed about the coincidence mostly. Said she couldn't believe how small a world it is. She spoke about you for about ten minutes over drinks before dropping the subject."

I braced myself. "I'm sure she didn't have great things to say…"

"She said while she'd really liked you back then, you weren't ready for a relationship. She ended things before you had a chance because she sensed it was coming. She wanted to beat you to the punch. But you probably know all this. She doesn't seem to have hard feelings, but I think she was disappointed by the way things turned out. In fact, I remember her talking about it back when it happened, even if I don't remember all the details since it was so long ago." Alex tilted her head. "How long did you and she date?"

"I honestly don't remember, but I think about three months. She's a great girl. I have nothing but respect for her. But she's exactly right. I wasn't ready for a relationship back then. It feels like a lifetime ago. I was so young. We both were. What she and I had ended before it really began."

"But you *did* have sex…" Alex chewed her lip.

I wasn't sure if it was a question or a statement. Either way, I couldn't deny it. "Yeah," I admitted, closing my eyes briefly. "I can only imagine how upsetting that is for you to hear."

She nodded, clutching her stomach as if she wanted to vomit.

Heck, I felt like vomiting myself.

"Do you have any idea how fucked up it is to feel jealous of your own child?" she cried.

I wanted to look her in the eyes and tell her whatever Kate and I had meant nothing compared to my feelings for her. I also wished I could tell her I hadn't so much as thought of Kate since college. But that seemed insensitive. This was her daughter we were talking about. Being dismissive was only going to make me look like an asshole. Even if the truth was that Kate meant nothing to me at this point in time and Alex meant…*everything*.

"When are you going to tell her?" I asked.

"Tomorrow morning at breakfast."

"Would it help if I went with you?"

"No." She shook her head. "I think that would make it much worse. I need to do this alone."

I ran a hand through my hair. "Okay. I know it will be awkward, but if you change your mind and need my support, I'm there."

Our eyes locked. She looked so damn beautiful tonight. She'd put on a sexy top that revealed more cleavage than she'd ever shown. She'd been comfortable enough to wear it around me, comfortable enough to finally let me explore all of her. Sex with her would've been incredible. But more than that, it would've been *meaningful*. But I'd never get to experience it.

"Shit." Alex looked down at her phone. "I have to go."

If she had to leave now, and if her morning was going to be occupied with that difficult talk, I knew I had very little time to say what was on my chest right now. Even if the timing wasn't right, I needed to do it before I lost the chance. "Before you go, I have to say something, Alex."

She licked her lips. "Okay…"

"I know it's not looking good for us right now. It feels like you were ripped away from me tonight. And like my heart got ripped out, too. I know you—you won't do anything to upset your daughter. And if that means erasing me from your life, that's what you'll do. I can't even blame you for it. I keep wanting to call her your stepdaughter, but really, you're the only mother she has now. Kate's your daughter. And I'm…well, I'm basically a stranger who blew into your life out of nowhere. There's no contest as to who has the upper hand here." I looked deeply into her eyes. "But I'd regret it if I let you go without telling you how much you mean to me. And I know that before this happened, I meant a lot to you, too."

"You *still* mean a lot to me," she whispered.

I moved in closer but stopped short of touching her. "You were going to give your body to me tonight, and I know you wouldn't have made that decision had you not already given a piece of your heart to me, too. Don't think I don't know that."

"It doesn't matter anymore," she said.

"I will never not wonder what might have happened if Kate hadn't showed up. I will *never* get over this. I'll never get over *you*. Because, Alex, I've never felt this way about anyone. And this unfortunate coincidence doesn't change the fact that you're the most incredible woman I've ever known."

She sniffled, fending off tears. "I have to go." Alex wiped her eyes and turned toward the door before slipping away.

I wondered if I'd ever see her again.

CHAPTER 14

Alex

I couldn't process words.

I stared at my daughter's mouth. Sound was coming out, but I could only catch fragments. The rest were a distant murmur, an incoherent language. I'd been up all night, unable to close my eyes long enough to sleep, so I was certain exhaustion had something to do with it. But I also had no focus. My brain couldn't latch onto thoughts about anything, other than how I was going to tell Caitlin about Brayden. *What the hell do I say?*

Caitlin spooned some of her yogurt parfait into her mouth and kept talking. After an undetermined amount of time, her brows puckered. She reached out and waved her hand in front of my face. "Earth to Alex...are you in there?"

I opened my mouth to apologize, to say I was just tired. But when I did, that wasn't what blurted out. Words raced fast and furious. "Brayden is the younger man I've been telling you about. I'm so sorry. I had no idea you two knew each other. Neither did Brayden." I closed my eyes, hating the way I'd delivered the news, yet relieved that it was out there.

"Brayden?" Caitlin said.

I peeked one eye open. "Brayden. Brady. They're the same person. My Brayden is *your* Brady."

She blinked a few times. "You're *dating* my ex-boyfriend?"

"Yes. No." I shook my head. "I mean yes, the man I've been talking to you about is Brayden, but we're not dating. I mean, we were, but we aren't anymore."

My daughter's forehead wrinkled. She averted her eyes, staring off into the restaurant dining room for a long time while I waited on pins and needles. Confusion was still all over her face when she turned back. "He's seen me naked. I've seen him naked. I *slept* with him."

I cringed. "I'm so sorry, Caitlin. I had no idea. I never would've gotten involved with him if I'd had an inkling of suspicion you two were somehow connected. I was hesitant enough because of his age. Even if you guys were *friends* it would've probably been too much for me to handle. I had *no clue*."

Caitlin had always been an easy read for me. I knew when she was upset, even when she tried to hide it. But at the moment, I had no idea what she was thinking. Her face was a cross between confused and something else—angry, maybe? She lifted the napkin from her lap and tossed it on the table in front of her.

"Did you sleep with him, too?"

"No." I shook my head. "*God no.* Thankfully things between us didn't get that far." It made me sick to think how close we'd come, though. If Caitlin had been five minutes later getting to the elevator, or if I'd been five minutes later to come down, Brayden and I would've gone along on our merry way to dinner and...*after dinner*. Though I wasn't about to share that.

"What are you going to do now?" she asked.

"Well, obviously whatever had been going on between us, whatever we'd started, is over. I haven't figured out what to do about the project we're working on together."

Caitlin looked anywhere but at me. It reminded me of when her father and I had first started dating. She'd seen me as a woman trying to take her mother's place. She'd resented me so much that it took almost a full year for her to look me in the eyes. It broke my heart to think we could be back there now, after all we'd had to go through to get to the other side. Caitlin wasn't just my husband's daughter; she was *my* daughter, and my very best friend. Or at least she was...

I reached across the table and took her hand. "Caitlin?"

Her eyes shifted to me.

"You believe me, right? That I had no idea who he was and would never do anything intentional to hurt you?"

"Why wouldn't I? That's what you said."

Her tone sounded more sarcastic than certain. But I'd had all night to let everything sink in. She was likely still in shock. I squeezed her hand. "I'm sorry this happened."

Caitlin frowned. "Yeah, me too." She looked over at my plate. I'd ordered an egg-white omelet and fruit, but hadn't touched a bite of it yet. "Are you finished with breakfast?"

My stomach was tied in giant knots. I couldn't possibly eat. "Yeah, I'm done."

"I need to get on the road." She pushed her seat from the table and stood. "I have a few conference calls this afternoon when I get back."

"Oh...okay." I looked around for the waiter and raised my hand. "I just need to pay the check."

"I'm going to wait for you outside the restaurant."

I forced a smile. "Sure. I understand."

After, we walked to the elevator bank. Neither of us said a word. Once we were inside and the doors slid closed, I turned to her.

"I'll meet you down in the lobby in fifteen minutes to check out? We can walk out together?"

She nodded but kept her eyes pointed at the ground. "Sure."

Inside my room, I was relieved to have a few minutes alone. It had been hard to breathe with the thick tension in the air. Since I'd been up all night, my things were already packed and ready to go. There wasn't much I needed to do before going back downstairs. I thought about calling Brayden, or maybe texting to let him know it was done. But that would inevitably cause an avalanche of questions, none of which I felt prepared to answer. So instead, I lay back on the bed, closed my eyes, and tried to meditate.

"Everything is going to work out," I whispered to myself. "Just breathe. In…and out."

I inhaled deeply, feeling my lungs fill with oxygen, then attempted to blow out all the tension from my body. But thoughts flooded my mind like a burst dam. *What if Caitlin can't get over this? What if she distances herself? Can I continue to work with Brayden at Ryan's House? If I don't, will I ever see him again?* That last thought made my chest ache.

I inhaled again, this time making an *ohmmm* sound. It might be impossible to clear my head, but I was giving it the old college try anyway. Finally, after a dozen inhales and exhales, I called it quits. If I didn't have to drive myself home, I might've resorted to alcohol to take the edge off. I used the bathroom before doing one last sweep of the room to make sure I wasn't leaving anything behind, and then I headed down to the lobby.

Still in a fog, I wasn't paying attention to how many floors the elevator car traveled down. So when the doors slid open, I started to exit, assuming we'd arrived at the lobby. But I stopped dead in my tracks when I got a look at the two people standing on the other side of the threshold, waiting to get on.

Caitlin.

And Brayden.

The three of us looked like a trio of deer caught in the headlights. "I, uh, thought this was the lobby," I said.

Caitlin pursed her lips. "Nope. Second floor."

Does she think I'm getting off to go to Brayden's room?

Brayden caught my eye. He looked as heartbroken as I felt, yet he gestured to Caitlin. "You two, go. I'll wait for the next one."

Brayden and I stared in awkward silence as Caitlin stepped into the elevator. I didn't think things could get much more uncomfortable, but they did, once the doors shut and my daughter and I were alone in the car.

"Caitlin, I'm so sorry. I had no idea he was checking out too. I haven't spoken to him since—"

She held a hand up. "Stop apologizing. I just want to go home."

Luckily, we only had to go down one floor. At the front desk, two clerks were waiting. Caitlin checked out with one while I settled up with the other. I looked around the lobby, anxious that Brayden might appear again, while trying my best not to *look* like I was scanning for anyone in particular. Probably didn't matter though, as my daughter never glanced my way. After we were done, we walked to the parking lot together.

Caitlin pointed to the left. "I'm over there."

I nodded. "I'm the other direction." I stepped forward, engulfing her in a hug I wasn't sure she wanted. "Thank you so much for coming all this way for my birthday. It meant a lot to me."

She gave me a piss-poor smile. "No problem."

"I'll call you tomorrow? After work?"

"Sure."

"Safe drive home."

"You, too."

A few minutes later, I watched Caitlin's white BMW pull out of a spot and drive toward the exit. My hands were still shaky, and I didn't feel ready to drive. But I was afraid she might check her rearview mirror to see if I was behind her. If I wasn't, she might assume I'd stayed behind to wait for Brayden. So even though I could've used another minute to collect myself, I started the car and followed. A mile or so down the road, I got caught at the light before the highway merge while Caitlin kept going. Up ahead, she turned right onto the entrance ramp, and then I lost sight of her. My shoulders drooped with relief.

Since she would now be a few minutes ahead and always drove faster than I did, I doubted she'd expect to see me behind her anymore. So I pulled into a gas station and called Brayden. I was curious about the conversation they'd had while waiting for the elevator.

He answered on the first ring. "Are you okay?"

I smiled sadly. He had to be hurting, too, yet it was just like him to worry about me.

"Not really." I sighed.

"I guess you told her?"

"She didn't say anything while you were standing at the elevator?"

"Nope. I smiled when she walked up, but she didn't reciprocate. She looked pretty pissed off. So I figured it was best to follow her lead. Neither of us said a word."

I took a deep breath and exhaled. "It didn't go so well at breakfast."

"I'm sorry."

"Me too. She put up a giant wall. I'm hoping she comes around a bit after it sinks in. If she feels anything like we did last night when we discovered how we're all connected, she's probably still shocked."

"Yeah, I'm sure."

"I'm *still* not over the shock."

"Neither am I."

We were quiet for a moment. Eventually Brayden spoke. "What are we going to do now?"

"There is no *we*, Brayden. Not anymore. There can't be."

I heard the sadness in his voice. "I didn't mean it like that. I meant what can I do to help? But…"

"But what?"

"Is this really the end for us?"

"You used to *date* my daughter, Brayden! You slept together!"

"It was a lifetime ago."

"It doesn't matter if it was a hundred years ago. It happened, and no amount of time can take that back. This is what being a parent is. You have to put your child first."

He blew into the phone. "Will you come on Thursday again this week? So we can talk?"

"I'm not sure I can come back at all, Brayden."

"But…"

Tears filled my eyes. "I need to go. I pulled over at a gas station to call you, and I don't want to get home too late after Caitlin, in case she drops by or something."

"Okay."

"I'll let you know whether I'll be back at Ryan's House."

"Okay. But I hope you come back."

"Goodbye, Brayden."

"Be careful driving."

I swiped my phone off just as my tears spilled over. I hadn't cried yet, but suddenly I couldn't turn off the waterworks. My shoulders shook as I sobbed and sobbed. It felt like my heart had been split in half. I wanted to turn my car around, drive back to the hotel, jump into Brayden's arms, and let him tell me everything was going to be alright. But it wouldn't be. That wasn't real. It was just a fantasy.

Maybe that's what thinking things could work out with Brayden had been from the start—a fantasy.

♥

"That…" Wells twirled his pointer finger, motioning to my face. "…had better be a look of exhaustion from banging all night, not from tossing and turning because of pent-up sexual frustration."

My eyes filled with tears as I stood across from him Monday morning at work.

Wells's face changed, and he pulled me into a hug. "Oh, sweetheart, you don't look *that* bad. Stop being so sensitive. Plus, we can do a laser eye treatment for those bags."

I sniffled, pulling back from Wells. "Brayden and me—it's over. We can't see each other anymore."

"Why? What happened?"

"He…used to date Caitlin."

Wells blinked twice. "Come again?"

I shook my head. "I know. It's crazy. But Caitlin showed up to surprise me at the hotel this weekend, and it turns out the two of them know each other. They dated for a while in college. For months actually. She was supposed to bring him on a family ski trip even, but it wound up getting canceled."

"Holy shit."

"I know."

"Damn, you two really do have the same taste. Remember that time you showed up at Richard's office party in the same dress?"

I closed my eyes. "You're not making me feel any better."

"Sorry, Kitten. I'm sure it was a shock to find that out, but does it really matter? College was a decade ago for Caitlin. What did she say when she found out?"

"She wasn't happy. She was as freaked out as I was."

"Well, give it some time. I'm sure she won't care."

I shook my head. "It doesn't matter if she cares. *I* care. They… were intimate."

Wells scrunched up his nose. "Okay, that is kind of weird. But it's better than sleeping with your cousin, right?"

"My cousin? What are you talking about?"

"I'm just saying, there are worse things than seeing the same man naked as your stepdaughter. For example, sleeping with your cousin, or your brother. Or…that really old guy in the Senate, the one whose ears hang down almost to his shoulders. He needs otoplasty. I read about different cosmetic ear surgeries the night of the last election when they kept showing that dude on the screen."

I frowned. "I really liked him, Wells."

"I know you did, sweetheart. I liked him for you, too."

"I don't know if I should go back to finish the Ryan's House project."

"What are you talking about? Of course you have to go back. That has nothing to do with whether you can be with the boy-toy."

I would hate to walk away from the commitment I made to the charity. That's not the person I was. "I know, but…"

"But what? I'm sure he'll be respectful. He seems like a stand-up guy from everything you've told me."

I sighed. "That's not the problem."

"Okay, so what is?"

"I'm not worried about Brayden's ability to keep his distance. I'm worried about my own self-control. I don't trust myself around Brayden."

CHAPTER 15

Brayden

I alternated between staring at the wall in my apartment and looking out the window at the busy street below. Despite having plenty of things that should've kept me occupied as I worked from home today, I couldn't concentrate on anything besides what had happened this past weekend. Or more specifically, what *never* happened this past weekend.

I'd been back in the City since yesterday after my most recent, miserable trip to Seneca Falls. Alex hadn't freaking showed up. I couldn't say I was surprised, nor could I blame her, but I'd really been hoping we could talk. Instead, I'd immersed myself in work at the house, probably one of my most productive times there. It was the first weekend since this project started that I hadn't been distracted by Alex, even if every corner of the house still reminded me of her.

My chest ached when I pondered the future. What if she *never* came back to Seneca Falls? What if I never saw Alex again as long as I lived? I couldn't imagine it, but it wasn't out of the realm of possibility.

On Wednesday of last week, Alex had sent me a text to let me know that while she didn't plan to abandon the Ryan's House project, she needed a week or two off to clear her head before facing me again. Still, I'd spent the weekend holding out hope that she'd change her mind and show up anyway. She'd surprised me before. I supposed in the end she'd done me a favor by staying away, because how was I supposed to handle myself around her now? All I'd want to do was reach out and kiss her, hold her, comfort her, and I wouldn't be able to do any of that. So maybe I should've been grateful she didn't show up.

My phone rang, interrupting my thoughts. It was a number I didn't recognize, but I picked up anyway.

"Hello?"

"Hey, Brayden. It's Wells…Alex's friend."

My heart nearly stopped. "Is everything okay?" *Why else would he be calling me?*

"Yeah. Yeah. Sorry. Didn't mean to alarm you, loverboy. She's fine…well, physically, anyway."

That hurt to hear, but it wasn't anything I didn't already suspect.

"I went into her contacts to steal your number because I thought you and I should have a talk about the latest…happenings," he continued.

I gulped. "Okay…"

"I know I may be overstepping here, but I'm doing so for her own good. Alex has been keeping everything bottled up inside."

I shut my eyes for a moment. "How is she doing overall?"

"She's really down. And I hate seeing it. She deserves so much happiness after everything she's been through. What you and she were cooking up made her happier than I'd seen her in a while. And as her friend, I'm having a hard time watching her throw all that away for nothing."

"I'd hardly call this dilemma *nothing*. It's fucked up, but it's not *nothing*."

"Yeah, I get the conflict. Believe me, I do. She loves Caitlin more than anything. But you're all adults, you know? It shouldn't be this difficult. She's sacrificing her own happiness for something that's long in the past. It wasn't like Caitlin was hung up on you or anything. You only came up again because you were dating Alex. Now all of a sudden, there's a problem? All of a sudden you exist again? It doesn't sit right with me that Alex should have to throw away her love life because of some college fling her daughter had a decade ago. I mean, I'm sure you're a totally different person than you were then."

"I am. But good luck convincing Alex she should disregard her daughter's feelings, regardless of how much time has gone by. She'll never do anything to upset her."

"I realize convincing her to put her own happiness first in this equation is a tough sell. But I'm also a huge believer that what people don't know won't hurt them."

I squinted. "What do you mean?"

"That brings me to the real reason I'm calling."

"What's that?"

"Alex and I are coming to New York City tomorrow."

My heart skipped a beat. "Really?"

"I figured she wouldn't have told you."

"Safe assumption. We haven't spoken since she texted last week to let me know she wouldn't be coming upstate. What's going on in the City?"

"A medical spa expo. We're driving in tomorrow, and only going to be staying one night."

Adrenaline coursed through me at the prospect of Alex coming to *my* city. The need to see her felt urgent. "Just one night, huh?"

"Yep," he said. "Blink and you'll miss us. I was thinking maybe you could, you know, *happen* to show up at the restaurant where we'll be eating dinner."

"I don't know, man. Do you think she'll want to see me if she's been actively avoiding talking to me?"

"I realize she'd never initiate this, but I do think once she sees you, she'll be happy you're there. It will give you an opportunity to properly talk about what happened. I feel like she ran off so fast the weekend Caitlin was there, you didn't have time to process any of this in private."

I sighed. "Well, that's the damn truth."

"No pressure. I just thought you'd want to know she's coming to town, because I knew she wouldn't tell you herself."

I nodded. "I appreciate you letting me know. Definitely text me where you guys end up going. I'm not sure yet if showing up is the right decision. I'll need to think on it."

"Will do."

"And hey, the offer still stands for me to introduce you to my friend Deek," I added. "Just let me know if you're interested. Maybe not this trip since you're only in town for one night. But next time."

"No. I'm not interested in meeting your big, burly, tatted friend—said no one ever." He chuckled. "Bring it on."

It wasn't like I'd been anxiously awaiting that text from Wells the following day or anything. I hadn't eaten all day, nor done anything productive—another useless day at work.

Around four PM, my phone chimed. I hopped out of my seat to grab it.

Wells: Alex and I will be dining at Le Poulet at eight.

My finger hovered over the keypad for several minutes. I wasn't ready to commit, so I bought myself some time.

Brayden: Thanks. I appreciate you letting me know. Gonna think about what's best and get back to you.

I wanted to take the risk and just show up. But then my common sense would kick in and remind me I was probably the last person Alex wanted to have turn up at dinner.

Better than my common sense, though, was my friend who always set things straight. I really could use Billie's advice on this situation. I went down to the tattoo shop to see if she had a moment to chat.

Billie held her hand up when she saw me standing there, and I waited while she finished with her client.

As soon as she was done, she walked over. "What's going on, Brayden? You never come down here in the middle of the day."

"I need your advice."

She smiled. "I figured something must be up."

"How much time do you have?"

"Half hour 'til my next client." She grabbed her black fringed purse. "Let's go grab coffee."

Billie and I walked to the coffee shop around the corner as I filled her in on the latest developments—from finding out Kate is Alex's Caitlin, to my dilemma over Alex being in New York.

She reached across the table. "Okay, first off, I'm so freaking sorry. What a shitty thing to happen." She frowned. "Are you okay?"

"Not really. I'm still shook up over the whole thing."

"So you haven't decided whether to go to the restaurant tonight?"

"I don't have a true sense of the right decision. I want to see her, but showing up also feels a bit stalkerish."

Billie ran her finger over the rim of her cup. "Whether or not you go tonight should depend on what you hope to achieve. Despite her friend's good intentions, if you don't think it will change anything right now, it's probably best that you not upset her this evening. On the other hand, if you feel her decision about you is not set in stone and she might weaken to your charms, maybe showing up will help. Don't kill yourself mulling it over." She leaned in. "Quick. Don't think about it for more than a few seconds. What's your gut feeling? Go!"

My gut feeling? *It's too soon.*

I shook my head. "If there's a chance in hell she'll see this situation differently, it's not going to be now. It will be down the road. So I think the main benefit of showing up would be to satisfy my own need to see her."

"Well, you have your answer. It won't achieve much. And might even upset her."

"Yeah." I sighed. "As much as I hate to admit it, I think it's best if I don't go."

Billie took a sip of her coffee. Then she shook her head. "Damn."

"What?"

"If only this Alex could see how down you look right now. She'd never doubt how serious you were about her."

After I returned to my apartment, I texted Wells to let him know I wouldn't be coming and thanked him for trying to help.

I spent the remainder of the evening second-guessing my decision and lamenting the fact that the woman I was crazy about was in my city, and I couldn't even see her.

The last thing I expected the following day was a certain name lighting up my phone.

Alex.

My heart sped up as I answered. "Hello?"

"Hi."

"This is a pleasant surprise," I said.

"How are you?" she asked.

"I've been better. How are you?"

"I'm…actually in New York."

"Really? What are you doing here?" I asked, feeling a bit guilty for faking my surprise.

"I'm here for a medical spa expo. Wells and I spent last night here, and we have to leave later this afternoon. I've felt strange being here without you knowing, for some reason. Everywhere I go, I keep thinking I'm going to run into you, though I know that's unlikely in a city of eight-million people. What are the chances, right?"

"About the same as having accidentally dated your daughter in college?"

"That was bad." She chuckled. "But true."

"Well, I have to laugh so I won't cry, right?" I blew out a breath. "How long 'til you have to leave?"

"A few hours."

"Meet me for coffee," I blurted. "Just coffee. Nothing more, Alex. Bring Wells."

"Wells has plans with someone he met at the expo today, so it would just be me."

"Okay, then I'd love to show you the building. We don't even have to go inside. I would just like you to see it."

After a brief pause, she said, "That'd be nice."

I exhaled. "Can I call a car for you?"

"Okay. Yes. Thank you. I'd appreciate that."

"There's a café right around the corner from here. We can go there and talk until you have to go."

A bit shocked that she'd agreed to meet me, I stopped short of leaping into the air for joy after we hung up. *Don't get your hopes up. It's just coffee. She felt guilty for not telling you she was in New York. It doesn't mean anything.*

Thirty minutes later, I waited outside my building until the car showed up.

A breeze blew Alex's long blond hair around as she exited the vehicle. She was so beautiful and looked amazing in a white peacoat and high-heeled boots. Her mouth curved into a smile when she spotted me standing there.

Instead of pulling her close and kissing her so damn hard, like I wanted to, I held out my hand. She took it. "Thank you for coming." I squeezed before placing my other hand over hers.

Alex smiled and looked up at the building. "This is it, huh? The famous building?"

"It is." I smiled proudly.

"It's bigger than I imagined."

If these were different times, I might've hit her with a sexual joke right then. But alas, I kept my mouth shut. "Come on. I'll show you inside."

Alex and I spent the next several minutes touring my property. I specifically didn't show her my apartment, but we rode the elevator to the top floor, hung out on the rooftop for a bit, and wandered the hallways before heading back outside. I'd wondered if we would run into any of the guys—at least Holden, maybe, since he worked in the building doing maintenance—but no one turned up.

"I'm so glad I had a chance to see it," Alex said as we stood together on the sidewalk after.

"Me too. I wish it were under different circumstances. But I'll take what I can get." I walked toward Billie's storefront as she followed. "One more stop I want you to see."

"Ah, this is the famous tattoo shop," Alex said.

We peeked inside, but Billie wasn't there. From the window, I pointed out Deek, who was busy inking someone. "That's the guy I wanted to hook Wells up with."

"Oh, he's definitely Wells's type."

"Pretty sure he might be everyone's type, and my type, too, if I swung that way." I winked. "Come to think of it, my life would be a whole lot less complicated right now if I were gay."

Alex smiled sadly.

"Come on." I winked again. "Let's get that coffee."

Over at the café, Alex grabbed a table while I went to the counter to order her coffee, prepared just the way she liked it. I also got a few different kinds of pastry in case she was hungry.

"Are you trying to fatten me up so you no longer want me or something?" she asked, looking down at the sweets I'd brought to the table.

Like I could ever not want you. "I wasn't sure what you felt like." I shrugged. "Bring them back for Wells, if you're not hungry."

After a few minutes of sipping our coffee, as we alternated between staring into each other's eyes and people watching through the window in silence, I finally asked, "So, tell me what's going on with Caitlin…"

Alex stared down into her cup. "Believe it or not, we haven't talked about anything since that weekend, and I haven't seen much of her. That's been unsettling. But at the same time, I don't want to be the one to bring it up."

I nodded. "I can understand why she'd want to forget the whole thing." For all I knew, this time at the café might be my last opportunity to set some things straight. I didn't want to waste it. "I didn't have much of a chance to explain some things to you," I told her. "Mainly, I've been holding back because I don't want to come across as a bigger asshole than I already seem, given the circumstances." I paused. "But I need you to know that the feelings I had for Kate back in college pale in comparison to what I feel for you. I don't want to seem insensitive, but I'm not sure if she's given you an accurate picture of what things were like between us." I shook my head. "She and I were never serious. At least, that's not where *my* heart was at the time. I never told your daughter I loved her. I never led her on." I let out a breath.

Alex fidgeted in her seat. "That doesn't make me feel any better, Brayden."

I raised my voice. "I still need you to know."

"Okay," she muttered. "I understand."

"I wish more than anything that things were different. But I can't expect you to disregard her feelings. I understand the type of person you are and why your relationship with Caitlin would be more important than your own happiness. I can't argue with that or ask you to change for me. But I want you to know that losing you will always be the biggest regret of my life."

Alex's eyes glistened as she looked down at her phone. "Shit. I have to go."

"I'll call you a car." I pulled up the app and arranged for her ride.

Alex placed the pastries in her bag to take back for Wells.

As we stood on the sidewalk, quietly staring at each other, I could see the hurt in her eyes. But there was also something else: desire—even if she'd never allow herself to act on it.

I don't know what came over me, but I suddenly voiced what I was thinking. "Do you ever dream about what might've happened if Caitlin hadn't shown up that day? Because I dream about fucking you every damn night, Alex," I rasped. "I probably always will."

She swallowed.

I inched closer. "I understand why you need to hold back. But I have *nothing* holding me back right now." I leaned in, taking her lips with mine before backing her against the wall of a building.

Alex panted over my mouth as she received my kiss.

"I'll stop if you want me to," I murmured.

Instead of saying anything, her tense body loosened as she succumbed, a moan escaping her. Alex raked her fingers through my hair as she pulled me close. I cradled her face as my tongue dove deeper into her mouth, tasting her coffee. The world faded around us. I couldn't have cared less about the droves of people passing by and getting a load of this spectacle. My cock grew hard as a rock as I pressed my body against hers.

She was the first to pull back.

We were both out of breath as I rubbed my thumb along her swollen bottom lip and looked into her glassy eyes. "I don't care if I go to hell for that. It was damn well worth it."

❤CHAPTER 16

Alex

"**Y**ou're scaring away the customers and making me depressed."

I looked up from the front desk and frowned at Wells. "Thanks. And I put in extra effort today."

I really had. This morning I'd gotten up early, forced a healthy breakfast into my belly, and done my hair and makeup like I was going out. I thought it might help my gloomy mood if I looked better. But apparently a little paint and hot rollers couldn't stop what was on the inside from spilling out.

"Oh honey, this is why I prefer one-night stands. Love sucks." He winked. "But a good one-night stand swallows."

I attempted a smile, but failed.

"Jeez, Louise. It's worse than I thought when I can't even make you smile with a good blowjob joke."

"I'm sorry. Even I'm confused by how hard I'm taking what happened. But I can't seem to shake this gray feeling."

Wells walked around the desk, pulled open the drawer where I kept my purse, and lifted it onto his shoulder. "Let's go, Kitten. I'm taking you for therapy."

"You made me an appointment with Dr. Mills?" I'd met with a psychologist a few times after Richard died. But I hadn't seen him since.

Wells extended a hand and yanked me to my feet. "Retail therapy, sweetheart. I asked Hallie to stay and close up tonight."

I wasn't much in the mood for shopping—wasn't in the mood for anything, really—but I knew better than to argue with Wells when it came to two things: shopping and taking care of me. So I nodded. "Thanks."

Our first stop was Nordstrom. We perused the expensive shoes in the ladies' department. I picked up a pair of sparkly silver Jimmy Choos. "These would look really cute with that black dress Caitlin has with the silver belt, wouldn't they?"

Wells plucked them from my hand and steered me to a pair of ridiculously high leopard-print Louboutins. "Now these are *hot*. You need *fuck-me* shoes. They pair great with a Brazilian, preferably the kind with a landing strip. Nothing else."

I smiled. "I don't know if they have them in your size."

Wells linked his arm with mine and started us walking. "Is down there still groomed to the nines?"

"Do you really need to know the current status of my pubic hair?"

"I do. Just humor me and answer."

I sighed. "I have a Brazilian right now."

"When did you get waxed?"

"I don't know. The week before my birthday, I think?"

"So that's what? Three weeks now?"

I shrugged. "I guess…"

"When was the last time you got waxed before that?"

"Is this conversation really necessary?"

"It is. Answer the question. I promise not to judge. When I went off that ridiculous six-month man cleanse I did a few years back, I had to use a sickle to cut down the bush before I jumped back into the dating pool."

I frowned, but answered truthfully. "I hadn't gotten waxed in a few years, not since Richard died. I'd shaved, but not gotten a Brazilian."

"That's what I thought. When you first get back into waxing, the hair grows in fast, so you must be starting to get stubbly."

I rolled my eyes. "You know too much about the intricacies of ladies' grooming. But if you must know, I have an appointment on Wednesday to get touched up."

"And when did you make that appointment?"

"This morning when I got to work, why?"

Wells's eyes sparkled. "Ah-ha! *I knew it.*"

"What do you know?"

"You might have closed the door, but you haven't locked it and thrown away the key yet."

"What on Earth are you talking about?"

"If there wasn't a chance someone might see that hoochie, you would not have made a touch-up appointment. Ergo, while your head is not planning on banging the boy-toy, your hoochie has other plans."

Wells directed us to the perfume counter. "Hello. We're looking for a scent that will drive a young man wild," he said. "What do you have that smells like sex?"

The woman smiled. "You want a sex-on-the-beach type scent?"

Wells twisted his lips. "Not quite that romantic. More like *talk dirty to me* and *take me against the wall of my hotel room.*"

The salesclerk chuckled. "Let me see what I can do."

Fifteen minutes later, I walked away with a ridiculously over-priced bottle of Baccarat, compliments of my best friend. We then headed up the escalator to the men's department. Wells loaded both our arms with summer clothes for him to try on, and I sat in a chair in the dressing room while he modeled for me.

"Doesn't my ass look good in these?" Wells turned his back

to the mirror and looked over his shoulder at the rear of a pair of aqua swim trunks.

"It looks like you do a lot of squats."

He shook his ass back and forth a few times and then parked it in the leather chair next to me. "She still hasn't called?"

I frowned. "She responds to texts politely, but that's about it."

"I love Caitlin, but she needs to get over herself."

"I'm not sure what to do. I want to clear the air, but I also don't want to push too hard. On the other hand, I don't want her to think I'm not concerned that she's upset."

"As long as we're talking about clearing the air, there's something I should tell you. You know keeping secrets gives me heartburn."

"What are you talking about?"

"I stole Brayden's number from your phone and called him."

My eyes bulged. "What? When?"

"The night before we went to New York. I thought you two should talk. So I suggested he *accidentally* show up at the restaurant where we were having dinner. He really wanted to see you, but he decided he didn't want to upset you with an ambush."

My chest grew heavy. That was just like Brayden. He'd jumped at the chance to meet when I'd called, but he was more concerned with my needs than his own. It was one of the things I loved about him.

One of the things I loved about him.

It felt like the wind had been knocked out of me. My eyes filled with tears, and I put my hand over the spot on my chest that ached. "Oh my God, Wells. I think I started to fall in love with him." I shook my head. "I feel so guilty even saying that, but it's true."

"You can't feel guilty for falling in love with a man before you knew anything about his past relationship with Caitlin."

"I wasn't talking about the guilt I feel toward Caitlin, though I do feel that, obviously. I feel disloyal to Richard. He's the only man I've ever said I love you to, aside from my family members. And I thought he would be the only man I said it to for the rest of my life."

Wells shook his head. "Jesus Christ, Alex. I have no idea how you manage to walk with so much guilt on your shoulders. Caitlin guilt. Richard guilt—for fuck's sake, you might as well steal that pair of Louboutins so you get something for all that guilt you're carrying."

I covered my face with my hands. "Wells, what am I going to do? I'm in love with Brayden."

"You need to have a conversation with Caitlin. Tell her how you feel. I can understand having guilt if you went after her ex *knowing* he was her ex. But this was completely innocent. She has to understand that."

"Even if she does accept it, I'm not sure *I* can."

"Well, that's your choice. But who knows how many loves we get in life. I would hate to see you regret letting yours get away."

My chest stayed heavy with that thought during the rest of Wells's try-on session. He wound up buying an armful of clothes, so I was glad the day had been productive for at least one of us. On the way out, we had to pass through the ladies' shoe department again. Wells picked up the pair of leopard-print stilettos he'd called fuck-me shoes and walked over to the clerk.

"What's the return policy on these babies?"

"Thirty days."

"Do you have them in a seven and a half?"

"I think we do. Let me check."

The salesclerk disappeared. I started to say I wasn't buying shoes, when Wells pressed a finger to my lips, cutting me off. "In thirty days you're either going to be miserable or getting laid. Either way, you need these. My treat. Just promise me, if you do wind up boning the boy-toy, you'll wear these and nothing else."

I figured it would be easier to come back and return them in a few days than argue right now, so I nodded and forced a smile. "Sure."

A few minutes later, we were buckling into the car when my phone buzzed from my bag. I dug it out, read the text, and showed Wells the screen. "It's Caitlin. She wants to stop over tonight."

I paced the kitchen like an expectant father. When the doorbell rang a few minutes after seven, I had to wipe my sweaty hands on my pants to open the door.

"Hi." I smiled and held my breath.

"Hey. Sorry I'm a little late."

I stepped aside and showed my nerves by babbling. "You're not late. I'm early. Well, I don't mean I'm early to arrive since obviously I live here, but the food is almost ready. Or maybe not. I should probably go check." I shut my eyes, feeling like an idiot, and power walked to the kitchen.

Caitlin followed. "Mmm… Do I smell your sauce?"

"I had some frozen, so I made breaded chicken cutlets, pounded thin, the way you like them." I opened the oven door to see if the mozzarella I'd put on top had melted, and Caitlin peeked over my shoulder.

"Umm… Is there an army coming?"

I glanced at the *two* trays, noticing for the first time that there were probably a dozen cutlets cooking. I shook my head. "I may have gotten a little carried away."

Caitlin chuckled. "You think?"

I was afraid to get my hopes up, but Caitlin seemed very much like herself, at least so far. I, on the other hand, was a nervous wreck. The chicken still had a few minutes to go, so I shut the oven door. "Would you like a glass of wine?"

"I'd love one. Thanks."

I busied myself pouring two glasses of chardonnay and passed one to Caitlin. We sat down next to each other at the kitchen island, and I tried to pretend I wasn't gulping. But there was a giant elephant in the room, and I needed to muster the courage to address it or I'd go out of my mind trying to tap dance around it. So I took a deep breath. "Caitlin, I'm so sorry."

She set her glass down. "No, Alex. It's me who needs to apologize. I acted like a spoiled brat. And I regret that it took me this long to get my ass here and clear the air. I know you. You've probably been stressing."

Hives had already broken out on my chest. That happened sometimes when I was upset. Caitlin zeroed in on them and shook her head. "Oh gosh. It's worse than I thought. I haven't seen you get that rash since Dad was diagnosed. I'm really an idiot for not coming over sooner."

"You were in shock. We both were."

"I'm sure I was at first, yes. But I acted possessive about something that happened a lifetime ago. It was immature of me." She sipped her wine. "If I'm being perfectly honest, it wasn't just about Brady. I think it took me this long because I didn't want to admit something to myself."

"What?"

Caitlin caught my eye. "I've always been a little jealous of you, Alex. It began when you started dating Dad, only I was too young to realize it back then."

"It's normal for a young girl to not want someone to come between her and her dad."

She shook her head. "It was more than that. I wasn't just jealous of the attention Dad gave you. I was jealous of *you*, Alex. You're so beautiful and confident."

"Oh gosh. I don't hold a candle to you, Caitlin."

She smiled sadly. "And that's another thing that makes you so amazing. You have no clue what you look like or the effect you have on people. I remember when I was younger, when my friends would meet you, they would always comment how pretty and sweet you were. But it got worse when the boys who came around would say it." Caitlin looked down and shook her head. "I used to tell everyone you'd had a shitload of plastic surgery."

I wasn't sure what to say, so I stayed quiet.

"Anyway, I thought I was past all that. But when I found out about Brady, it felt like I was thirteen with braces and acne all over again, and you were the beautiful stepmother."

"I'm sorry I made you feel that way."

Caitlin looked up. "That's the thing, *you* didn't ever make me feel that way. *I* felt bad because of my own insecurities. But it was easier to blame you than to look inward."

"Oh, Caitlin." I stood and hugged her. I'd thought nothing could be worse than having my daughter dislike me, but I was wrong—I'd rather have her dislike me than herself.

After a long embrace, she pulled back. "Can you forgive me for acting like such a brat?"

"There's nothing to forgive."

"I hope I didn't mess things up with you and Brayden too badly."

"There is no me and Brayden."

"What? No! I saw the way your eyes lit up when you talked about him, before we knew about the connection. You really liked him."

"It was a bad idea from the beginning. He lives in New York and is too young for me. It was just…" I shook my head. "Exciting to have a handsome man interested. That's all it was."

"You're so full of it. When I asked you if he had a six pack, you told me what you liked best about him was that he was humble. You *liked him*, liked him."

"Sure, he's a nice guy, but there are plenty of nice guys out there—ones my own age who live here in Connecticut."

"Really? Can you introduce me to a few, because I can't seem to find any who are handsome, humble, and kind. How many have you met since Dad died?"

When I went to respond, I realized I didn't have an answer.

Caitlin pointed to my face. "That's what I thought. Trust me, if you find a good one, you're lucky. I'm thirty years old, not a kid anymore. So I realize how hard it is to find a good man—one you connect with and has the qualities you want in a partner." She paused. "A man like Dad."

"Your dad was one in a million."

"I agree. But this is about you, Alex. Not him. He's not here anymore. So if you're lucky enough to find *another* one-in-a-million man, you shouldn't let him go."

Wells had said something similar to me earlier, but right now, I thought a change of subject might be best. So I hugged my step-daughter and took dinner out of the oven. By the time we started eating, it felt like there hadn't been a two-week rift between us. I was so relieved and grateful to enjoy our time together. Somehow we managed to keep away from the subject of men for the rest of the evening, at least until I was walking her to the door…

"Are you going upstate to Ryan's House this weekend?" Caitlin asked.

"I'm not sure yet."

"Alright, well, let me know after you and Brayden have done the deed. We can compare notes."

My eyes flared wide.

Caitlin laughed and bumped shoulders with me. "I'm kidding. Too soon?"

"I don't think it would ever *not* be too soon."

She kissed my cheek. "Love you, Mom."

"I love you, too, sweetheart."

A half hour later, I was staring up at the ceiling, going over everything Caitlin had said tonight, when my phone buzzed on the nightstand.

Wells: Are you alone?

Alex: Yes.

My phone rang seconds later. I sat up and flicked the light on before answering the FaceTime call.

"Are you in bed? You were seriously going to go to sleep without calling and giving me the deets of what happened tonight? How could you?"

"I'm sorry. My head is still spinning."

"What happened with Caitlin?"

"She apologized and gave me her blessing to go out with Brayden."

"That's great!"

I frowned. "Yeah."

"Jesus Christ, woman. What now? Why aren't you happy that Caitlin is over it?"

"I am. I definitely am. It's a huge relief that she's not upset with me anymore."

"So why do you still look like someone pissed in your Cheerios?"

My shoulders slumped. "Because I don't think it changes anything between Brayden and me."

"Why not?"

"Because I think it would still hurt her if we were together. Plus, what would happen down the road? If Brayden and I were a couple, the three of us would inevitably spend time together." A thought hit and made me a little queasy. "What if we were to get married someday? Then Caitlin would've slept with her stepfather."

Wells smiled. "And I always thought it would be me on one of those daytime talk shows..."

I sighed. "I need to get some rest."

"You do that. You're going to need all the strength you can get."

"For what?"

"To get your ass up to Ryan's House this weekend and have a conversation with Brayden in person. You at least owe the dude that much."

❤CHAPTER 17

Brayden

I rolled into Seneca Falls early on Friday afternoon. There was no sign of Alex yet. For all I knew, she would decide to back out. If so, maybe I could concentrate on getting some freaking work done again this week. Her ghosting me might be easier than having to face her. *Who am I kidding?* I'd be crushed if she didn't show up. I wanted to see her. I *needed* to see her.

The only way to describe this feeling was nervous exhilaration. I was both excited to see Alex and dreading having to hold back. What I'd done when she visited the City—pushing her up against the wall of that building and kissing the hell out of her— had to be a one-time deal. I couldn't lose control like that if she wasn't mine. That would be torture.

Needing to expend some nervous energy, I decided to go to the hospital to visit Will. It had been a while since I'd checked in on him.

After getting set up with my volunteer badge, I went to his room. Peeking through the door, which was cracked open, I found him in bed. He was looking out the window. It made me sad to think of all the things he was missing, the normal kid stuff that people like me took for granted when we were younger. At least Ryan hadn't gotten sick until he was a bit older. Still too young, of course, but our childhood had been unscathed, filled with so many precious memories that didn't involve a single hospital stay among us, from what I could recall. Will couldn't have been more than ten or eleven. He deserved to be making memories outside of this damn place.

I knocked lightly.

He turned, smiling. "Brayden…"

"Hey, man, how's it going?"

He struggled to sit up. "I finished the books you gave me. They were really good."

"You enjoyed them? You can tell me the truth if you didn't. I won't be offended."

"I wouldn't lie. Life's too short to read bad books. Trust me, I wouldn't have finished them if I didn't like them."

"Well, I'm glad."

"It felt good to get lost in that world. So, thanks." Will stared out the window again.

"You seem kind of down." I took a seat. "Everything okay?"

"Not really."

My heart sank. "What's going on?"

"There's this girl from school. I really like her, and she wants to come visit me. We're neighbors, actually. But I don't know about her coming. I don't want her to see me like this, not looking my best. But I also don't want to tell her not to come. That's kind of rude."

"You want to see her?"

"Yeah. Just not…like this."

While I was relieved that his news had nothing to do with his health, I wasn't sure what advice to give him. I scratched my chin. "Do you like her?"

"What do you think?" He glared at me. "I wouldn't give a crap if I didn't like her."

"Got it."

"I *wish* I didn't like her, though. It would make things easier."

"I feel that more than you know, buddy. Right in here." I patted my chest. "When we like someone…it makes us self-conscious, sometimes more than we need to be. You look good, considering all you've been through as of late. You don't have hair, but anyone who looks at you can still see your handsome face and your bright blue eyes."

He seemed to perk up a bit, then shrugged. "I guess I could always wear a hat."

"Exactly. I can't relate to having no hair, but I know when I have a bad hair day, hats always save me."

"Do you have a favorite hat?" he asked.

"My friend Ryan's Eagles cap. He had a few of them. And I got one of them when he…" *Shit.* I stopped myself from finishing the sentence. But Will knew who I was referring to.

"Ryan is your friend who died?"

Swallowing, I nodded. I always had mixed feelings bringing up Ryan to Will, since I never wanted him to lose hope. But he'd asked me why I was involved with the hospital a while back, and I'd told him all about Ryan.

Will sighed. "I guess I shouldn't be overthinking the Caitlin thing."

My eyes widened. "Did you say Caitlin?"

"That's her name."

I chuckled. "Ah…" I'd thought I was hearing things. Can't escape *Caitlin*, I guess.

"Well, if you like this girl, Caitlin, it's totally understandable that you're nervous about what she thinks. Believe me, I get how you feel."

Will smirked. "What about that woman I saw you talking to here that one time? Is she your girlfriend?"

"That's Alex."

"Cool name for a lady. Isn't that a guy's name, though?"

"Funny enough, that's sort of how we met. I thought she was a dude when I met her."

"You thought she looked like a man?"

"No." I laughed. "Far from it."

"I don't get it."

"I'd been corresponding with her via email and thought she was a guy the whole time—until I saw her in person."

"No way." He laughed. "What did you do?"

"After I got over the initial shock, I fell for her pretty quickly. I've been making a fool of myself ever since."

His mouth curved into a smile.

It was nice to see his mood lighten up. "Anyway, Alex is someone I wanted to be my girlfriend. But...things are complicated with us now. Although, I'm supposed to see her this weekend—*if* she shows up—so I can relate to what you're feeling, being nervous about seeing a girl and not knowing what to expect."

"Why don't you just wear a hat?" he teased.

"I wish it were that simple, buddy. Not sure a hat's gonna fix *my* problem."

I would spare Will the details of my relationship drama. As always, though, being around him reminded me that there were far worse problems than my own. I'd continue to pray each day that Will's outcome would be different than Ryan's.

A nurse came in to see Will, so I said goodbye and promised to visit him again soon, making a mental note to buy him a cool hat.

On my way down the hall, a soft voice stopped me. "Brayden."

I turned to find Alex. Her blond hair was tied up, showcasing her slender neck. Her beautiful face held a serious expression.

I cleared my throat. "Hey... I was wondering if I would run into you here."

She smiled hesitantly. "Hi."

"Were you visiting Ashlyn?"

Alex shook her head. "Ashlyn is not here anymore."

My stomach sank. "Is she okay?"

"Yeah." She nodded. "Discharged."

I breathed a sigh of relief. "Thank God." A long moment of silence passed. "It's good to see you." My eyes dropped to her neck. "You look amazing. But that's nothing new." I balled my fist, resisting the urge to reach out and hug or kiss her. *Don't do it.* The longing was real, though. I'd replayed that last kiss we shared in my head too many times to count. I still had no idea where things stood or what she was expecting out of this weekend. But I knew I needed to let her take the driver's seat. She was the one with the decision to make, not me. For me, the decision was clear: I wanted to be with her. End of story.

"Do you think we can go somewhere and talk?" she asked, fidgeting with her ring.

"Definitely. Why don't we get coffees and take them to a park or something? It's pretty mild out."

"Sounds good."

Alex and I said nothing else as we exited the hospital together. The afternoon breeze blew a whiff of her flowery scent toward me, that hint of her essence enough to drive me crazy. Mainly because there wasn't a damn thing I could do about it.

She drove behind me as I headed to a local café. Alex waited in her car as I ran inside. I ordered her the usual coffee with oat milk and cinnamon, along with a few different pastries. She followed me to a park, where we sat on a bench with our coffees.

Alex pulled the flap back on her lid and blew on the coffee. "So…" she said. "Caitlin came by the other night."

I licked my lips. "Okay…"

"She and I talked about the situation for the first time."

I felt a glimmer of hope in my chest. "What did she say?"

"She spent much of the time trying to convince me I should

go for it with you. She said enough time had passed that it didn't matter anymore. She claims it wouldn't bother her, and that her initial reaction was just out of shock."

My hopes probably should have gone up upon hearing that, yet the look on her face said *not so fast*. "Why don't you look like that's good news?"

"I don't really think it is." She shook her head. "Caitlin loves me, and she wants me to be happy, so she's sacrificing her own feelings. I don't trust that she's truly okay with it."

Sacrificing her own feelings. Sounded familiar. "Why should *you* have to be the one to sacrifice?"

"Because that's what you do for your children." She exhaled. "Think about the long-term reality of this situation, Brayden. She's the biggest part of my life. Things like spending holidays together? It would be awkward for both you and her."

I raised my voice. "That's not true. It would *not* be awkward for me. The only reason I would ever feel uncomfortable is if I thought *you* were uncomfortable."

"Have you really stopped to imagine it, though?"

"No." I shook my head. "Because I don't need to. But if *you* can't accept the situation, we're destined to fail."

I couldn't believe this. Caitlin had given her blessing, and Alex was still scared? Here I was thinking the only obstacle was that Caitlin hadn't come around. Maybe this was about more than just Caitlin's feelings. Then again, I didn't have a child and couldn't relate to how deep Alex's guilt must be. If Alex wasn't going to budge, though, we were a lost cause. As much as I wanted to, I wasn't going to beg.

I sat across from her stone faced, my coffee getting cold because I could no longer stomach it.

Her eyes watered. "I'm sorry, Brayden."

"Yeah, me too." I stood, needing to get away before I said something I'd regret. "There's nothing more to say, I guess."

My original plan had been to invite her to have dinner with me tonight. That wasn't going to happen. For the first time I realized how badly I needed to distance myself if Alex didn't think we had a future. The challenge would be figuring out how to do that while continuing to support this project.

"I'm gonna head back to the hotel," I announced as I started to walk away, leaving her sitting on the bench.

She called after me. "Brayden…"

Refusing to turn around, I kept on walking. That was one of the hardest things I'd ever done. But the sooner I learned to walk away, the better I'd be.

I got in my car and took off.

Later that night, holed up in my hotel room, Owen's name lit up my phone. It had been a while since I'd caught up with him.

I answered. "What's up, Dawson?"

"Hey, man. Long time no speak."

"How's everything going?" I asked.

"Can't you hear how everything's going?"

The sound of a baby crying was pretty much *all* I could hear. Owen's fiancée, Devyn, had just had a baby boy. So they had their hands full.

"Earlier today, Holden filled me in on everything that's been going on with you," he said. "You've been hooking up with that woman from Ryan's House, and I didn't know about any of it."

"What made him tell you today?"

"Well, I told him I'd spotted you practically mauling some woman outside our building the other day. He said that was Alex. You hadn't even mentioned you were dating anyone. God, I've really been out of the loop, haven't I?"

"You've had some things on your plate. And there's nothing happening anymore anyway." I shut my eyes for a moment. "It's over, and I don't really feel like talking about it tonight." I sighed. "It's been a day."

"Shit. I'm sorry. Holden told me about the whole daughter thing, too—that you used to date her in college. That's some shit luck. It's not her biological daughter, though, right?"

"Stepdaughter, technically. But it doesn't matter. She considers her a daughter."

Owen's fiancée had a younger brother and sister he'd become a father figure to. "Think about how close you've become to Heath and Hannah in the short time you've known them. Now, imagine if several years went by on top of that. There's no way I'm ever gonna be more important to Alex than her daughter. And she's decided it needs to be a choice."

"Well, that just sucks, Brayden. Truly. It's so rare for you to have these kinds of feelings for a woman. And to have this happen…" He let out a long breath into the phone. "Each one of us has ended up with the person we're meant to be with, and the same thing will happen to you. I'm sure of it. If Alex is the one, she'll come around. And if not? Someone better will come along."

I stared out my window at the dark parking lot below. "I thought I'd finally found my person." My voice cracked. "Thought I was gonna finally join the ranks with you guys. Finally settle down." I paused. "I used to feel pressure about joining your club, though deep down I didn't want to. But what I had with Alex was easy. There was no pressure. It all fell together very naturally. And I'm sorry you're not gonna get to know her. Because she's really special."

"I'm sorry, too."

"Thanks," I murmured.

"Brayden, if I haven't said this already, I'm damn proud of you. I mean, we're all involved in Ryan's House to some extent, but you've really taken the reins on that. He would be so proud of you, too."

I looked up at the ceiling. "This whole Caitlin thing better not be Ryan fucking with me from up there."

"I do think he'd find it pretty ironic." Owen chuckled.

"Thanks for calling, but I'd better let you go. Say hi to Devyn—and Heath and Hannah."

"By the way, speaking of my honorary brother, Heath, I should probably let you know something."

"What?"

"He happened to take some *footage* of you and Alex kissing outside the building the day we drove by and saw you. We were at a red light. So just be on the lookout for that on the Internet—or potentially a blackmail letter."

"Great." I rolled my eyes. "Thanks for the heads up, but that doesn't really faze me right now." *Nothing does.*

After Owen and I hung up, I felt a tiny bit better. Talking to him had been a step up from staring blankly at my uneaten room-service food, like I had for the majority of this evening.

I decided to take a shower. Under the water, I pondered how strange it was to know Alex was in the same hotel tonight, yet we weren't together. I had no idea what to expect from the rest of this weekend. But this was the way it had to be.

When I exited the bathroom, I'd just put on gray sweatpants when there was a knock at the door. I'd been in such a funk that I couldn't remember if I had ordered something else from room service or not.

I opened the door and found her standing there. *Alex.*

"What are you doing here?"

She looked flushed. Her chest heaved. The hair that had been tied up neatly earlier looked almost like she'd been pulling on it, wispy pieces framing her gorgeous face.

"I needed to see you," she said, her tone breathy.

"Why?" I asked. "I told you earlier, there's nothing more to say. You shouldn't be here."

The look on her face was a mix of torment and...lust. Her eyes fell to my bare chest. Her breathing quickened even more.

Then she finally said it.

"We can't be together." She paused. "But I need to know what it's like, Brayden."

CHAPTER 18

Alex

Brayden's eyes jumped back and forth. "Are you saying what I think you're saying?"

"I want you, Brayden. It won't change my mind about our future, but I *need* you. I need you so much, it physically hurts. And I'm well aware it's incredibly selfish of me to show up like this and ask you to be with me the way I want when I won't be with you the way you want, but I don't care. My desire for you is stronger than my ability to do the right thing tonight."

His gaze stayed locked with mine as he shook his head. "I'm so fucking mad at you right now, for not giving what's between us a chance. Even if on some level I understand why you're doing it, the anger is still there. I'm afraid if we were together right now, I wouldn't be able to set that aside."

My heart pounded. "So don't. Don't even try. *Be* mad at me. Hate me for doing this. But take that anger out on me tonight. I *want* you, Brayden."

His jaw clenched, and his green eyes darkened to almost gray with anger. For a second, I thought he was going to throw me out. But then he swallowed. "Turn around," he growled.

My body felt like it had been plugged into an outlet; an electric current raced through me. I would've done anything he said. I'd take him however he would give himself to me. So I turned and faced the wall.

Brayden came up behind me and pressed his body to mine. "No condom," he said. "I'm clean. Haven't been with anyone since you turned my fucking life upside down. If I'm only getting one night, I want to feel you. Want you to feel me. I'm going to bury my cum so deep inside you, it'll take days for it to seep out."

Oh, God. Was it possible to have an orgasm without someone even touching you? I nodded. "I'm okay with that. I've had an IUD for years."

Brayden pushed against me harder. He wrapped my hair around his hand and made a fist, giving a good, firm tug. My neck jerked back, and he leaned in and sucked along my pulse line. "Is this what you want?" he growled. "I'm going to leave bite marks the way I'm feeling."

My eyes rolled to the back of my head as he nipped his way up to my ear. "Go ahead," I breathed. "I want you to."

Brayden's big hand wrapped around me, slipping inside my blouse. When he felt my skin, he stilled. "No bra. You *knew* I wouldn't be able to resist you."

That wasn't actually true, but I didn't think this was the right time to debate it. Instead, I pushed my ass against him. "I don't have any underwear either."

He groped my chest, pinching one nipple then the other— hard. A jolt of pain shot through me, but it only heightened my desire. "More," I gasped.

He reached between my legs. "Are you wet for me, Alex?"

I opened my mouth to respond, but the words fell away as his hand slid inside my pants. Brayden's long fingers stroked up and down over my center and then plunged inside. "Spread wider," he commanded.

Whatever shame I had about coming here to make this man have sex with me was long gone—left outside his hotel room door. I spread my legs as wide as they could go, feeling desperate.

"So fucking wet," he growled next to my ear. "So fucking needy. I'm going to finger you until you're about to come, and then I'm going to stop, show you what it feels like to have something you want so badly taken away from you. That's how you make me feel by taking *you* away from me." He pumped in and out once, twice, then added another finger. "I want you to *beg* tonight."

I moaned and shut my eyes. "Yes. Please. I'll beg. I'll do anything."

The sound of his hand slapping against my wetness grew louder as he glided in and out. It was sensory overload—feeling him inside me, the smell of sex, the echo of my arousal bouncing around the room. I was so on edge, I didn't think I'd last longer than a few more pumps. My breathing hitched, and I felt the ebb before the wave and then…he *stopped*.

I was mid breath and almost choked on air. Brayden withdrew his fingers. I was still facing the wall, my head turned to the side. My eyes fluttered open just in time to watch Brayden lift his fingers to his mouth and suck my wetness off.

I whimpered.

A wicked smile spread across his face. "Take off your pants so I can finish eating."

I shimmied out of my joggers and waited for what would come next. But it wasn't an instruction this time. Brayden dropped to his knees, dipped down, and came up with his mouth directly between my spread legs. As it had been from the start, there was no easing in, no gentle licks and sucks—no, he buried his entire face in my pussy. It was rough and angry, desperate and unapologetic. Brayden moved his face back and forth, lapping at my arousal like he was starving and I was his last meal. The scruff on his cheeks caused a sweet ache in my tender flesh.

"*Brayden…*"

"So sweet. *So fucking sweet,* just like you are. But you're cruel, too." He sucked hard on my clit and pushed two fingers back inside me.

My cries grew louder, more desperate. "Brayden…" I gyrated my hips, riding his face. "Brayden, please…*please* don't stop."

He answered by once again pulling away, just seconds before I was about to come. Tears welled in my eyes, and I panted as the bastard's eyes gleamed. He stood and pushed down his sweatpants in one swoop, stepping out. Brayden grabbed my wrist, pulled my arm back, and wrapped my fingers around his cock.

Oh, Jesus. He was so gloriously hard, his skin so smooth and hot. Not to mention, my fingers could barely fit around his girth. I licked my lips, salivating at the thought of taking my turn. But I was *not* the one in control right now. Brayden's face still glistened with the evidence of that.

"Bend at the waist." He placed his palm on my back and pressed, guiding me down. "Two hands on the wall. Eyes forward."

Once I was folded in half, he wrapped an arm around my stomach and hoisted me up to my toes. I held my breath, waiting for him to enter me from behind. But like everything that had happened since I walked into this room, he caught me by surprise once again.

This time, it was a loud crack, the palm of his hand connecting with the bare skin of my ass. It stung like hell, but before I could complain, Brayden thrust inside me, knocking the wind out of my lungs. He buried himself so deep that his hips were flush against my ass. A vibration spread between us, and I wasn't even sure which one of us was shaking.

Brayden's fingers pressed into my hip, and he thrust harder against my ass. "Is this what you want? Me to angry-fuck you?"

"Yes," I breathed. "Yes."

"You might not want anything to do with me tomorrow, but I'm going to make you so sore you'll feel me for days." He grabbed a handful of my hair and tugged as he pulled almost all the way out, then slammed back in. Again and again. Over and over. It was harsh and punishing, but I couldn't remember anything ever feeling so good. Once I found my bearings, I moved with him, pushing back when he burrowed in, gripping him tight as he slid almost fully out. My orgasm hadn't gone very far, so it came barreling back with a vengeance. If he didn't let me finish this time, I thought I might lose my mind.

"Fuck," Brayden said, his voice hoarse. "You're squeezing me so tight, I'm going to explode." He pumped with a roar—once, twice—and before he could get to three, my body flew over the edge, pulsing with an intensity I'd never felt before.

"Brayden!"

He kept pumping, mumbling a string of curses. My knees weakened, and I worried how much longer I'd be able to keep myself upright. Then, with a roar, Brayden sank deep and stilled, unloading inside of me. I could feel heat seeping through my body.

After, our panting was the only sound in the room. Brayden pulled out and wrapped me in his arms from behind. We stayed that way, in silence, for a long time. Tears prickled at the corners of my eyes, but I refused to let him see them since I'd gotten what I asked for.

"I'm sorry," he eventually whispered.

I tried to make light of it. "For what? We both finished, didn't we?"

Brayden turned me around in his arms. It hit me like a punch in the gut when I saw tears streaming down his face. "I'm so sorry. I shouldn't have done that."

"Oh God, no. Don't apologize. I asked you to."

He shook his head, looking down. "It doesn't matter. I shouldn't have taken my anger out with sex. You mean more to me than that."

I cupped his cheek. "You mean a lot to me, too, Brayden. That might be hard to believe, but you brought me back to life."

"I can't let you go like this. I'll never forgive myself if the last moments we spend together are filled with anger. Will you stay with me tonight?"

I was so far gone for this man, a couple of hours couldn't possibly make it harder to walk away. I didn't want to leave him feeling guilt for something I'd caused. So I nodded. "I'd like that."

He half smiled. "Maybe we should move away from the door then?"

Until now, I hadn't noticed that we were still standing in the hall and hadn't made it into the actual room. I smiled. "That might be a good idea."

"How about I give you one of my shirts to change into, and we order some room service?"

"That sounds perfect."

I was wrong.

I hadn't thought it could get any harder to walk away, but after a night like this one—it was going to be hell. Brayden and I had stayed up until all hours—eating, talking, sharing a bottle of wine. We laughed, we held each other, somehow we pretended it wasn't the end.

But now the sun was coming up, and it was getting harder to breathe. My head lay on his bare chest while he stroked my hair. Neither of us had said a word for the last half hour. I'd forced us to where we were now, so it was going to have to be me to end it— even if it was the absolute last thing I wanted to do.

"I should probably get going," I whispered.

Brayden's hand stilled. "No, not yet. I need to do something first."

I turned, propping my chin on top of my fist. "What?"

He sat up, gently turning us so I was on my back, and kissed my lips gently. "I want to make love to you, Alex."

I swallowed, tasting salt in my throat, and nodded.

Brayden reached for my hand, brought it to his mouth, and kissed it. "I will never regret the time we've had together. You've taught me what love is—it means someone else's happiness is more important than your own. And because of that, I'm not going to bother you or make things harder. I will let you go. Because it's what you need. But I want you to know, there won't be a day that goes by that I won't be thinking of you."

Tears welled in my eyes again. When he pressed his lips to mine, it was unlike any of the other times we'd kissed. It was filled with more emotion, more passion, and...love. I made a conscious decision to let go of all of my worries, of all my concerns about protecting myself and everyone else, and let myself get lost in this man. Even if it was only this once.

Brayden climbed on top of me as our kiss heated up, and I spread my legs wide, inviting him in. He rocked back and forth, working his bare cock against my clit, and spreading my arousal between us. When things built to a frenzy, he pulled back, never taking his eyes from mine as he pushed inside.

"I swear, Alex." His eyes closed briefly. "Nothing has ever felt so good."

We moved in unison, our bodies growing slick with sweat, kissing each other like we were the air we needed to breathe. Never in my life had I experienced such a connection—we were one in mind, body, and soul.

But too soon, the tension built. It might've been the first time I didn't want to have an orgasm, because I knew at the end, it would be over. I wanted this moment to last forever. But of course, it couldn't. Brayden's jaw clenched, the speed of his thrusts increasing, and I knew he was trying to prolong it just like I was.

"Fuck," he gritted. "I can't hold back much more. You feel too good."

Those words were all it took for my body to fly over the edge. My muscles began pulsing on their own, squeezing his cock tight as I let out a loud moan.

"I can feel you," he groaned. "Feel you coming all around me."

He bucked a few more times before he finally let himself go, gazing into my eyes. It was a moment I would remember forever.

Long after, Brayden continued to glide in and out, still semi erect, even after such a powerful orgasm. He kissed my lips gently and pushed my hair from my face. "I need you to know something, Alex."

My voice was barely a whisper. "What?"

He looked back and forth between my eyes. "I am totally and helplessly in love with you."

My heart clenched, and I cupped his face. "*Oh, Brayden.*"

He smiled sadly. "I might've learned that true love is self*less*, but right now, I needed to be self*ish* and tell you my truth."

"Thank you. Thank you for always giving me your honesty."

Too soon, Brayden had to get out of bed to get to Ryan's House. The only other person with a key wasn't going to be there today. The mood was heavy with melancholy as we got dressed. I was at least grateful this wouldn't be the last time I'd see him. I wasn't sure I could handle a clean break quite yet.

"Take your time getting to the house," Brayden said. "We're waiting on a few deliveries anyway."

"Okay." I tried to force a smile, but failed. "I'm going to go back to my room and shower. I'll probably be there in about an hour."

He nodded, pushing his hands into his pants pockets. A half hour ago, we'd been connected in a way I didn't know existed, yet suddenly the interactions between us felt awkward, like neither of us knew how to end the night. This was my fault, so it had to be me. I pushed up and kissed his cheek. "I'll see you later."

Walking out of that hotel room felt nearly impossible. It didn't get any easier over the next forty-five minutes either. I took a shower in a fog, couldn't even remember drying my hair, and barely had the energy to put on a little makeup. Just as I was getting ready to leave, there was a knock at my door. I opened it to find Brayden standing there.

"I was just about to head out."

He frowned. "Don't bother. When I got to the house, I found this on the door."

Brayden held up a piece of paper, the top three words in big, bold letters:

STOP WORK ORDER

I felt panic in my chest. "What is this?"

"The city building department also slid some papers under the door, violations for not having proper work permits. Apparently the electrician I hired didn't file the paperwork he was supposed to, and the town is now saying we have an environmental issue. Some cesspool under the ground wasn't filled in right years ago."

"Years ago? But none of that is your fault. Can they do this? Make us shut down?"

"It's a fifteen-hundred-dollar-per-day fine if we do anything more on the house and get caught. I can't risk it."

"What are you going to do?"

Brayden raked a hand through his hair. "I'll call my lawyer first thing Monday morning and then go down to the building department, see how I go about getting this taken care of."

"What about the volunteers? What will they do?"

"There's nothing any of them can do this weekend. We're done until I can get this fixed. I already sent out a group text, hoping maybe I'd catch some of them before they drove over." Brayden looked into my eyes. "I guess everyone who's already here can just go back home."

CHAPTER 19

Alex

Three months.

That's how long it had been since I'd looked into his eyes. Since I'd smelled him. Touched him. Heard his voice. Three months since he'd…been inside of me. Just thinking about the weekend Brayden and I had sex sent shivers through my body.

Not a day went by that I didn't think about him. That's for damn sure. Actually, not an *hour* went by. Brayden was still the first thing that popped into my mind when I woke up in the morning and the last thing I thought about as I drifted off to sleep at night. I missed him more every day. And I didn't know if it would ever get any easier.

That last weekend in Seneca Falls, Brayden and I had gone our separate ways shortly after we got the stop-work order. I'd taken that unexpected development as a sign that ending things was still the right decision—even after the best sex of my life. Even after he'd told me he loved me. I'd kept those three words inside of me instead of returning them, despite longing to blurt them out before I left. There was still an ache in my chest from having to hold them in. And those words were still there, begging to come out. The love was still there. It was burning a hole in my heart.

What surprised me most about the past few months was that neither Brayden nor I had given in and contacted the other. I'd expected him to call or message me, but he hadn't. It wasn't that I *wanted* him to call, because that would complicate things. Lord knows I'd had to stop myself from calling or texting him multiple times. Every time I got the urge to contact him, I reminded myself that it would only make the current situation harder. We were done. There was no need to torture ourselves.

One of the things that worked best to remind me that I'd made the right decision was spending time with Caitlin. I'd been making more of an effort to schedule with her lately. Today she and I had gone to a local nail salon for mani-pedis.

Caitlin sat next to me, immersed in a magazine as we both got our feet done before we'd eventually move over to the manicure stations. Before this, we'd gone to lunch at her favorite sushi place. As the woman worked on my feet, I found myself deep in thought. Not meditating, as I'd hoped to in this seat, but mostly thinking about everything I'd kept secret from Caitlin.

The friction from the loofa gliding across the bottom of my foot wasn't enough to snap me out of it. As much as I loved spending time with Caitlin, guilt always crept in that I hadn't told her Brayden and I had slept together. I'd convinced myself she didn't need to know, since I'd vowed to stay away from him. Why make her uncomfortable with that information if we were truly over?

Over. If only it were that simple. Maybe this would be easier if Brayden hadn't told me he loved me. Those words haunted me. I hadn't been expecting a declaration of love. I'd known his feelings were strong… But love? He *loved* me. I realized I'd known I loved him for some time before that, even if I couldn't fully admit it to myself. But I'd never imagined that he felt the same way. It made ending things so much more bittersweet. Though we couldn't be together, I'd always be touched that he'd cared so much.

Caitlin's voice snapped me out of my thoughts. "Hey, what are you thinking about over there? You're totally spaced out."

I turned to find she had closed her magazine and was looking at me—for God knows how long.

"Just enjoying this quiet time." I cleared my throat.

"You're in la-la land. We usually talk while we're here, use the time to catch up. It's one of my favorite things about getting our nails done together."

I shook my head. "Sorry… I suppose I *was* caught up in my thoughts."

"Is something going on?"

I swallowed. "Nothing bad or anything."

"Is it about Brayden?"

I tensed. "Why would you think that?"

"Because I'm not stupid. You told me you'd ended things the last time you saw him, but I know you downplayed it—for my sake. Which I truly hate, by the way." She raised a brow. "Did you hear from him again? Is that why you're preoccupied?"

"No. We haven't spoken since Seneca Falls…since we lost the permit."

"It's a shame that happened," she said. "I have a feeling if you had kept seeing him, the two of you would have ended up together."

"Actually I was thinking the opposite," I told her. "It was a damn good thing they stopped work on the house because it basically solved my problem for me. The dilemma was never whether I needed to stop seeing him, but rather *how* I was going to make that work while having to see him week after week."

Caitlin looked down at the man working on her feet for a moment, then back up at me. "I don't understand why you didn't listen when I told you it didn't bother me. It was a shock at first, and I didn't handle it well—I'm sorry for that. But I would've been okay with it. Your happiness is worth any little discomfort that was left."

The two nail techs seemed to pause at the same time to look up at us before returning their attention to our feet. This soap opera had apparently garnered their interest.

I lowered my voice. "I do believe you felt okay with it when you said that. If I had moved forward with that relationship, though, once the reality set in—you had to see us together and spend time with us—it would've bothered you, whether you realize that now or not. But it's all a moot point, Caitlin, truly. It's over."

Her eyes lingered on mine. "I don't know. I don't feel like it's over in your head. It's especially not over in your heart. I still see the look on your face when you talk about him. It's not like any other expression you have. You really care about him."

I sighed. "I'm sorry if I'm not very good at hiding it. But I made a decision, and I'm sticking with it, okay? I need you to respect that. I'm not gonna lie. It hasn't been easy. But I'm hoping as time goes on, it *will* get easier. It's been three months." *Three excruciating months.* I pressed a button to turn on the massage chair. "For all I know, he's dating someone else now. The sooner I can move on, the better. You insinuating that I made the wrong decision isn't helping. It doesn't change anything."

She frowned. "I'm sorry. You did what you felt you had to do. I don't agree, but I know it was a sacrifice for me…because you thought it's what I needed. I just wish things were different. I want you to be happy."

"I know," I muttered, looking down as the woman applied a bright pink polish to my toes. I shook my head. "I think we need to move on to a lighter subject."

"Okay. Lighter subject." Caitlin grinned. "We've got to get you on a dating app."

"Ugh. That's not lighter." I laughed. "That's torture."

"Well, it's something we should talk about. I agree that it's not exactly fun out there—believe me, I know. But it's kind of necessary if you're going to get over him."

I sighed again. "Wells has been trying to convince me too. I'm certain one of these days he's just going to set up the dating profile for me, if he hasn't already."

"Count me in on that. I can help him. I'll tone down his crazy write-up. Because you know Wells will go off the rails with that shit."

"Can you imagine if he had total control? These men would think I liked my nipples clamped and my ass whipped."

Caitlin laughed. "Maybe I should have him set up mine."

I chuckled. "I'll be seeing Wells tonight, so I can pass along the message."

She wiped the corner of her eye. "Are you guys going anywhere good?"

"I'm meeting him at Casablanca's. He's dating a new guy. Name is Winston. He wants me to meet him."

"Winston sounds like a dog's name." She giggled. "So, third wheel, then?"

"Yeah. *Winston* will be the third wheel." I winked.

"Yeah. That's always the way with you and *Funcle* Wellsy." She smiled.

The nail techs moved us over to the manicure station where we spent the rest of our time quietly enjoying our pampering while we watched the Food Network show they had playing on multiple televisions. As I looked up at a woman decorating a cake, I thought about what to wear later to meet Wells's new boy-toy. A simple black dress seemed like the right fit. Maybe a pop of red.

Ever since Brayden and I had ended things, I'd felt a little guilty around Wells, too. I hadn't told him that Brayden and I had slept together back in Seneca Falls either. Wells would think I was absolutely crazy for ending things if he knew Brayden had told me he loved me. Wells had always advocated for me to put myself first, even before he knew Brayden felt that way about me. With more details, he would most definitely lecture me on making a huge mistake. I didn't want to hear it. So as of now, my last *amazing* night with Brayden remained my secret. Someday I'd tell Wells everything. Just not anytime soon.

After our manicures, Caitlin and I moved to the nail drying station. She admired my bright pink nails. "I love that color. What's it called? I want to find it online."

I got the tech's attention. "Excuse me. Can you tell me the name of this color?"

The woman went over to the shelf to retrieve the hot pink polish and looked at the bottom. "It's called Mrs. Robinson," she yelled over.

Mrs. Robinson?

My mouth fell open. Caitlin burst into laughter, and I couldn't help but crack up myself.

It felt good.

The second I spotted Wells's table as I entered Casablanca's later that night, I regretted agreeing to come out. There were *two* men with him, one sitting on either side. *Is this a setup?* This dinner was supposed to be about me meeting *his* new guy. This other guy had better be one of their gay friends.

"You're late, Kitten," Wells chided.

"Yeah, well, I figured I'd give you two some alone time before I crashed your dinner, but I see you *aren't* alone."

Wells pointed to his new boyfriend. "This is Winston." He gestured to me. "Winston, meet my best friend, Alex."

Winston offered me a hug. "It's a pleasure, sweetheart. I've heard so much about you."

He had red hair and freckles and was a good bit shorter than Wells.

Winston turned to the other dude. "And this is my big brother, Everett. He came to hang with us tonight."

Everett stood. He, unlike his little brother, was really tall and dressed in a suit, more formal than the rest of us. Also unlike his brother, he had sandy brown hair.

Everett held out his hand. "It's so great to meet you, Alex."

"You as well." I nodded. "I've heard so many wonderful things about your brother."

"That's how it always goes." Everett smacked Winston on the arm playfully. "Little bro here gets all the glory. Thankfully, we've never had to compete for the ladies."

"I didn't realize you were coming out with us tonight," I told him, giving Wells a look. I sat down and placed a napkin in my lap.

"Wells tells me you're his rock," Winston said, pointing his wine glass toward me. "I've been excited all day to meet the famous Alex."

I wanted to kill Wells, but I smiled over at him. He looked happy, which made *me* happy.

I dug deep and sucked it up over a glass of wine, and then I did my best at getting to know both of the guys during dinner.

But I was still pissed that Wells had caught me off guard. So when my BFF got up to visit the bathroom, I excused myself as well and waited for him outside the men's room. The moment he came out, I crossed my arms. "What the hell do you think you're doing?"

"Trying to help you get some, what any caring friend would do."

"You could've given me a little warning. I had no idea this was a blind date tonight."

"A warning? Why? So you could've made up an excuse to not come? That's *exactly* what you would've done, Alex. You know it."

I looked over my shoulder and back at him. "You're right. Because I have no interest in dating right now. I've already told you that."

"Do I have to remind you that it's been *ages* since you've gotten laid?"

Not exactly. Flashes of the rough sex I'd had with Brayden ran through my mind. My body tingled. *Jesus.* My face suddenly felt flushed.

Wells's eyes widened. "You little wench."

I cleared my throat. "What?" God, apparently, I had no ability to hold this in any longer.

"You had sex…"

It was one thing to keep it a secret. It was another to lie to his face. I couldn't do it. "Maybe." I bit my bottom lip.

"It's a yes or no answer, Alex."

I sighed. "It hasn't been ages, okay? So I'm…not in need of any help."

"I don't care if Winston thinks I'm screwing that hot waiter in the bathroom. I'm not returning to the table until you tell me what happened."

"Brayden and I slept together the last time we were upstate," I confessed. "There. You have it."

"Holy shit." He put his hands on my shoulders and shook me. "You've been keeping this from me for three fucking months?"

"I didn't realize I was obligated to tell you *every* last detail about my life."

"Woman, I know more about you than you do." He scratched his chin. "But if you were keeping this a secret, there's a reason. You wouldn't normally hide something this monumental from me."

"I didn't want you to tell me I was making a mistake," I admitted.

"You didn't want me to tell you what you already know. Because me telling you that wouldn't bother you if it wasn't *the truth*."

My neck felt hot. "Can we not discuss this here?"

"Fine. We have to get back to the table. I just want to say one last thing."

"What?"

"If you're going to be stupid about Brayden and throw away something that means a lot to you, at the *very* least, please entertain the idea of Winston's perfectly handsome, successful, eligible brother."

"There's nothing wrong with Everett. It's just that…" My words trailed off.

He smirked. "He's not Brayden. That's what you wanted to say, right?"

I sighed. "What do you want from me?"

"I want you to be honest with yourself. It doesn't matter what you're telling me. But when you're lying to yourself, Alex, that's a huge problem. That will always come back to bite you in the ass. What if you wake up in two years and realize you made a mistake, but then it's too late? A guy like Brayden isn't gonna stay on the market for very long—I'll tell you that. And no offense, but you're not getting any younger."

I rolled my eyes. "Thanks for that, Captain Obvious."

"You can always count on me for the truth, babe."

"I can always count on you to screw with me, too, which is what you did by tricking me into this date!"

"Everything I do, I do because I love you." He smiled. "You know that, right?"

I sighed. "I do know that."

He put his hand on my shoulder. "Try to have some fun tonight, okay?"

I shrugged. "I'll see if I can find it in me."

He wriggled his brows. "There was a major thing *in you* I apparently didn't know about."

Laughing, I smacked him.

"Was it as good as I imagine?" he asked.

"Far, far better."

"Damn." He exhaled, putting his arm around me as we walked. "One can dream…"

After we returned to the table, I forced myself to engage in conversation with Everett and try to think about something besides Brayden.

Before we left the restaurant, Everett and I exchanged numbers. It turned out he was quite nice. He owned a furniture store and was divorced with two children. Everett also indicated he was done having kids. That was another plus in his column. I didn't want to get involved with anyone who wanted children. *Like Brayden.*

My heart clenched. There I was thinking about him again.

CHAPTER 20

Brayden

I really didn't feel like being here tonight, not even when a super-hot blonde sidled up to me at the bar.

"Hi. I'm sorry to bother you," she said. "I need to ask a big favor."

"Okay…"

"You see that table of ladies behind me?" She motioned with her eyes for me to look over her left shoulder. "The ones who are probably staring at us right now and smiling like loons?"

I glanced over. Sure enough, three sets of eyes were glued to us. "Yep. I see 'em."

"Okay, so…a year ago today my fiancé ended our engagement. Those are my three best friends, and they are never going to leave me alone until I talk to someone tonight." She sighed. "They mean well. I know that. But I'm not ready to jump back into the dating pool. Do you think we could just talk for ten minutes? They'll sleep better tonight not worrying that I'm going to die an old maid."

I smiled and lifted my chin toward the stage. "You see that drummer up there? The one watching us with a dumb-ass smile right about now?"

The woman looked over and back. "Yes?"

"That's the male version of your three ladies. I didn't make it to engagement, though I'm pretty sure the woman who dumped me recently was *the one*. And it's only been three months, not a year. But I agreed to come out tonight just so my buddy would stop making up reasons to pop in and check on me."

"Perfect." She smiled and extended her hand. "I'm Lacey."

"Brayden." We shook. "Nice to meet you. Can I buy you a drink?"

"How about a shot of tequila?" she said. "And I'm buying."

"Even better."

I glanced over at her friends again. They looked equal parts excited and nervous. "I'm going to look left and hold my hand up to call the bartender over. Why don't you give your friends the thumbs up on the sly while I do that? Might help them relax a little."

"Oooh… Good idea."

A few minutes later, Lacey and I clinked tequila-filled shot glasses. I held mine up in a toast. "To moping around and getting teary-eyed when we see other couples looking happy."

Lacey chuckled. "To being miserable for as long as we want."

We both knocked back the shot, following up with a lick of salt and a suck of lime. Lacey set down her glass. "So what went wrong in your relationship?"

I frowned.

"Oh gosh." She saw my face and put up her hands. "I'm sorry. It's too soon for you to talk about. I wasn't thinking. I'm sure I wouldn't have wanted to talk about it after only three months."

"It's fine." I shrugged. "Though nothing really went wrong. It's kind of a crazy story, actually."

"Well, that's a very intriguing statement. Now you have to tell me…"

I chuckled. "I think I might need another shot if we're going to swap war stories. How about next round on me?"

Lacey smiled. "Good idea. I find alcohol makes it easier for me to talk about the hard stuff."

I raised my hand to call the bartender, and we knocked back another round. The second one slid down smoother than the first. I wasn't much of a drinker, so between the tequila and the two beers I'd had before she walked over, I was feeling a fuck of a lot more relaxed. The alcohol apparently also helped improve my vision, because I noticed a few things about Lacey for the first time—like how big her blue eyes were, and how full her pouty mouth was. When she sucked on the lime, my gaze took a dip lower—appreciating her feminine curves.

With our liquid-courage tanks topped off, Lacey turned and straightened in her seat, giving me her full attention. "Feel more talkative now?"

I smiled. "Yeah, I'm good."

However, telling my story turned out to be more difficult than I'd thought. I couldn't seem to find the right place to begin. After a few minutes, I decided to stop overthinking things and just spit it out. "I slept with my girlfriend's daughter."

Lacey's jaw dropped, and her eyes went wide as saucers.

"Shit. That didn't come out right." I shook my head. "I didn't sleep with her after I started seeing Alex. I slept with her before."

But Lacey only looked more confused. "You slept with your girlfriend's daughter and then your girlfriend?"

"Yes, but it sounds worse than it is. Let me back up, start from the beginning." I explained how Caitlin—Kate—and I had briefly dated in college, and that Alex and I had no clue about that when we'd met by chance. When I was done telling the story, Lacey looked almost as shocked as when I'd blurted out that I'd slept with my girlfriend's daughter.

She shook her head. "That's the most insane thing I've ever heard. What are the chances you would date someone in college in one state, and then randomly meet her stepmother a decade later in a different one and fall in love?"

"I told you it was a screwed-up story."

"Is it weird that I almost feel like it was fate working in some odd way?"

"Working against me, maybe."

"So the daughter couldn't get past it?"

"That's the hardest part for me to swallow. Caitlin, the step-daughter, was pretty upset at first. In the end, though, she said she was okay with it. She wants Alex to be happy. But Alex is too afraid to risk her relationship with Caitlin. She doesn't really believe Caitlin would be okay with it."

"Do you think maybe Alex is hiding behind her daughter, using her as an excuse?"

"Because she's afraid of a serious relationship with someone younger?"

"Oh. Yeah, I guess it could be that, too."

I tilted my head. "What did you mean?"

"I meant maybe she used it as an excuse so she wouldn't hurt you."

My face fell. "Oh."

Lacey put her hand over her heart. "I'm so sorry. I just keep sticking my foot in my mouth, don't I? I shouldn't have suggested that. I don't know what the heck I'm saying."

But the seed had been planted, and my brain was already nurturing it, watching it grow. How the hell had I never considered that maybe Alex didn't feel the same way about me that I did about her? I'd spent hours thinking about what I could've done differently, how I could've convinced her to take a chance with me. Never once did it occur to me that she just…didn't love me. But she hadn't said the words back when I'd told her how I felt.

I swallowed and cleared my throat. "Alright, your turn."

Lacey chewed on her lip. "I need another shot."

"Coming right up."

If the second shot relaxed me, allowed me to appreciate the view, the third loosened me a little too much—emotions bubbled up as I listened to Lacey's story.

"So, yeah…" She sighed. "We'd been dating for three years when I got pregnant. Henry proposed the night we went for our first sonogram appointment and heard the heartbeat. A few days later, I miscarried. After that, I threw myself into planning the wedding—trying to focus on the happy things in life. But Henry changed. At first I thought he was sad about losing the baby, so I gave him some space. As time went on, though, it became apparent that Henry wasn't into the wedding. One day I asked him, '*Are you sure you even want to go through with this?*' I mean, we only got engaged when we did because I was pregnant. Still, I never expected him to say he didn't want to marry me. He said he loved me, but not the way a man should love a woman."

"I'm sorry."

Lacey shrugged. "Deep down, I know it's a good thing. I would rather have a year of heartache than a lifetime of not being my spouse's person. My parents didn't have a happy marriage. I want more than that. But it still stings that he couldn't love me the way I loved him. It makes me feel like I'm not enough, you know?"

"I'm really sorry."

She forced a smile. "Nothing to be sorry about."

Holden walked over. He slung an arm around my shoulder and offered his signature cocky grin. "Hi. I'm better looking and musically gifted, but my friend Brayden here is rich as hell. Did he mention that yet?"

Lacey arched a brow. "He actually didn't."

"He's also philanthropic as fuck. Runs a giant foundation and puts smiles on the faces of sick kids."

Lacey turned to me. "Is that true?"

I shrugged. "The foundation isn't that big. We do what we can."

Holden slapped my chest. "I knew it. He's been sitting here telling you his tale of woe for the last twenty minutes instead of talking himself up, like he should be."

Lacey smiled. "I think we've been going woe for woe."

"Well, let me finish the hard sell, and then I'll be out of your way." Holden mussed my hair. "My buddy Brayden here has some pretty great qualities. He's loyal—been friends with this idiot since kindergarten. Smart—I can't even spell the shit he's gotten patents on. And he owns a piece of real estate in Manhattan." Holden leaned in and flashed a grin. "I also own a piece of the apartment building, so that's two selling points in one—you get me as the sidekick for this handsome hunk of man."

I gave my idiot friend a shove. "I think you can put a sock in it now, jackass. Peddle that junk somewhere else."

"Speaking of junk—did I mention he's hung like a horse? Now, I haven't seen it since seventh grade, but once I pulled his swim trunks down at our buddy Ryan's pool party, and his thing put mine to shame. I'm sure it's only grown since then."

I chuckled, shaking my head. "It was actually *me* who pulled down *his* swim trunks, and I started wearing my underwear in the boys' locker room right after that. But thanks for the effort, buddy."

Holden winked. "My wife is a pretty lucky lady."

With that, my friend disappeared to play another set, leaving Lacey and me both laughing. I couldn't help but notice her lips again. "You have a great smile," I told her.

Lacey pushed hair behind her ear. "Thank you. And you have beautiful eyes."

"Look at us," I said. "Are we flirting?"

"I think we are!"

"This sounds like cause for celebration. Another shot of tequila?"

"Definitely."

A few hours later, it was just the two of us left at the bar. Holden was home with his family, and Lacey's friends had happily left her behind. We were both pretty drunk, so I hailed a cab, figuring I'd make it a two-stop ride home. To my surprise, Lacey lived only a block away from me. So when we stopped at her place, I got out to make sure she got in safely and would walk home from there.

At her apartment door, Lacey dropped her keys. We both reached for them at the same time and bumped heads. Lacey wobbled, so I grabbed her to keep her from falling, and she somehow wound up wrapped in my arms. She looked up at me with her big blue eyes, her hands pressed against my chest.

"Oooh…you feel good," she whispered. "I haven't had sex in a year."

It had been three months for me, but I definitely missed the feeling of a woman in my arms. "That's a long-ass time."

She bit her bottom lip and fluttered her lashes. "Too long. Do you want to come in? Maybe we can help each other forget?"

I was tempted. *Sort of.*

Lacey wrapped her arms around my neck. "I know neither of us is emotionally available. But it doesn't have to be more than it is. I like you. You're hot. I miss the physical part of a relationship."

I *wanted* to want to, so damn badly. But I couldn't. It would feel like I was cheating on Alex. Which was absolutely ridiculous, because in order to *cheat*, you have to be *in* a relationship, and I hadn't even spoken to Alex in three months. For all I knew, she'd met someone and moved on. Yet I couldn't do it. Besides, even if there were no Alex, Lacey and I had had a lot of tequila. The last thing this nice lady needed was regrets on top of the other shit she was already carrying. But I didn't want to make her feel bad, make her feel *rejection* again. So I needed to handle the situation delicately.

I lifted Lacey's hand and brought it to my lips. "You are gorgeous. And funny and smart. And your ex is a goddamned dumbass. But you've also had too much to drink. So as tempting as the invitation is, I'm going to head home."

She pouted. "But I don't want a gentleman right now. I want someone to do *bad things* to me."

I groaned and kissed the top of her head. "You're killing me."

Lacey dug her phone out of her pocket. "Give me your number at least. Maybe we can try this again when we're sober?"

I smiled. "You got it."

❤

Holden knocked the next morning. When I opened the door, he looked over my shoulder and grinned. "Bad time?"

I opened the door wide and stepped aside for him to enter. "I'm alone, jackass. I also knew you'd be down here today. I'm surprised it took this long. You can't help yourself when it comes to gossip."

"Well, you owe me a shitload of it. All you've done the last few months is mope around this place." He plopped down on my couch. "So…Lacey was nice. Cute, too."

I sighed. "You want some coffee?"

"Coffee? Dude, it's eleven o'clock. I've already had three cups, fixed Mrs. Denton's sink, changed two diapers, and sang a lullaby to my princess."

I refilled my mug. "Hope likes it when you sing to her?"

Holden smirked. "I meant I sang for my wife. Me singing Lala a lullaby is her version of Viagra. She gets turned on when I croon."

I shook my head. My buddy's wife was also our best friend's little sister. Even though they were married and had a kid, I still felt protective of her. "That's Lala you're talking about, dickhead. I don't want to know."

He stretched his arms across the back of the couch. "So what happened with Lacey?"

"She invited me inside at her place."

"Nice."

"Not really." I frowned. "I couldn't do it."

"Why not?"

I sighed. "I couldn't do it to Alex."

Holden's eyebrows pulled tight. "You guys are talking again?"

"No. But that doesn't make me feel any less for her."

He smiled. "I know the feeling, man. Remember when Lala showed up in town? She was engaged to that dude, yet I couldn't be with another woman. It was the longest dry spell of my life."

"Yeah, but you and Lala always had something going on. In your hearts, you knew it was meant to happen. I'm holding out for a lost cause."

"Is it?"

"Is it what?"

"A lost cause. Because I don't see you doing shit to try to win her back."

"What are you talking about? She made a decision, and I'm trying to respect that."

"And Lala made a decision to marry Dr. Douchebag. All's fair in love and war, my friend."

"It's not the same."

Holden shrugged. "If you say so. But if you want my two cents, I don't think you fought the good fight long enough."

"You don't understand. It's not going to happen."

"If you really believed that, you'd have taken Lacey up on her offer last night. Your head might have given up hope, but your heart hasn't, my friend."

"I wish my dick was aligned with my head."

"Maybe you should give yourself a deadline. If things don't work out with Alex by a certain date, you move on. Set a fire under your own ass."

My phone vibrated from the counter. Wanting a distraction from this conversation, I walked over and picked it up. I was surprised to find Lacey's name on the screen.

Lacey: Hey. Just wanted to say thank you for last night. For the drinks and...for being a gentleman when you walked me home.

I typed back.

Brayden: No thanks necessary. I had a really good time.

Lacey: Me too. You made me realize there are other fish in the sea. A year has been way too long.

Brayden: Good for you.

Lacey: I'm leaving for a work trip tomorrow, but I'll be back next Saturday. Maybe we could hang out?

I wasn't sure what *hang out* meant, and I didn't want to lead her on, so I stalled. My fingers were still hovering over the keypad when a second text came in.

Lacey: I know you're not over your ex. So no hard feelings if you're not up for it. But if you are, I'll be at my apartment at 8. Naked and sober.

My jaw dropped open. I'd completely forgotten Holden was still here until he spoke.

"Everything okay?"

I raked a hand through my hair. "Yeah. Except apparently, my deadline is next Saturday."

❤️CHAPTER 21

Brayden

The following Tuesday, it was my poker night with the guys. We always took turns hosting, and tonight Holden was in charge while his wife and daughter hung out with Billie over at Colby's.

Holden arranged pizza boxes on his kitchen counter while Colby set up the table for our game. As always, he'd set up a fifth chair, which would remain empty in honor of Ryan, the fifth member of our crew. With the exception of my night out with Holden last weekend, I'd kept to myself lately, so it felt good to be here and away from my empty apartment.

Owen was the last to stroll in. He was the only one of the guys who'd moved out of our building after getting engaged. Between the new baby and his fiancée's teenage siblings always being over, Owen had a lot going on. Whether he realized it or not, he probably needed the break tonight.

When we'd all assembled, Colby shuffled the cards and looked around the table. "How's everybody doing?"

"Same." Holden shrugged. "Handsome, charming, and hung as ever."

Colby rolled his eyes. "How 'bout you, Owen? What's new with you, dude?"

"Devyn and I are making progress with the wedding plans. Which reminds me, you guys need to go get fitted for your tuxes."

I sighed. "Wasn't it just yesterday that we got fitted for tuxes when Holden got married? Don't they have our info on file?"

"Doesn't work that way. They said you have to go in to get accurate measurements."

"Who's your best man, by the way?" Colby asked.

Owen smiled over at me. "Brayden, of course."

My eyes widened. "I am? That's news to me."

Owen laughed. "You don't sound thrilled."

"It's not that… You just never *asked* me."

"What, do you need flowers and a quartet? Consider this me asking you."

"I'm surprised, I guess."

"Who else would it be?" He gestured to Colby and Holden. "These two assholes chose each other. They left us out. So, I choose you, Brayden." He batted his eyelashes. "I choose you."

"That's so romantic," I teased.

"You win by default," Owen said.

"Gee, thanks. When you put it like that… You're making me all emotional," I said sarcastically.

"And therefore, you'd better pick *me* when you get married," Owen noted.

That comment felt like a joke. *I won't be getting married.* Not any time in the next decade, at least. I might've felt differently if you'd asked me a few months ago. But now? I was pretty damn bitter about love and marriage.

"I wouldn't hold my breath on that one," I told him.

Owen squinted. "Who else would you pick for your best man?"

"That's not what I meant. I was referring to there being a wedding in the cards for me. Especially with my track record lately."

Holden pointed his beer bottle toward me. "I think your track record is pretty damn good. He met this girl the other night, in fact. She's basically begging to ride him this coming Saturday. Absolute sure bet. And he's debating *not* doing it. Help your brother out here, because he's going insane. Knock some sense into him."

Colby turned to me. "You're hesitating because of Alex? Dude, she's gone. She closed the door. That's the harsh reality. You owe her nothing."

I looked down at my cards, mindlessly arranging them. "I didn't say it was because of Alex."

"You don't *need* to say it." Holden frowned. "Sadly, we all know it's the truth."

"Let's get started with the game, please." I took a long drink of my beer.

Thankfully, the guys did, in fact, turn their attention to the poker game at that point. The conversation drifted away from me, much to my relief.

I ended up the loser of the evening, which pretty much mirrored my place in the game of life compared to my buddies. With the three of them now settled, it put some unwanted pressure on me. But that was the thing about what I'd had with Alex—it had never felt like pressure. I'd wanted to settle down for the first time in my life. I'd never thought I'd feel that way about anyone. Heck, I would've even considered moving to Connecticut. That's how bad I'd had it. Maybe I still did.

When I went over to the fridge to grab another beer, Owen followed me.

His voice was low. "You okay? You seem down, although I understand why. I thought I might be able to cheer you up with the best-man thing. Because seriously, you should be stoked about that—especially having to write a speech." He winked.

"Don't get your hopes up for anything eloquent. I feel like a chicken with its head cut off lately." I cracked open the bottle. "But I'm good. Don't worry about me. And thank you for asking me to be your best man. I'll do my best not to fuck it up."

"Feel free to go easy on me in your speech. I don't need to be roasted."

"Can't make any promises." I shrugged.

"So what's with this new prospect Holden mentioned? Is she cute? What's her deal?"

I took a drink of the beer. "Just someone I met out one night when Holden was playing. She's going through a bad breakup, too, so we bonded a little. That's about it."

"You should force yourself to go, even if you don't feel a hundred percent about it yet. You have nothing to lose."

I sighed. "It's hard for me to move on physically when my mind is still stuck on Alex. I know that's unhealthy, and I'll have to force it at some point, but it hasn't felt natural yet."

"I get it. When Devyn was dodging my efforts back in the beginning, I met up with Tarryn. I've mentioned her before, the realtor?" When I nodded, he continued. "She threw herself at me, offered me what was sure to be a *great* time. But even though Devyn and I weren't together, I was so hung up on her that it still felt like cheating. So I get it." He paused. "I mean, Alex was your first love basically, right?"

I pondered that. "Yeah. I had my first real love in my thirties, which is pretty damn pathetic."

He shook his head. "No. What would be pathetic is never experiencing that feeling. At least you can say you did."

With that, my mind went to Ryan. He hadn't experienced that kind of love before he died. I supposed I should feel grateful. That reminded me of something my grandmother used to say. "*Better to have loved and lost than never loved at all.*"

"However, it would've been nice if out of all of the people in the universe, the person I fell in love with wasn't my ex's stepmother."

"Touché." Owen laughed. "Not like you can choose who you fall in love with, though, right?" He sighed. "At some point, you're going to have to pull the Band-Aid off and just fake it 'til you make it. You know?"

Holden approached. "Fake what?"

Owen turned to him. "Interest in women other than Alex."

"The girl he met the other night is hot. He shouldn't have to fake much." Holden smacked me on the head. "Wake up!"

"You're one to talk," I snapped. "When you were into Lala— even back when she was still *engaged*—women were throwing themselves at you and you didn't bite."

Holden wriggled his brows. "Now I bite *Lala* whenever I want."

Owen cringed. "Can you not talk about her like that?"

"She's my *wife*. I'll talk about her however I want."

"Ryan might beg to differ," Colby said as he joined us in the kitchen. "I still can't believe you married his little sister. If he were alive, I'm convinced he would've beaten your ass over it at least once."

"We would all have been front and center for that one," Owen added.

With the subject momentarily elsewhere, I tried to go back to the table, but Owen stopped me. "Hey, we're not done here. You gonna accept that date with what's-her-name or what?"

"Her name is Lacey. And I haven't decided yet."

"He has until Saturday." Holden chuckled.

Colby patted me on the shoulder. "Well, my vote is to go for it. It's been long enough."

"I know everyone's feelings on the matter, thanks."

Just then Lala entered, carrying Hope. "Is the game still going on? Are we back too soon?"

"Game is over, and it's never too soon, baby. I missed you guys." Holden kissed Lala's cheek and the top of Hope's head.

Lala handed the baby to Holden and walked straight over to me. "What's going on, Brayden? I feel like I haven't seen you in forever."

"I've been busy. It's good to see you, though, Lala."

"*Busy* is code for moping," Holden cracked.

I glared at him.

She flashed me a sympathetic smile. "I heard about…everything that happened with that woman from the project upstate. Billie and I were just talking about it, actually."

I rolled my eyes. "Great."

"Nothing bad." She chuckled. "We were saying life has some crazy twists and turns." She looked around the room. "Each of you guys has had crazy things happen when it comes to women, but you all came out on the other side. You won't be any different, Bray."

Holden arched a brow. "What did I have happen that was crazy?"

"*I'm* your crazy." She winked. "But I mean, look at the way Devyn and Owen met, for example. They had a one-night stand, and he didn't even know she lived in the damn building. Crazy coincidences *do* happen." She looked at me. "Although, *your* coincidence was something else."

"Pretty sure my coincidence takes the cake."

Lala leaned against the counter and crossed her arms. "Well, if you'd known you'd dated her daughter, you never would've pursued Alex. In some ways, it's kind of nice that you *didn't* know, as hard as it was to find out the truth. Because I think this whole experience has really helped you grow as a person, Brayden. You're like a big brother to me. I've known you for a long time, and honestly, out of all of the guys, I thought you were the least likely to settle down, to fall in love. You proved me wrong."

I pointed to Holden. "Pretty sure your husband was the least likely to settle down for a long while."

She smiled. "That's what it looked like on the surface, but I think even Holden was more open to love than you. But you're a changed man now. Consider the Alex thing as a learning experience. Whoever gets you next might actually have a chance they didn't before. Now you know what it's like to form a connection with someone."

"Well, I appreciate your insight, Lala. But I feel no more ready for a relationship than I did before. If anything, I'm more hesitant to have my heart broken like this ever again."

"You can't see it, but you did grow from this," she insisted.

It was hard to see the bright side of any scenario that didn't involve Alex and me together. Growing and maturing for some nameless, faceless woman I hadn't met yet brought me no comfort.

Holden laughed. "You're trying to get him to recognize his emotional maturity, and I'm just trying to get him laid. He has an opportunity this weekend. You should be encouraging him to take it. That's what he needs to get over things. Forget love right now."

Her face lit up. "Oh, you have a date?"

I shook my head. "I haven't said yes yet."

"She asked *you* out? Confident girl."

"Yeah. She's great, but…"

Her eyes widened. "You're making her wait for a response?"

"I don't want to mess with her if I'm not serious."

Lala smacked the counter. "See? I told you. The old Brayden wouldn't have thought that way. You wouldn't have cared if you used her for sex. You have *totally* matured, Brayden. This is proof."

I sighed. Maybe I had matured. But what good was maturing and being ready for a relationship when the one person you wanted that with was gone?

A little while later, I went back to my apartment no clearer on whether to take Lacey up on her offer, despite the well-meaning encouragement of my friends.

I took a shower before bed, and as the warm water rained down on me, I closed my eyes and thought about her—not Lacey, of course. That would have been too good to be true. *Alex* consumed my mind. My dick grew hard the moment I conjured the memory of fucking her against the wall. The two times we'd had sex in Seneca Falls were very different experiences—the first angry and frantic, the second slow and emotional. The second was *goodbye*. We'd both known it. That would always be bittersweet.

I usually tried not to think about the sex. It was too damn painful. But moments like this, alone in the shower, my body aching for her, the memories came flooding back. When Alex had come to my hotel room that night, it was the last thing I'd expected. I'd never forget that shock. There were *many* things I'd never forget—the look of hunger in her eyes when she'd told me she wanted to know what it was like to fuck me, the urgency I felt to take her right then and there. I'd never forget how wet she was as I sank into her, as if she'd been aroused before she came to see me—the way her beautiful blond hair felt in my hands as I fisted it, her incredible smell, the sounds she made. God, I missed her. Not only because my body needed her, but because she was the only person who made me feel whole.

I'd always avoided thinking about my mother in the context of Alex. While some had said my attraction to an older woman had something to do with my mother's abandonment when I was younger, I knew that wasn't true. It wasn't like I'd gravitated toward older women my whole life. I was drawn to Alex because of *her*. Not her age. Fuck, I still didn't know her actual age because she never told me, nor had I tried to look it up online. Nothing had ever mattered less to me. But age aside, it *was* true that Alex had made me feel wanted in a way I'd been missing. Perhaps that was the only connection to my mother, that she'd given me back something I'd lost a long time ago.

After my shower, I lay in bed, scrolling on my phone. A while back, Alex's friend Wells had found me on Instagram and followed me, so I'd followed him back. In retrospect, that was a big mistake, as right now, I wished I was looking at anything other than his post. Staring me in the face was a photo of *Alex*. Not only did she look hot as hell, but the man next to her had his arm around her. They were sitting next to Wells and his boyfriend. I might've tried to convince myself that the guy was one of Wells's gay friends were it not for the caption:

Double date with these two.

Fuck. Double *date*?

She's on a date.

Not that I hadn't expected her to move on... I swallowed, still staring down at the photo. Alex wore bright red lipstick and a fitted black dress that hugged her beautiful breasts perfectly. She looked absolutely stunning.

Why did I have to see this tonight?

Maybe it was a good thing.

Maybe this was *exactly* what I needed to move on and accept that date with Lacey on Saturday.

My stomach felt unsettled. I unfollowed Wells. It took me several minutes, though, before I could force myself to move past the post. But once I did, before I could change my mind, I texted Lacey.

Brayden: We're on for Saturday night.

That should have felt good, but it didn't. It felt like a desperate act, trying to forget something that would gnaw at me for days to come.

A few minutes later, she responded.

Lacey: Awesome. I can't wait to see you again.

CHAPTER 22

Brayden

Lacey snort-laughed, then covered her mouth. "Oh my God. You made me snort."

I smiled and pointed to her cheek. "You also have some ketchup over there."

"Why didn't you tell me?"

"I was going to, but I got distracted by the hyena that walked in."

She crumpled her napkin and tossed it across the table at me. "You suck."

We both laughed. Today was our third date. Things had started out rocky for us, commiserating about our breakups and all, but the more time we spent together, the more I liked her. But we were taking it slow. I hadn't taken her up on her offer to come over for a no-strings-attached evening. Instead, I'd texted the day before and asked her out to dinner. I was upfront from the start, explaining that I wasn't sure I was ready for something with anyone, but I liked her. So I thought we should proceed slowly. So slow, in fact, that I didn't even kiss her goodnight on the first date. After the second date, though, we made out like two teenagers at her door.

"What time do you have to be at the hospital?" I looked at my watch.

"Eight."

Lacey was a third year OB/GYN resident, so she worked ninety hours a week. Which was why tonight, and on our last date, we could've qualified for an early-bird discount.

"What made you pick obstetrics anyway?"

"In my first year of med school, I found out that babies are born with three-hundred bones."

"I thought we only had something like two hundred."

She picked up a fry and shook it at me. "We do. Two hundred and six, to be exact. But a baby skeleton has cartilage that becomes bone during ossification, and some bones fuse together. That got me interested, and then I watched a birth. A woman's body is a walking miracle."

"I don't want to get ahead of myself. But I have to admit, it's a little intimidating to date someone who has more experience with vaginas than I do. You surely know how to handle one better."

She laughed. "Like the average man doesn't have more experience with his dick than a woman?"

I leaned forward and bit the French fry from her fingers. "I suppose you have a point."

Lacey wiped her mouth. "I want to ask you something, but I don't want an answer today."

"Okay…"

"My friends have a house share in East Hampton. They invited me out next weekend, and I'm off Saturday and Sunday. Some of them are single, and some have partners, so it wouldn't be weird if I went alone. But if you'd like to come, I think you'd have a good time. Zero pressure, though. I know we agreed to take it slow."

"Do *you* feel like you're ready for an overnight trip?"

"I haven't had sex in a *year*, Brayden." She bit her bottom lip. "And I'm attracted to you. *Very* attracted to you. Think it over and let me know. If you decide to come, I promise I won't be looking for a proposal after."

I smiled. This was exactly what I liked about Lacey—she was open and honest, not afraid to say what was on her mind. "Alright, thank you."

The hospital where she worked was only a few blocks away, so after I paid the dinner check, I walked her over. When we got to the entrance, we kissed. Last time, an overwhelming sense of grief had hit me almost as soon as our lips unlocked. Grief, not guilt. So I braced myself when I pulled back, waiting for it to come again. But...it didn't.

"What are you grinning about?" Lacey asked.

"Nothing."

She smiled back, swiping at my lip with her thumb. "You have a little lipstick."

"What's your schedule like this week?"

"I'll be waking up and going to sleep in this building for the next six days. One of the other residents lost her dad and had to fly out to California for a while. But I'll text you, okay?"

"Sounds good."

She pushed up on her toes and pressed her lips to mine with a smile. "Did I say *very* attracted to you or just attracted earlier?"

I smiled back. "Have a good shift."

"Thanks. Let me know about the Hamptons when you can."

"You got it."

As I walked away, I realized my steps felt a little lighter. I even noticed some birds chirping nearby. I felt...good. Damn good, in fact. And there was clearly only one reason for that. So I made a split-second decision and turned back around. "Hey, Lacey?"

She turned, already halfway through the door. "Yeah?"

"I'm in for next weekend."

The next morning, I ran into Holden in the lobby of our building as I was heading to my office for a meeting.

"Hey," he said. "I was going to come upstairs to see you later. I'm playing another gig next weekend, if you're up for it. Saturday night at The Scope."

"Thanks, but I can't. I'm going out to the Hamptons."

"Nice. Golfing?"

"Nope. With Lacey. Her friends have a house."

A smile bloomed across my buddy's face. "Sleepover? *Nice.*" He patted my shoulder. "Thatta boy."

I nodded. "I figured it was time to move on. Though, I gotta admit, it still feels like I'm doing it with a piece of my heart missing."

"It'll get easier."

"Yeah? Did it ever get easier when you thought of Lala and couldn't have her?"

"That's different. We kept finding our way back to each other. I'm a strong believer that the man upstairs puts us where we're supposed to be."

I blew out an exhale. "Welp, my enlightened friend, I'm heading to East Hampton next weekend, so I guess that's where the big man wants me."

Fifteen minutes later, I jogged up the stairs from the subway around the corner from my office. Cell service was always spotty on the A train, so as I reached the street level, a bunch of messages came through on my phone. I opened and sorted through them as I walked.

Ad for overpriced monogrammed socks. *Delete.*

Bank notifying me that my monthly statement is ready. *Save for later.*

Credit-monitoring company telling me my score went up by two points. *Delete.*

Letter from Seneca Falls Building Inspector informing me the stop-work order has been lifted. *Freeze in place.*

I came to such an abrupt halt in the middle of the sidewalk, a guy crashed into my back.

"What the fuck?" he grumbled.

I held up my hand. "Sorry, man." I stepped out of the flow of foot traffic to stand against the front window of a deli and reread the email.

Dear Mr. Foster,

We have approved your application for the missing electrical permit and completed our inspection of the underground fill-in. A certificate of occupancy will be issued within three business days. After such time, you may remove the posted stop-work order and resume construction on your property.

If you have any questions, please feel free to contact this office.

Regards,

Inspector David Arnoff

My stomach sank. It was, of course, great news for Ryan's House and the people who needed free housing so they could be with their loved ones during treatment. But for me, it was terrible. Because it meant there was a very good chance I'd have to see Alex again. And now that I knew she'd moved on, that would be torture.

Though…I'd moved on, too, hadn't I?

It sure as hell had felt that way a half hour ago. But suddenly, the only thing I could think of were Holden's words. "*I'm a strong believer that the man upstairs puts us where we're supposed to be.*"

On Thursday evening, I pulled into the parking lot of the hotel up in Seneca Falls. I'd canceled my trip with Lacey to the Hamptons, since I needed to be here instead. I felt terrible letting her down, but I needed to get things up and running here as soon as possible.

My chest felt tight as I walked to the entrance, trying not to glance around the parking lot, searching for Alex's car. Of course she had no reason to be here this early. The only contact I'd had with her was the group email I'd sent to all the volunteers telling them we were back in business and starting on Friday. Most had responded to say whether or not they were coming, but not Alex.

I checked into the hotel, eyes darting around the lobby, even as I hated myself for getting my hopes up. The clerk slid the key-card to my side of the counter with a smile.

"Welcome back, Mr. Foster. You're in room three-oh-two."

"Thank you."

"If you need anything, please let us know."

I nodded and took a few steps away, then turned back. "Actually, could I trouble you to see if someone has checked in yet? We're here for a volunteer project, and I have the keys, so…"

She hesitated. "Oh, you're with that group from Ryan's House, aren't you?"

I smiled. "I am."

She looked down at her keyboard. "What's the volunteer's last name?"

"Jones."

My heart raced as she tapped the keys. When she squinted at the screen, I held my breath.

"Hmmm… How do you spell that?"

Seriously? Jones? "J-O-N-E-S."

"That's what I thought. I can't find a reservation under that name, though."

"Maybe she's not checking in until tomorrow?"

The clerk clicked a few more keys, then a few more. "I don't have a reservation at all. Is it possible she might be staying at a different hotel?"

My heart sank. "That must be it. Thanks anyway."

"No problem."

Hours later, I lay in bed, staring at the ceiling in the dark. I felt like I'd gotten my ass kicked. *She's not coming.* I'd told myself I'd moved on, closed the door on that part of my life, but I guess I'd been keeping it a crack open. This slammed the door in my face. And it hurt. It hurt like hell. Even if I knew it was for the best.

I tossed and turned half the night, finally conking out somewhere around two. That's probably why I overslept the next morning. I grabbed my cell and wiped sleep from my eyes.

9:35.

Shit. I ripped the covers off. I'd told the volunteers I'd be there by nine. And the only other people who had keys were the team leaders. One couldn't make it until tomorrow, and it seemed Alex wasn't planning on making it at all. I jumped in the shower for three minutes, got dressed, and ran out the door with my hair wet. Pulling up to the project house, I expected to see everyone milling around outside, but no one was there.

Fuck. Is *no one* coming?

I checked the time on my phone again after I parked, wondering if maybe I'd misread it earlier. Sure enough, it was 10:15. This wasn't good.

But the front door was unlocked when I approached. And when I stepped inside, Charlie greeted me. He looked great—clean shaven, clean clothes. It lifted my spirits.

"Hey, Charlie." I shook his hand. "It's good to see you. I'm glad you could make it."

"I told my boss I was coming here this weekend, and he told me to take the day today."

"Your boss? You got the job?"

He lifted his chin with a smile. "I did, indeed. Thanks to you. I'm going to repay you for the suit and hotel as soon as I'm back on my feet."

"You are absolutely not going to do that. It was my pleasure. Pay it forward someday, if you can."

He nodded. "Alright. I'll definitely do that."

I looked around, still trying to figure out how the team had gotten in. "Is Jason here? I didn't think he was coming until tomorrow."

Charlie shrugged. "Not that I saw."

"Was the door open?"

"It was when I arrived. But Alex was here before me."

I froze. "Alex is here?"

Then I turned and caught a flash of blond hair in the kitchen. I immediately forgot my conversation with Charlie, and my feet started moving toward the other room. As I approached, our eyes met.

"Hey." Alex smiled. "There you are. I was starting to worry."

I frowned. "Why?"

"Because you said in the email you'd be at the house by nine, and you weren't here yet."

"And you didn't say you'd be here at all."

She looked down. "Sorry. It was a last-minute decision. I drove in early this morning."

Alex looked beautiful. Her hair was piled on top of her head in a big messy bun, and her blue eyes seemed somehow bluer than I'd remembered. And that...only pissed me off. The new guy from the photo on Instagram probably liked gazing into those eyes as much as I did. I looked away, clenching my teeth so hard it gave me an immediate headache. I needed to put some distance between us.

"It's fine," I said. "But I've got shit to do so...whatever."

I left Alex standing in the kitchen and went for the stairs. I would've preferred to put a few states between us, but at the moment, a floor was going to have to do. I needed to get my head on straight and get things going here. That wasn't going to happen while I was smelling her perfume—the same perfume I'd inhaled from her neck while I was buried inside of her.

Upstairs, a few volunteers were getting ready to cut moldings—using the wrong saw. I helped them out, and then a delivery came. I had to run out to get new bolts to install the bathroom fixtures, and one of the volunteers cut her finger. Luckily, she didn't need stitches, but that definitely got my mind back in the game. When lunchtime rolled around, I ordered a few pizza pies, and everyone took a break. I went outside and sat on the front stoop with my slice, trying to keep to myself, but Alex came out to find me.

"Do you mind if I sit for a minute?"

"To be honest, I would prefer you didn't."

She blinked a few times. "Oh, okay." She turned away but then turned back. "Are you mad at me because I didn't respond to the email or just mad at me in general because of what happened between us?"

"I'm not mad."

"It sure looks like you are."

"Well, I can't help the way I look."

"Do you want me to not come anymore?"

"You should do whatever you want, Alex."

"Well, I would like to be here. But I don't want to make you uncomfortable."

I stood and crumpled the paper plate in my hand, brushing past her to go back into the house. "Don't worry about me. I'm a big boy."

The rest of the day, I managed to keep busy. We had a lot to do at the house. At one point, I went into the second-floor bedroom and found Alex huddled in the corner on her phone. She had an ear-to-ear smile on her face. "Alright. Maybe we can do that next weekend. But I gotta go." A pause, and then she said, "I love you too."

It felt like a hot knife sliced through my heart. I stood there, practically foaming at the mouth. I couldn't keep my anger inside anymore. "Seriously?"

Alex's head snapped up. She lifted her hand and covered her heart. "You scared the crap out of me. I didn't realize anyone had walked in."

"Obviously." I shook my head. "I can't believe you're in love with him already. What did it take you, two days to get over me?"

Alex squinted. "What are you talking about?"

"I heard you on the phone, making plans for next weekend. Telling him you love him. Flirting."

"Flirting?"

I held a hand up. "Whatever. I don't care."

"Brayden, who do you think I was on the phone with just now?"

"The guy from Instagram, I assume. Or maybe you dumped him and found another boyfriend already."

"Instagram?"

"I used to follow Wells, Alex. I saw the picture of your double date."

Her face fell. "Oh."

"Yeah...*oh*."

"It's not what it looks like. He and I—"

I shook my head. "I don't want to hear about it."

"Brayden—"

"You know what? Maybe you *shouldn't* come anymore."

Alex's eyes welled up. But I didn't care. I turned away. "I got shit to do."

Hours later, I was still in a piss-poor mood, sitting in the hotel bar nursing my second glass of whiskey. I'd come in to take the edge off, which the alcohol had done, but now I'd slid from anger to fucking depressed. I raised my hand to ask for the check just as the woman responsible for my shitty mood walked in.

Alex came over. "Can I sit for a minute?"

I stood. "It's a free country. I was leaving anyway."

"No!" She raised her voice, then leaned in. "I'm sorry. I didn't mean to yell. And I don't want to sit at the bar alone. I came to talk to you."

I took a deep breath and blew it out before sitting back down. "Fine."

The bartender approached. "What can I get you, ma'am?"

"Nothing for me, thank you."

I lifted my glass. "I'll take one more. I feel like I'm about to need it."

The guy looked between me and Alex and nodded. "Coming right up."

We sat quietly for a long time. Eventually she spoke. "I won't come again after today, but I need to say a few things before I go."

The idea of never seeing her again crushed my soul, yet I stayed silent.

She took a deep breath. "I'm assuming you thought I was on the phone today with a man I'd fallen in love with over the last few months. But I wasn't. I was on the phone with a man I fell in love with when I was eight." She turned to look at me. "It was Wells, Brayden."

I looked over and met Alex's eyes.

"I'll walk away, but I can't do it with you thinking what we had was so insignificant that I could fall for someone else so soon. The photo Wells posted on Instagram? That was his boyfriend and his boyfriend's brother. Wells tried to fix me up because I'd been moping around. He meant well. And to be honest, I thought about going out with him. Everett was a very nice man. But he wasn't you, so I never did."

"So you're not dating that guy?"

Alex shook her head. "No, I'm not."

"Are you dating anyone else?"

"No." She stood. "Anyway, it was important for me to tell you that. What we had meant something to me, Brayden. And it will take me a long time to move on. I didn't want you to think anything less."

I swallowed, tasting salt in my throat. "You don't have to leave the project."

She smiled sadly. "Are you sure?"

I nodded. "I'm sure. I know it means a lot to you."

"It does. Thank you."

My cell phone vibrated on the bar, the caller's name flashing on the screen. Alex's eyes jumped to mine. "Lacey?" she said.

I felt like a deer caught in the headlights. "It's new."

♡CHAPTER 23

Brayden

The following Tuesday night, I was over at Owen's brownstone back in the City. He and Devyn had invited me to have dinner and catch up. This was probably only the third time I'd been over to his new place. The aroma of seafood and onions cooking on the stove swirled around me in the living room as Owen and his fiancée worked in the kitchen to prepare the meal.

Devyn's teenage brother, Heath, sat on the couch opposite me. His sister Hannah was in her room doing homework. Devyn's siblings technically lived with their mother, but my understanding was that they were at Owen and Devyn's the majority of the time. They each had their own room here, too.

Heath stood and moved closer to show me something on his phone. "Hey, remember this?" He faced the screen toward me, revealing the video he'd taken of me and Alex kissing against the building the time she'd visited Manhattan. My chest tightened. It was painful to watch—especially after this past weekend. But *damn*. That was some memory. I'd been so into her that day.

Devyn's brother was known for posting shit on the Internet, and several of his videos had gone viral. Owen had warned me that

226

Heath had this footage, but Heath had never mentioned it to me before now.

"I do remember that day, yeah," I finally said once I'd managed to pry my eyes away. "And I'd prefer you erase it from your phone."

"Why would I do that?" He smiled. "It's too much fun being able to threaten you with it."

"There are much more interesting things than two people kissing on the street. People aren't going to care about that."

"You don't think this would go viral?"

"I would hope not."

He shrugged. "Only one way to find out."

"Please don't."

"If I add some interesting music or a funny caption to it, it might do well. Plus, chicks love sappy kissing stuff like this."

I gritted my teeth. "Can you please...not?"

Heath crossed his arms. "How much you gonna give me if I don't post it?"

"If you don't post it, I won't tell your sister you're trying to extort me. Pretty sure she wouldn't be too happy if she knew."

"She already knows how I operate. Heck, I've threatened *her*. She still loves me." He laughed. "The other day she was singing in the shower, and I recorded it from behind the door. Her voice could kill the birds outside. Saving that one for collateral."

Begging wasn't going to stop this kid. I had to try a different route. "I know you're pretty young, but have you ever had your heart broken, Heath?"

He looked away, seeming to ponder. "Yeah. Once."

"When?"

"When I was in middle school. There was this girl, Ava. She's my friend's sister. She sort of made me think she liked me, and then did a total one-eighty. I don't really want to talk about it."

"Oh, you don't want to talk about it? Because it sucked, right? So why relive it?"

"Right."

"Okay, well, imagine if on top of everything else, I had some video of you kissing Ava. And I threatened to plaster it all over the Internet—not only for you to see, but everyone else, too. Then every time you saw it, you'd have to think about how things had turned out between you and her. How would that make you feel?"

His smirk faded, and he exhaled. "That woman in the video broke your heart?"

"It's a long story, but we're not together anymore. And that thing going viral—or even a hundred people looking at it—would really suck. It's not that I don't want you to have your fun or grow your following. And I can normally take one for the team and laugh at my own expense. But that video? I don't want to see that ever again, let alone a million times."

Heath hung his head. "Damn. Now I feel bad."

I arched a brow. "Bad enough to delete it?"

He narrowed his eyes. "I don't know."

I reached for my wallet. "How about bad enough to delete it with twenty bucks?"

He scratched his chin. "Fifty makes me feel particularly bad for you."

"Done. But I need to see you get rid of it myself."

I watched as he deleted the video.

I pointed to his phone. "Go into your deleted files and re-move it from there, too."

He sighed but did as I asked.

I reached into my wallet, took out a crisp fifty, and handed it to him.

Heath smiled. "Nice doing business with you."

"I sure as heck hope you can put that ballsiness of yours to good use someday."

Devyn walked into the living room. "What did my brother do now?"

"Nothing." I slipped my wallet back into my pocket. "He's good."

She flashed him a skeptical look before announcing, "Dinner's ready."

"Thanks, Dev."

I walked into the kitchen to find Owen at the table feeding their baby boy, named Devon after Devyn—same pronunciation, different spelling.

Owen looked up from the small jar of sweet potatoes he was feeding Devon. "So, how was your weekend in the Hamptons?"

I'd told Holden I was going to the Hamptons and never clarified the change in plans. He must have told Owen. I shook my head as I took a seat next to him. "I didn't end up going."

His eyes widened. "You chickened out?"

"Not exactly."

I filled him in on the Ryan's House project resuming, canceling on Lacey, and finished up with my intense encounter with Alex in Seneca Falls.

Owen scraped the bottom of the glass jar with a spoon. "So, you told her you're seeing someone else?"

"Yep. I kind of had to when she saw the name pop up on my phone."

"That's not true. You could've lied."

"What's lying going to achieve at this point? It's not like Alex and I have a chance. There was no reason to hide anything."

"So that's good that she found out, right? Don't you think it will help you both move on?"

"Well, Alex isn't currently seeing anyone, so not sure how much this is going to help her. It certainly didn't help me move on when I *thought* she was seeing someone else. It just made everything harder to swallow."

"How did you leave things with her?"

"She looked hurt after I admitted I was seeing Lacey. She went quiet after that, and I let her be. There wasn't anything I could do to make the situation easier. If I'd told her my feelings for Lacey were nothing compared to how I still felt about her?" I shook my head. "I can't be around her without wanting to reach out and touch her, either." I rubbed my temples. "It's so damn hard."

"You never saw each other besides at the house?"

"Well, just for a minute at the bar that one night. We worked at the house during the days and went back to our respective hotel rooms." I looked away. "She was hurt. And it was hard to see that. But if she's not going to change her mind about us, maybe it is better if she thinks things are more serious with Lacey than they are."

"Speaking of that, what *is* the deal with Lacey?"

"Well, I agreed to go to the Hamptons with her when I thought Alex had moved on, because I was forcing myself to do the same. Now I'm not sure what the deal is, but Lacey and I are gonna see each other tomorrow night."

"So you're not really ready to *go there* with her."

"I need to take it one day at a time. I got the email about the project resuming right after I'd told her I would go away with her." I sighed. "The timing of that was kind of strange."

"Definitely," he agreed.

"Was that fate? I don't know. I have some thinking to do—though not about Alex. Because nothing has changed there. More about how long I can string Lacey along before she kicks me to the damn curb. I also don't want her to get hurt."

"Who would've thought you'd become so damn conscientious?" He patted me on the shoulder. "I'm proud of you. You could've taken advantage of the situation—used Lacey for gratuitous sex and Alex would've never known."

"It needs to feel right, you know? It hasn't yet."

"My boy is growing up."

I shook my head. "'Bout time at thirty-one."

The following evening, Lacey and I were headed to dinner in the West Village after meeting for coffee first. We walked hand in hand down the street. She'd picked a restaurant I'd never heard of, so I was unsure where we were heading both literally and figuratively now.

I really liked her as a person, and under different circumstances, I'd bet we would've stood a real shot. But more times than I could count tonight, my mind had returned to the look on Alex's face when I'd told her I was seeing someone. And that had me distracted, unable to give Lacey my all.

"I'm sorry again about missing the Hamptons trip," I said as we strolled.

"No biggie. Your work upstate is important."

"Thanks for understanding. We're getting to the end of the project, and it's gonna be nice to finally see it finished. What's the point of all that work if we can't complete it, right? I'm really grateful, but I still can't believe they reinstated our permit."

I'd told Lacey before that the woman I'd been involved with also volunteered in Seneca Falls, so I was expecting her to ask whether I'd seen Alex this past weekend. But she never did, and I certainly wasn't going to offer that information.

"Tell me more about your trip," I finally said, happy to change the subject.

"Have you ever played pickleball?" she asked.

"I haven't, but it seems to be all the rage lately."

"I played a couple of times while I was there," she said. "It was so much fun, like a cross between tennis and ping-pong."

"I feel like I'm hearing about it left and right. I might need to try it."

"That's definitely a sign you should try it. It's actually been around since the sixties. But it's only gotten popular recently. Don't laugh, but I think I'm gonna join a pickleball club here in the City."

"Why would I laugh at that? Because it's the modern-day version of a bowling league?" I knocked into her playfully.

"That's exactly what it is." She giggled. "And I'm not even ashamed."

"You shouldn't be. Anything to blow off steam."

"I'm not doing much *else* to blow off steam lately." She winked.

Ugh. There it was. The elephant in the room. The fact that I hadn't initiated sex yet, while she'd made it clear more than once that she was down to have some fun with me. She wasn't even asking for a commitment. Was I crazy not to jump at the chance?

I pretended I didn't get her innuendo and pushed forward. "So, besides pickleball, what else did you do?"

Lacey told me more about her trip until we finally got to the restaurant, an Asian-fusion place that had been recommended to her by a co-worker. The food was perfect. The ambience was perfect. Everything was perfect except for the fact that I still didn't know how to approach the evening once we left this place.

I had officially reached the shit-or-get-off-the-pot portion of this courtship. It wasn't fair to keep playing dumb when Lacey had been nothing but clear with me this entire time. So as we exited the restaurant, I decided to make the first move for once. "We're closer to your place than mine," I blurted.

"I was thinking that myself." She batted her lashes. "Are you saying you'd like this night to continue?"

"Well, it's too late for you to teach me how to play pickleball, but I'm sure we can find something else to do."

She beamed. "I think we can."

That was it. I was going to do it. There was no way I could back down now—because that would be fucking rude. My stomach was in knots as we hopped on the subway and headed toward her neighborhood. I tried to convince myself it was something I'd eaten, rather than my lingering uncertainty.

When she opened the door to her place, I realized Lacey had a tiny apartment. It was one of the smaller studios I'd seen in the City.

I looked around. "This is…"

"Small." She laughed.

"How do you fit all your stuff?"

"I'm sort of forced into minimalism. My couch turns into a bed, and then there's storage underneath." She blushed. "Don't worry. There's plenty of room for two."

"I wasn't too concerned." I laughed nervously, feeling like an inexperienced teenager. I didn't even recognize myself right now. I was the same guy who'd fucked Alex into oblivion against a hotel room wall, and yet with my nerves right now, you'd think I hadn't had sex in years.

I can do this.

It'll be good for me.

I need to move on.

Before I could think any more, Lacey had wrapped her hands around my face and brought me in for a kiss. I opened my mouth and let her tongue in. She pressed her little body against mine. My heart began to race. She could probably feel it, and she would likely misinterpret the reason.

You're doing this.

You can't stop it now.

My heart beat even faster as she led me over to the couch and pulled me on top of her. I willed myself to kiss her faster, to feel more, to get into it. But the faster and deeper I kissed her, the more forced it felt. My body was tight, and everything was stiff—except my dick. She moved to sit on top of me.

How could I not be hard right now? I had a beautiful woman straddling me.

Then Lacey lifted her top over her head, revealing her black satin bra.

It felt like a virtual timer had been set. Past experience told me I didn't have too much time before I'd be expected to stick my dick inside of this woman. And considering my dick seemed to be taking a break tonight, that was a problem. The larger problem, however, was the realization that even if somehow my dick were able to get hard, this didn't feel right.

I shut my eyes, and all I could see was Alex. Her blond hair. Her eyes, filled with concern the last time I saw her—concern that perhaps I'd moved on and found someone else. That couldn't have been further from the truth.

I sat up under Lacey. Panting, I swiped the back of my hand across my mouth. "I'm so sorry."

"What's wrong?"

"It's not you. God, you're beautiful, and smart, and charismatic…"

Her expression dampened as she figured out where this was going—nowhere.

"The problem is…I'm still in love with someone else. As much as I don't want that to be true, it just is." I paused. "I saw her this past weekend at the worksite, and it made me realize my feelings are as strong as they always were. She and I aren't together, but I can't shake her." I looked into her eyes. "I thought I could move on with you tonight. I'm so sorry I can't."

Lacey's expression was hard to read, a mix of sympathy and disgust. "I don't know what to say, Brayden, except I'm glad you stopped things when you did. Because while I don't mind sleeping with someone who's getting over a breakup, wasting my time on someone who doesn't even want me is a whole different story." She sighed. "I hope you can get her back, if you can't move on."

I'm more likely to end up alone.

And that would be exactly what I deserved.

I stood and adjusted my shirt, shaking my head. "I must be crazy for walking away from you."

She closed her eyes and bent her head back in frustration. This girl had already been hurt by her ex, and I'd hurt her again. I felt sick. Lacey deserved the world, but I wasn't going to be the one to give it to her. So the sooner I got out of her sight, the better.

I left awkwardly and vowed never to do this again. I needed to be absolutely sure I wasn't wasting someone's time before I got involved. Walking down the street as I left her apartment, I'd never felt so alone. Not only did I not have Alex, I was incapable of making a connection with anyone else. I wanted to call someone, but it was late, and I didn't want to disturb the kids by calling any of the guys.

A few minutes later, though, my phone rang. Owen.

"Hey, man," I answered.

"Everything okay?" he asked. "I just thought I'd check in. Wanted to see if you ended up going on that date."

"It didn't go well." I exhaled, my voice shaky. "I know it's late, but…what are the chances I could steal you away? I'm all fucked up. I could really use a drink and a friend."

He hesitated. "Brayden, I've known you most of my life, and this is the first time you've ever asked me for a damn thing. Name the place, and I'm there."

I asked Owen to meet me at a bar midway between his brownstone and the building. Once he'd agreed, I caught a cab. He'd texted me that he was there while I was still on the way, so when I walked in, I expected to see him sitting in the corner alone.

But instead, there were three: Owen, Colby, and Holden.

CHAPTER 24

Alex

"**S**o, what's new?"

I stirred the pot of sauce on the stove. "I think I overcooked the pasta. Though I suppose that's not new, is it?" I pointed to the cabinet next to my stepdaughter. "Can you grab the strainer for me, please?"

Caitlin took the metal strainer out and placed it in the sink. Grabbing the potholders, I walked over and dumped the pot of angel hair. I'd made her favorite meal—meatballs and braciole. She usually came early and helped me cook, but tonight she'd worked later than usual. Together we brought everything to the table, and before I sat, I refilled our wine glasses.

"What did you do last weekend?" I asked, filling her plate with pasta.

"Friday night I went out for drinks after work and…I met someone."

"Really? Tell me more."

She smiled from ear to ear. "Well, his name is Justin. He's a few years older than me. He's never been married and doesn't have any kids, but he wants them. And he's handsome and sweet. Oh, and he's an orthodontist."

"Oh my. That all sounds fantastic. Especially the sweet part."

Her eyes sparkled. "We went out Saturday night and Sunday night, too."

I couldn't remember the last time Caitlin had sounded so excited about meeting a man. It made my heart full. "I can't wait to meet him."

"I told him all about you, and he can't wait to meet you, either." She rested her fork on her plate. "This might sound weird, but something about him reminds me of Dad. He's just sort of doting and goofy."

My eyes welled up. "Your father was definitely both of those things. I'm so happy for you, Caitlin. He sounds amazing."

She cut into a meatball. "What did you do last weekend?"

"I actually wound up going to Seneca Falls. The missing permits that had stopped work on the Ryan's House project came through, so things started back up again."

"Oh, wow. Did you see Brayden?"

"Yes, he was there." I tried to keep my face impassive, but I guess I failed.

Caitlin sighed and set down her fork. "I don't understand why you're torturing yourself. I told you I'm okay with it. And I am. What happened between Brayden and me was a long time ago. We were just kids, really."

"I know, but…" My eyes welled with tears. "It doesn't matter anyway. He's moved on. Brayden's dating someone."

She frowned. "Oh no."

"It's fine. Really, it is."

"Is it serious?"

I shrugged. "I didn't ask."

Caitlin wiped the corners of her mouth with her napkin. "Maybe he just told you he's seeing someone to make you jealous? A last-ditch effort to get you to change your mind?"

I shook my head. "I saw her name come up on his phone when she called. The only reason he told me about her was because I asked when I saw it."

It was my stepdaughter's turn to sigh now. "Alright, well, I'm sure he's only moved on because you cut things off with him. It might not be too late. Tell him how you feel. I want you to. I told you, I reacted the way I did because I was shocked. It was immature and brought back old feelings of the silly competition I used to have in my head with you. But I know we're not competitors." She rested her hand on my arm. "You're my biggest cheerleader, Mom. You could never be a competitor."

I smiled sadly. "Thank you for saying that. But I'm moving on. I think it was just seeing him for the first time after a few months and finding out he's with someone that made it hard. It will get easier."

Caitlin gave me the side-eye. "I don't know about that. I hope you know I'm being sincere when I say I want you to go after this."

"I do, sweetheart. And I appreciate that."

She swirled pasta around her fork. "But…if you're really moving on, that means you have to put yourself back out there. Have you joined any dating apps or anything?"

"Not yet."

She frowned. I didn't want her to worry, so I shared something I thought might make her feel better. "But I did get asked out recently."

Her eyes lit up. "You did?"

"Wells's boyfriend has a brother. His name is Everett. The four of us had dinner one night, and at the end of the evening, he asked me on a date."

"Excellent. When are you guys going out?"

"Soon," I fibbed.

"Maybe we can double date with my new guy!"

I smiled. "That would be weird. But fun."

We managed to not talk about Brayden for the rest of dinner, but thoughts of him were never far from my mind. After Caitlin left, I curled up on the couch with a blanket and flicked on the TV, but after a while, I picked up my phone and started scrolling through social media. I'd been staring at the screen, yet somehow not really paying attention to the photos until one hit me like a freight train.

Brayden. Holding a baby.

My heart pounded. He hadn't been dating this new woman long enough to have a child, yet I couldn't help but think how I'd feel if he did.

Brayden. A dad.

He'd make a great father, that much I knew. I'd witnessed his tenderness and parental skills with the kids he visited at the hospital. I imagined he'd be a hands-on dad, too—the kind who wore a baby carrier on his chest and went to Mommy and Me classes. He'd make up silly songs and let the kid eat a whole cake with his hands. Picturing it made me smile, until I remembered Brayden's baby would have to *belong to another woman.* Then it became hard to breathe.

I scrolled down and read the caption. He'd been tagged by Owen. *Uncle Brayden does his first diaper duty. Next time, he might not even put it on backwards!*

It made me sad to think I'd never have any of those firsts. When Richard and I had married years ago, he'd already had a vasectomy. I'd never felt like I missed out because I had Caitlin. And she and Richard were always enough. But seeing the photo of Brayden holding a baby made me yearn for a child.

I stared down at the phone for a long time before finally forcing myself to swipe away. I was just lonely. I didn't really want a child. The picture was a stark reminder of how different my and Brayden's lives were. We were in such different places. He'd get married, have three, maybe four kids, and probably a dog and a pet goldfish. Whereas I had…my work.

I swallowed and forced myself to keep scrolling. Just like before, I wasn't really *looking* at the photos, at least not until another one stopped me in my tracks. This time it was Everett—Wells's boyfriend's brother.

He was at the beach, standing in front of a volleyball net, mid-jump as the ball came toward his raised hand. It was impossible not to notice his six pack. *Brayden's was more like an eight pack.* But I forced that thought from my head and pinched the screen to zoom in on his face. Everett was smiling. Having fun. Living life. Unlike me, who had been sitting home practically every night for the last few months, moping.

I attempted to swipe away more than once, but each time something stopped me.

Maybe it was time.

Time to move on.

Brayden had. The only way to get on a new path was to take a first step. And what better way to do that than with someone I'd already met? That would definitely be easier than meeting a stranger on a dating app. Plus, Everett was nice. And handsome. So I took a deep breath, swiped over to my text messages, and scrolled down until I found the chain where we'd exchanged messages a few times. I nibbled on my nail as I considered.

It had been three weeks now, and I'd never answered his last message asking me to dinner.

Could I just message him again out of the blue?

Should I?

Yes, yes, I absolutely should.

Brayden's moved on with Lacey.

It was *time*. Long past time.

So I tapped out a quick text before I could reconsider.

Alex: Hey. Sorry it took me so long to respond. But if the offer is still open, I'd like to have dinner sometime.

I forced myself to hit send.

There. I'd done it. I'd moved on. At least I'd taken a big first step.

Maybe he wouldn't answer. Maybe Everett was already seeing someone himself. But I'd done it. I'd put myself out there.

Less than a minute later, my phone buzzed.

Everett: Hey! Great to hear from you. How about tomorrow night?

I was a nervous wreck. Sitting at the bar waiting for my date, I looked around. The woman a few seats down was wearing jeans. Was I overdressed? I'd put on a little black dress, thinking that was a safe bet. But now I wondered if I should've gone with jeans—or at least worn flats instead of these heels. *God, I'm so out of touch. Maybe I should go home and change…*

But a minute later, Everett walked in looking frazzled. "Sorry I'm late. I got rear ended on my way here."

"Oh my gosh. Are you okay?"

He nodded. "Yeah, just a dent. But we had to exchange insurance information and stuff. Last time I had a dent, it cost me almost four grand for a new bumper. What happened to the days when they just popped out dents and repainted? Now they replace everything."

"I know. I feel like even appliances are disposable these days."

He leaned in and kissed my cheek. "Anyway. I'm sorry to keep you waiting. Have you been here long?"

I pointed to my empty glass. "Long enough to calm my nerves the old-fashioned way."

He smiled. "What are you nervous about? We go way back. It's been what, like three weeks now?"

I smiled back. "We're practically childhood friends."

"Plus, I've been warned to be on my best behavior. Winston might be younger, shorter, and skinnier, but that guy fights like a ninja. I'll swear I never said it, but he could kick my ass."

I couldn't imagine that to be true, but Everett's self-deprecating humor put me at ease. "He and Wells are really cute together," I said. "I can't remember the last time I saw Wells check his phone so often and smile—except maybe when his favorite Real Housewife announced she was getting divorced. Then he was scrolling gossip for weeks."

Everett laughed and gestured toward the hostess station. "You want to see if our table's ready?"

I got up. "Sure. I told her I was here when I walked in, and she said to let her know when you'd arrived."

He looked me over and shook his head. "Wow. I know I'm supposed to be on my best behavior, but can I say you look freaking amazing?"

I blushed. "Thank you."

Once we were seated, Everett asked if I liked red wine, and when the server came by, we decided to share a bottle. He folded his hands on top of the menu. "So…I was surprised to get your text. Happily surprised, but surprised, nonetheless."

I took a deep breath and nodded. "I'm sorry it took me so long. I was…" I considered lying and saying I'd been busy or traveling, but I didn't want to start out on the wrong foot. So I was honest. "I was getting over someone."

He nodded. "Well, his loss and my gain. And I appreciate that you took your time and made sure you were ready."

I felt a little guilty because I wasn't actually *sure* I was ready. In fact, I was starting to question whether I'd ever feel ready to move on from Brayden. But there was a limit to what I thought I should share with my date. So I smiled and lifted the menu. "I've never been here before. What are you going to have?"

"This is actually my first time here, too. I have this dumb rule that the first time I go on a date with someone new, I go to a place I've never been. I think it's nice to start fresh and not have a memory of someone else lingering."

I smiled. "I love that."

The waiter brought our wine and poured. Everett held his glass up. "To something new?"

"To something new." I smiled again.

Conversation came easily, and Everett told me how he'd gotten into the furniture business. I told him all about the spa I owned with Wells. Things couldn't have gone much better. Everett was the full package—handsome, independent, divorced with a good relationship with his ex and his kids. If I were making a pros and cons list, there wasn't much I could think of to put on the con side. Except for the big one: *He isn't Brayden.*

But even so, it turned out that a hundred things on the left side of the list couldn't offset that single thing on the right, no matter how hard I tried. After we finished dinner, Everett walked me to my car.

"I had a really good time tonight," he said.

"Me, too."

"Do you think you'd like to do it again sometime?"

It would've been easier to say yes and make up an excuse later. But Everett was a nice guy and deserved honesty. Plus, he was Wells's boyfriend's brother. I smiled and met his eyes. "Earlier, when you went to the men's room, I was thinking about what a great guy you are."

Everett frowned. "Uh-oh. I hear a *but* coming."

I sighed. "I think you're amazing. But unfortunately, I don't think I'm ready to get back into dating after all. I realized that I'm not over the guy I was seeing. You're a man who goes to the trouble of finding a new restaurant just to make sure you give a relationship a fresh beginning, so you deserve a person who's ready to give you the same in return. I wish I could do that, but my head is stuck somewhere else."

He nodded. "I get it. And I appreciate the honesty. Wells wasn't exaggerating when he said you're something special."

"Thank you."

"I'll tell you what, if something changes, give me a call. Maybe our timing is just off."

I kissed his cheek. "I'll do that. Thank you for understanding."

❤CHAPTER 25

Brayden

I slipped a shirt over my head as I spoke to Billie on speakerphone. "What can I bring tonight?"

"Just bring yourself," she insisted.

Billie and Colby were having everyone over for a group dinner. Weekends had been busy lately, so they'd chosen to do it on a Tuesday.

"I usually bring wine, but you and Colby always seem to have so many bottles you don't know what to do with them."

"I'm pretty sure all of the bottles we have are from you, Brayden. It's all you ever bring. Not complaining, just stating a fact."

I sighed. "That's because I never know what *else* to bring. Bringing wine means I don't have to think. Since I don't cook, I'm limited in terms of options."

"Well, Owen and Holden don't cook, either. It's always Lala and Devyn who make whatever they bring. Therefore, technically, the other guys don't bring shit. So don't feel bad."

"I guess I could buy something from the market, since you're sick of my wine."

"Brayden! Dinner is in fifteen minutes. Just bring yourself. Truly. And don't be late. You know how I hate it when the food I make gets cold."

I glanced out the window. "There's still time to go to the store…"

"Brayden, if you show up with anything, I'm gonna strangle you."

I chuckled. "Well, since you put it like that. Jeez…"

I heard a knock at the door. "Someone's here, Billie. I'll let you go. See you in fifteen." I hung up.

When I opened the door, my heart fell to the floor. On the off-chance I was hallucinating, I blinked. *She's here.*

She's here?

"Alex…"

Her cheeks were red. Was that the cold January air outside or nerves? Her long, blond hair was wind-blown and wild. And she looked more beautiful than I'd ever seen her in the nearly five months since we'd met.

Perhaps I should've thought of something more eloquent to say, but nothing came out of my mouth.

She fidgeted with her hands. "Is this a bad surprise?"

I shook my head. "What the heck are you doing here?"

"Can I come in?"

Jesus. I was an idiot. I moved aside. "Of course. Sorry about that. Come in."

Alex looked around my apartment and licked her lips. "Can I have some water?"

She seemed exhausted, like she'd just run a marathon. Had she run here? "Sure, yeah." I couldn't get to the kitchen fast enough. I grabbed a glass from the cabinet and filled it with filtered water from the fridge.

After I handed it to her, Alex downed the entire glass.

"Damn. You were thirsty."

She wiped her mouth with the back of her hand and exhaled.

Maybe it was just nerves. I couldn't blame her. I felt it, too. "Are you sure you don't need something stronger?"

"Actually, I would *love* something stronger."

"Coming right up."

Alex followed as I returned to the kitchen. This was surreal. She stood several feet away as I fumbled with the wine opener, then nearly let the glass slip from my hands. *Okay, who's the most nervous here? Her or me?* I made sure to pour the chardonnay slowly so as not to spill it all over the damn floor. As I filled the glasses, I could see her reflection in the bottle.

I can't believe Alex is standing in my kitchen.

I turned toward her. "Here you go."

"Thank you." She took a sip.

I crossed my arms. "What brought you here tonight?"

"I have a meeting with a potential spa partner here tomorrow," Alex explained. "Someone who owns a company that makes red-light saunas. We're thinking of having them installed. It was sort of a last-minute thing. Wells was supposed to come with me, but his grandmother is not doing well, so he went to Massachusetts to visit her."

"I'm sorry to hear that."

She nodded somberly. "So I came alone."

"When did you get into town?"

"A few hours ago."

"You already checked into your hotel?"

"Yeah. I got here this afternoon, checked in…then sat in my room alone and thought about how much I wished I could come say hello to you." She paused. "And then I figured, what's stopping me from doing that?" She looked down at her wine glass. "Things were quite tense between us the last time we saw each other, but I thought I'd take a chance that you were alone and might not mind the surprise visit."

"I'm really glad you didn't let what happened in Seneca Falls stop you from coming by." I forced myself to look at her. "I'm sorry...about everything. I felt awful that you were caught off guard by seeing Lacey's name on my phone. And I regret not seeking you out before I left. But I didn't want to make things worse by chasing you down when you were already upset."

"You don't have to explain, Brayden. We're not together." She let out a shaky breath. "Honestly, if you're happy...then I'm happy."

I should've told her then and there that I wasn't seeing Lacey—and there was nothing in my life as of late to be *happy* about. But for some reason, I chose not to. I just let her speak.

"You're right, though. I was surprised, though I shouldn't have been. I mean, a virile guy like you isn't going to stay single."

Unable to hold back a second longer, I stepped forward. "There's no one, Alex."

Her eyes widened. "What do you mean?"

"Absolutely no one. The woman whose name you saw on my phone was someone I really *wanted* to like, mostly because I'd assumed you'd moved on with someone else." I shook my head. "But I couldn't fall for her, even as much as I wanted someone to help me move on. I didn't sleep with her, either. We just went on a few dates, and then I admitted to her a week ago that I wasn't ready."

She set her wine glass aside and rubbed her hands over her arms. "So...you're not seeing anyone?"

"No, I'm not."

"Wow," she breathed. "Okay. I need to let that soak in for a moment. I wasn't expecting that."

"What were you expecting when you came here tonight?"

"The worst." She laughed nervously.

I tilted my head. "Were you expecting to find me with her?"

"I wasn't sure."

"What about you?" I asked. "Have you started seeing anyone?"

She sighed. "I tried to go on a date with Wells's boyfriend's brother recently. But I wasn't into him at all." She chuckled. "He was too nice for me. He deserves someone who likes him for him, not someone who merely wanted a breathing human who could distract her from someone else. It was over before it even started."

"Well, look at us…" I grinned. "I guess we're both batting zero right now, huh?" I squelched the need to cup her cheek. "I'm so glad you came by. I know it wasn't an easy decision, especially if you thought I might not be alone."

"Even if you had been seeing someone, I didn't come here for any other reason than to talk. Nothing has changed. I just… wanted to make things right between us. At the very least, I want us to be friends, if possible. I know that sounds crazy after everything we've been through, but I don't want you to disappear from my life. I think that's been the hardest part of this. So much of our relationship took place before we ever had sex, before everything turned crazy. Before we found out about Caitlin. You were a good friend to me and made my life better."

I stared into her eyes. "Right back at you, sweetheart." I took a breath. "I want you to be happy, to have no regrets. And I certainly don't want to erase you from my life. It felt terrible being in Seneca Falls and not speaking to you." I glanced over at the time. "Shit."

A look of alarm crossed Alex's face. "What's wrong?"

"I forgot about dinner at Colby's. He and Billie are hosting the entire crew, and Billie gets pissed when we're late and the food gets cold."

Alex pointed her thumb behind her. "No worries. I'll get out of your hair. I said what I had to say."

I reached out to stop her. "Are you kidding? Alex, you came all the way here. You can't leave." I laughed. "I mean that in the *least* creepy way possible."

"Well, I don't want you to cancel on your friends."

"I won't have to." *I can't believe I'm saying this…* "You can come to dinner with me. Come meet them."

She bit her lip, seeming unsure. "Wouldn't that be terribly awkward?"

I shrugged. "I think my friends will be happier than pigs in shit to see you. It'll probably be the biggest surprise I've ever given them."

"What will you tell them?"

"The truth, that you're in town for business and came by to say hello."

"Are most of them current on where things stand with us? I won't have to explain?"

"Not unless you want to. I've told them everything. They know we're not together anymore and all that."

"Won't they think it's odd for me to show up with you?"

"They sure will. In fact, I can't wait to see the looks on their faces when we walk in."

She shrugged. "Okay. I'll just throw myself right into the fire."

Alex followed me into the elevator. Being in that tight, enclosed space with her brought back painfully sexy memories. Thankfully, the elevator doors opened again quickly, and before I knew it, we were standing in front of Colby and Billie's apartment door.

I took a deep breath. This was the strangest scenario I could have imagined for how all my friends would finally meet Alex. This was going to be interesting.

When Billie opened the door, she looked to my right, and her jaw dropped. "Oh my God…*Alex*! What the hell are you doing here?"

Alex's mouth fell open. "How did you know it was me?"

She cringed. "Well, I've cyberstalked you since Brayden first told me about you. Hope you don't mind."

"Not at all." Alex smiled over at me.

Billie held out her hand. "Billie, by the way."

"I know. I remember your beautiful face from when it popped up on Brayden's phone. It's great to finally meet you. I cannot tell you how many wonderful things I've heard about you, Billie."

"Likewise, but are you gonna tell me why you guys are together right now?"

"Would you believe me if I said I don't really know?" Alex laughed.

Billie looked to me. "I guess you decided what to bring tonight, huh?" She winked. "You two have some explaining to do."

Before I could say anything, Alex interjected, "I surprised Brayden. He didn't know I was in town for business. And I only stopped by his apartment fifteen minutes ago. It's as awkward of a surprise as you could imagine. Then he told me he was late for dinner with you guys, so here I am tagging along."

Billie took Alex inside and introduced her to everyone. It was a full house tonight. We'd been the last to arrive. Sitting around the dining room table were Owen, Devyn, baby Devon, and Devyn's two siblings, Heath and Hannah. Then Holden, Lala, and baby Hope. And lastly, Colby, and his daughter, Sailor, and son, Mav.

"If there's one thing about us, Alex," Holden said, "we like to bust balls. But most of the time we're busting each other's, not other people's." He winked. "So you're safe."

"You can expect to hear many embarrassing stories about Brayden, though," Owen added.

"All you need to do is sit back, relax, have some wine, and leave the entertaining to these guys," Lala explained.

"That sounds like a plan." Alex took a seat, seeming more relaxed.

Throughout dinner, I couldn't take my eyes off her. But Alex wasn't looking at me. And she certainly hadn't been sitting back and saying nothing, either. She'd seemed to grow more comfortable with each minute that passed. I'd watched her talk science with

Lala, and then she got into a friendly argument with Billie over the value of artificial intelligence. Alex had faced the fire tonight and come out the other side.

There was one awkward moment, however. Heath finally recognized Alex as the woman from the video he'd shot, the one I'd made him delete. "Isn't that the woman you were kissing on the street corner," he blurted. "The one who broke your heart?"

I then explained to Alex that I'd been overly dramatic in my explanation so he would delete the video, rather than posting it on the Internet. Hopefully, she believed me...

All in all, throughout the evening, Alex seemed like part of the group, like she'd always been a member of our crew. I'd gotten one night to experience what things would have been like had everything not gone to hell with us.

When all the people with kids—basically everyone—started to gather their things to leave, I knew Alex and I should do the same. So we said goodbye to my friends and headed back toward the elevators.

I didn't want Alex to go back to her hotel just yet, but I knew she wouldn't agree to come to my apartment. That wouldn't have been a good idea for either of us if "nothing had changed." But that didn't stop me from trying...

My heart sped up. "Do you wanna come back to my place and hang out? I promise I'll be on my best behavior."

When her face turned serious, I knew the answer. "It's better if I go back to my hotel," she said. "My meeting with that vendor is early in the morning. I wanna make sure I get some sleep tonight."

"When do you return to Connecticut?" I asked, deflated.

"I'm heading back right after my meeting."

I thought of insisting that she have lunch with me tomorrow, but decided against it. The happy mood of this evening was just one night in time. Our larger reality remained the same. Alex had closed the door on the possibility of us being together, so it was still in my best interest not to spend time with her, no matter how tempting.

I called her an Uber and waited outside with her until it showed.

Despite my self-talk about distancing myself, I needed to know when I'd see her again. "Will you be in Seneca Falls this weekend?"

"Yes. I'm planning on working."

I was such a hypocrite, because suddenly the weekend couldn't come fast enough. "Okay, good," I said. "I'm happy we had this time together so things won't be weird."

She smiled. "Me too, Brayden. Well, better not make him wait."

Just as she was about to get into the Uber, I stopped her. "Alex…"

"Yes?"

"Thank you for not being afraid to knock on my door tonight."

She flashed a beautiful grin. "I've knocked on your door several times since I've known you. And I've never regretted it."

♥CHAPTER 26

Brayden

It was late, only a few minutes until the end of visiting hours, but I couldn't wait to show Landon the attachment I'd made for his prosthetic Spider-Man arm. Well, I might have made two attachments—one for myself as well—because you're never too old for superpowers, and you never know when you might need to catch someone in your web.

I walked into Memorial Hospital and went straight to the volunteer coordinator's office to speak to Liz. Last time I'd visited, I had to wear scrubs and a mask because Landon's treatment had left his immune system compromised. Hopefully that wasn't the case anymore, but I figured I'd double-check before going up to the ward. But Liz's office door was closed. It was almost eight. She was most likely gone for the day, so I decided to check in with the nurses' station upstairs, instead.

Peyton, a PA I'd met a few times, was behind the desk when I arrived. "Hey, Brayden. It's been a while."

I nodded. "Yeah. The house we're building had some permit issues, so the project was put on hold for a few months, but things are full steam ahead again. I'm hoping we'll be able to start booking families sometime next month."

She smiled. "That's great news."

"But in the meantime, I came to deliver a new toy. Actually, it's more of an add-on to something I already made."

"You make the coolest stuff. Can I see what you have?"

I set the box down on the counter and took out one of the wrist attachments. Landon's would connect to his prosthetic arm with a magnet so he could take it off and on easily. But mine strapped around my forearm. I wrapped it on and held my arm up. "This is how Spider-Man catches the bad guys." I positioned my fingers into the usual Spidey stance—thumb, pinky, and forefinger pointed out—and used my other hand to press the button on my wrist. A net launched out of a concealed hole, shooting at least ten feet in front of me.

Peyton laughed. "I wish you could've seen your face when that net shot out. You're really a big kid at heart, aren't you?"

"What guy isn't?"

She chuckled. "So who's the lucky recipient of this gadget?"

"Landon Wilkes. I configured his so it attaches to the arm I already made him."

Peyton's face dropped.

I knew immediately that things hadn't improved like I'd hoped. My stomach sank. "His immune system is still compromised?" I asked.

Peyton shook her head. "I'm sorry, Brayden. We should've called you. Landon passed away a week ago."

My heart lurched to my throat. "What?"

She nodded. "I'm really sorry. He was very sick."

"Peyton!" A nurse called from down the hall. "Can you give me a hand for a minute?"

Peyton patted my hand. "I'll be right back."

I bit back tears, unable to move as my eyes darted around the unit. To my left, a guy in a gray housekeeping uniform mopped the floor, whistling. He smiled when our eyes met. To my right, two kids who couldn't have been more than nine or ten years old came down the hall laughing, pushing their IV poles. Peyton and the nurse who'd called her were a few feet away trying to figure something out on the computer they always rolled around on a cart. Everything seemed ordinary. Like any other time I'd visited.

Except it wasn't. Landon was gone.

I looked around for a few more minutes. Life just kept rolling on. When I tasted salt in my throat, I decided I didn't need to wait for Peyton to come back. There was nothing more to say or do. So I left the box on the counter—with my contraption and the one I'd made for my little buddy—and returned to the elevator.

"Brayden?"

I looked up, but not even finding Alex standing in the lobby of the hotel a day earlier than I'd expected could lighten my mood. "Hey."

She frowned. "What's wrong? What happened?"

I thumbed over my shoulder. "I just got back from the hospital. I made Landon this…" The words clogged in my throat, and the tears that had been threatening since I left the hospital spilled out.

Alex closed the distance between us and wrapped me in her arms. "Oh no."

I couldn't do it. I couldn't keep it together anymore. I cried like a damn baby as she held me.

"Let it out," she whispered. "Holding it in doesn't do us any good."

Somehow we went from standing in the middle of the lobby to sitting on a couch in a quiet corner, yet I didn't remember walking there. It had been a long time since I cried, and evidently all the tears I'd held back over the years had been waiting for their moment.

Alex rubbed her hand up and down my back. "I'm so sorry," her voice cracked. "I'm so sorry, Brayden."

Hearing her sadness might've been the only thing that stopped me from blubbering for hours. Once I knew Alex was in pain, a switch flipped. I went from self-pity to protective mode. "I'm okay." I sniffled. But tears were now silently streaming down Alex's cheeks. I wiped them away with my thumb. "Please don't cry. I can't bear to see you upset."

She smiled sadly. "Don't worry about me."

"Like that's ever going to happen."

Alex rested her head on my shoulder and sighed. "You made his life brighter."

"It's not fair. He was just a kid."

"I know. At least he's not in pain anymore. He went through so much."

I stared out into the lobby. People were coming and going, just like any other evening, the same way everyone had been at the hospital. "It just feels wrong that the world doesn't stop, even for a moment, to grieve."

Alex laced her fingers with mine. "We can grieve together."

We stayed that way for a long time, sitting hand in hand in silence, stopping our lives in honor of Landon. Eventually, I took a deep breath and squeezed her fingers. "I didn't know you were coming tonight."

"I wasn't sure if I should. But now I'm glad I did."

I nodded. "Me too."

"I didn't check in yet. I saw you when I was on my way to the reception desk. Did you eat dinner? I don't think the hotel's restaurant has closed."

I shook my head. "I couldn't possibly eat."

Alex nodded. "Yeah. I understand. You should get some rest. Would you want to have breakfast in the morning?"

"I'd like that."

She smiled. "Me, too."

It seemed neither of us wanted to be the first to move, but when my phone buzzed with a call from Liz, I showed it to Alex. "It's the volunteer coordinator at the hospital. Why don't you go check in while I answer?"

"Okay. Good idea."

Alex came back just as I'd ended the call.

"Everything okay?" she asked.

I nodded. "I left a box at the nurses' station with something I'd made for Landon's prosthetic arm—a Spider-Man web shooter. The PA must've called Liz at home to let her know I'd come by. She wanted to apologize for not calling me last week, and she asked if it would be okay to send what I'd made to his parents. Apparently his older brother has taken an interest in prosthetics, and she thought he might appreciate the add-on."

"Oh, that's really nice."

"That's how I became interested in the field, too, through my buddy Ryan."

"The world may not stop, but it changes. Because of your friend Ryan, you've made the prosthetics industry a little better with your technology. Maybe Landon's brother will do the same."

"I hope so."

Alex and I walked to the elevators together. Inside, I pushed the button for the fifth floor. "What floor?" I asked.

"I'm on five, too."

We both turned right as we exited, and Alex stopped at room 519. I pointed to the door right next to hers. "Seriously? I'm right there, five twenty-one."

She swiped her keycard. "It seems like the universe knew we might need each other today."

I had to bite my tongue to stop myself from saying, *I need you every day*.

"Is eight okay for breakfast?" she asked.

"Yeah, sounds good. I'll meet you downstairs."

"Morning." I was already on my third cup of coffee when Alex came downstairs at ten before eight the next morning. I'd also already finished my breakfast.

She looked at my empty plate. "Am I late? I thought we were meeting at eight?"

"We were. But I was up early and wanted to get on the road. Sorry. I thought about knocking since I know you're an early riser, but I listened at your door and didn't hear anything. I thought maybe you slept in."

"I did. I had trouble falling asleep last night, so I slept until almost seven thirty. But if you want to get on the road, I don't need to order anything for breakfast. I can just grab a cup of coffee to go. I always keep a protein bar in my purse."

"Actually…I'm going to get on the road to Philly. That's why I waited for you. I wanted to ask if you would mind running things for Ryan's House today, in my absence."

"Oh. Of course. But is everything okay?"

I wiped my mouth with my napkin. "Yeah. I just need to take a quick road trip to visit Ryan."

"Ryan?" Alex's nose scrunched up. "Your friend who…"

I nodded. "I go there sometimes to talk things out. That's what Ryan and I were to each other—sounding boards. He might be gone, yet he's oddly still here for me. I didn't sleep so well last night, but I woke up with clarity this morning—I need to go visit him today. It's been too long."

"How far is the drive from here?"

"It's a few hundred miles, should take about four-and-a-half hours. So I'll be gone all day."

"Do you want me to take the ride with you?"

I smiled. "It's nice of you to offer, but it's something I need to do on my own. Plus, I need someone to fill in for me at the house. I already typed up a list of things that need to be done, in case you didn't mind. I can text it to you."

Alex waved me off. "Alright. You should get going. Don't worry about the project at all. I've got you covered."

I stood and kissed Alex's forehead. "Thank you."

"Hey, buddy." Later that day, I dusted some dirt off the top of Ryan's headstone. "It's been a while. Sorry about that."

There was a heavy feeling in my chest, but Ryan's gravesite could always make me smile. He'd made sure of that. After he passed, his dad had handed out letters he'd written to everyone important in his life. They all ended the same way. *P.S. Don't come to my grave empty handed. Bring me something to eat.* It had seemed like a bizarre request at the time, but it was always fun to see what random things were here when I arrived. Usually I could guess the recent visitors by the snacks they'd brought. Like today, I could tell Ryan's mom and Lala had both been here in the last few weeks. The potato that leaned against the gravestone had sprouts growing out of it. Mrs. Miller always brought a potato since Ryan's favorite food had been her homemade mashed potatoes. The dude could eat five pounds by himself. Lala must've come more recently since the bag of fortune cookies sitting opposite the old potato wasn't even dirty yet.

Ryan's little sister was a few years younger than us and the smartest person I knew, but she'd also been the most gullible when we were kids. When Ryan was maybe ten and Lala probably eight, he'd convinced her that the fortunes in fortune cookies came true if you believed in them enough. For the longest time, he had replaced all the fortunes in her fortune cookies with ridiculous shit—

Girl with blond hair, must dye pink to live long life.

(Lala used red Kool-Aid to dye her hair pink the next day.)

Woman who speaks three languages solves world hunger.

(She's fluent in Spanish and Mandarin to this day.)

Lala wasn't much of a cook, so every time she came to visit, she brought the same thing—a bag of fortune cookies. It was their thing. Which reminded me… I reached into my pocket and took out the small bag of Oreos I'd brought. Ryan and I used to devour an entire package, along with a gallon of milk, while watching Saturday-morning cartoons together.

"Here you go, buddy. Enjoy."

I took a seat on the grass and looked around for a long time. The cemetery was pretty empty this afternoon, but people wouldn't have stopped me from talking to my friend anyway.

"I'm not sure if you met him yet, but I'd appreciate it if you could keep a lookout for my little friend Landon." I pulled a few pieces of grass from the ground and shook my head as I threw them back at the Earth. "*Fucking cancer.* It's still kicking people's asses here. He was just a damn kid." I didn't like my visits with Ryan to be completely depressing, so I decided to tell him about my life. A lot had happened since I'd been here.

"So…I have some news. Are you sitting down? You might not believe me, but I met someone. Her name is Alex, and she's freaking incredible." I paused and smiled, picturing her beautiful face. "I know, I never thought I'd see the day either. But you'd like her. She's warm and caring, smart and funny—and of course, smokin' hot. I'm in love, man." I took a deep breath. "I'm pretty sure she feels the same way about me, though she won't admit it. There's one hell of a crazy story behind why. Actually, before I tell you—let me clarify that this is *Brayden* speaking and not Holden. Because this shit is gonna sound like something Holden would've gotten his ass into—before the lovely Lala, of course."

261

For the next half hour, I sat there spilling my guts. I told him the entire story about Caitlin, and even brought him up to date about Lacey. "I wanted to do it, but I just couldn't. I felt like I was cheating, even though Alex and I weren't together, and I hadn't seen her in months. I'm not sure what to do, how to move past it. Maybe you could help me out, give me some guidance, because I have no damn idea which way to turn."

I scanned the quiet cemetery, searching for some sort of sign from my friend. Finding nothing, I closed my eyes and took a deep breath. Maybe there wasn't an answer, and the best I could do was try to find peace within. But then suddenly, a gust of wind stirred, blowing something into my lap. I opened my eyes and looked down, finding the bag of fortune cookies Lala had left behind.

I smiled. "I'm not as gullible as your little sister was, but okay… I'll give it a try."

Unfurling the bag, I reached in, pulled out the top cookie, and snapped it in half. The tiny slip of paper had the familiar series of lucky numbers printed on the back, and I flipped it over to read my fortune.

Never let no be the end of your story. Make it a chapter in your journey to yes.

"Seriously?" I looked over at the headstone, a smile tugging at my lips. "How the hell did you do that?"

I wasn't sure I'd ever get that answer, but Ryan had given me what I needed—a swift kick in the ass. The answer had been obvious the entire time, though, hadn't it? I'd sat here telling Ryan I was in love, and I thought she loved me, too. Yet I couldn't figure out what to do. Had my head been up my ass or something? Because the answer was so damn obvious now—*never let no be the end of your story*.

I climbed to my feet in a hurry, shoving the slip of paper into my pocket. "Thanks, buddy. I know what I need to do now."

My heart raced as I climbed into my car and took out my phone. I debated calling Alex, but I didn't want anything to mess up what I was about to do. So I went with a text and jumped right in without any preamble.

Brayden: I'm madly in love with you. Be ready at 8 tonight.

I hit send and then realized she might think I was drunk or be confused about what she was supposed to be ready for. So I tapped out another message.

Brayden: In case you're wondering, I'm perfectly sober. And dinner is at eight. Wear something sexy.

I hit send again, but then reconsidered telling her how to dress. She was in upstate New York for a construction project. She probably didn't have anything sexy with her. I'd have to fix that. Some overpriced store must deliver. But first, another text…

Brayden: Something will be delivered for you to wear.

I might've lost my mind, but excitement pumped through my veins, so I didn't give two shits. And screw it—since Alex was likely going to think I'd hit my head on something, I might as well jump in with both feet.

Brayden: And don't wear anything underneath.

The little dots started to bounce around. *Oh shit.* Alex was typing back. She might tell me no—which I wasn't going to accept. So before she could do that, I quickly tapped out one last text.

Brayden: Also, I'm blocking you right now, so I won't get any texts or messages. Sorry/not sorry. See you at 8, beautiful.

CHAPTER 27

Alex

There was a loud knock on my hotel room door.

I looked out the peephole to find a woman holding a large package. "Delivery for Miss Jones?" she said as I opened the door.

Oh my God.

He really did it.

"Yes, that's me. Thank you."

She handed me the white box. It had a black satin bow. My hands were practically shaking as I took it over to the bed to open it.

Inside was the most gorgeous black-lace mini dress. From the label, I knew it was also quite expensive. The box also contained a shoebox, which I opened to find the perfect pair of black stilettos with peep toes. Both the dress and the shoes were exactly my size. I'd never mentioned either to Brayden, so this entire transaction had Wells written all over it. I was certain he must have been utterly amused to help.

Who knew I'd come to Seneca Falls to work and end up feeling like something out of *Pretty Woman*? I'd worked my butt off at the house today and had just showered, intentionally staying in my robe since Brayden had offered to send me something to wear. Still, I couldn't believe he'd actually made that happen.

More than that, I didn't understand what had gotten into him. It was like a switch had flipped while he was out in Pennsylvania. I wasn't sure how to handle that, but no way was I going to disappoint him after the days he'd had—finding out Landon had died and then visiting Ryan's grave. I would be what he needed me to be tonight.

Removing my robe, I took the dress over to the mirror and slipped into it. It had a straight neckline and cap sleeves. It was fitted at the waist with a subtle flare to the skirt, which ended just above the knee. The dress fit my curves perfectly—though I had underwear and a bra underneath despite Brayden asking me to go bare. I'd have to think on that one for a minute.

The shoes elongated my legs even more and went perfectly with the outfit. I turned around, checking out how the dress made me look from behind. I smiled, realizing just how sexy, wanted, and loved Brayden had made me feel today. And with that, something inside me shifted.

I closed my eyes a moment, feeling emotion rush through me. I knew in my heart I couldn't deny this anymore. Just like everyone around me had been saying, I needed to stop running away from Brayden and deal with any possible fallout later.

When he'd texted me earlier that he was madly in love with me? My heart had nearly combusted. I'd been trying to figure out the perfect way to respond, but then he'd blocked my messages, taking away the responsibility of having to say anything at all. It was just as well, because I hadn't been able to put into words how he'd made me feel. I still didn't know how I was going to handle being with him tonight, but I was certain I wouldn't be fighting my feelings anymore.

A knock at the door startled me.

I checked my phone—still an hour before Brayden and I were supposed to meet for dinner. Nonetheless, I peeked through the peephole to find him standing there.

My heart skipped a beat as I opened. "Hey," I said, my voice breathy.

He smiled. "You look absolutely beautiful, better than I could have imagined you in that dress."

"You're early. My hair and makeup aren't even done yet."

"You don't need a damn thing. You look perfect."

"How did you and Wells manage this?" I asked, looking down at my dress.

He chuckled. "It was that obvious that I had a little help, huh?"

"Yeah, just a bit." I laughed.

"On my way home, I stopped at a mall and FaceTimed him. He helped me pick everything out. Then I had it wrapped up and paid a hotel worker to deliver it to you."

"I can't believe you did this. But thank you."

"You're welcome, sweetheart."

Brayden wore a black blazer over a button-down shirt. He looked so delicious, I wanted to scream. "You look very handsome. But you're early."

He nodded. "I know. I couldn't wait to see you."

"What happened to you in Pennsylvania?"

He took a step toward me. "I lost all the fucks I had left to give, Alex." His eyes sparkled as he looked into mine. "Hearing about Landon's passing reminded me that I don't have forever. I already knew that, but it was yet another harsh reminder. There's one thing I want in this life, more than anything right now. And she's standing in front of me. And I know with every fiber of my being that you feel the same. Alex, I'm done trying to live my life as if you don't exist. I can't erase you. I've tried."

"I know," I muttered.

"And if you're worried about Caitlin, think of it this way: Being apart isn't going to change the situation. Does it matter if we're apart if I still love you each and every day? You can change situations, but you can't change feelings. I love you whether we're together or not. So I'm guilty no matter what." He paused. "I love you. And no one else's feelings are ever gonna change that. I'm done taking no for an answer."

Chills ran through me. He'd left me speechless. My chest heaved.

"Say something," he insisted.

There was *so much* I wanted to say, but nothing would come out. No words could encompass my feelings in this moment. Nothing could explain what it felt like to comprehend just how much Brayden loved me. Or how much I loved him. All I wanted to do was *show* him how I felt.

I ran my fingers through his hair. Brayden bent his head back, letting out a long exhale as if he'd been craving my touch. "My beautiful Brayden," I finally said. "I can't fight this either." I pulled him close, opening my mouth at first contact, desperate to taste him.

"Do you have any idea how much I've been dying for you?" he mumbled over my mouth. Our kiss grew deeper. "I don't want to stop," he rasped, threading his fingers through my damp hair.

"Don't," I insisted as I kissed him.

"What do you want right now, baby?"

"I want to ride you," I hissed.

He pulled back, his eyes filled with mirth. "Well, okay, then."

Brayden unzipped my dress as we continued our kiss. When it fell to the floor, I slipped out of it.

He removed his jacket, tossing it aside before we stumbled together onto the bed. His cock strained so tightly against his pants, I thought it might burst through. I licked my lips just thinking about taking him into my mouth.

We broke our kiss for a moment, and Brayden panted as he looked up at me. "You're so fucking beautiful, Alex."

"You make me feel beautiful."

He lay back and stared up at me in wonder. I unhooked my bra, playfully wrapping it around his neck and using it to bring him up toward me again, our mouths meeting as I straddled his hips. I began grinding against him with my panties still on. The heat of his cock made me wetter by the second. I couldn't wait to have him inside of me.

As he lay back again, I scratched my nails over his chest through his shirt, continuing to push my clit against his erection. He'd let me take the reins tonight, but from the look on his face, he wasn't going to take this cock teasing much longer. And quite frankly, neither was I.

I lifted my body off of him for a moment to unzip his pants. Brayden groaned as I lowered my mouth over his cock and licked the wet crown in slow, sensual circles.

"Fuck," he breathed. "I could die a happy man right now."

Taking him deeper, I massaged his slick shaft while I moved my mouth up and down, savoring the salty taste of his precum. I took him deeper down my throat, as far as he could go one last time, then moved back for a moment.

Brayden looked up at me with glassy eyes, continuing to let me run the show. I worked to remove his pants and boxers, then slipped out of my thong. Brayden tore off his shirt, so we were both now entirely naked. His dick stood straight up, begging to be ridden. I positioned myself over him and sat down slowly as he sank into me. Brayden let out a guttural sound as I bucked my hips. He wrapped his hands around my waist as I moved up and down over his cock.

I'd never taken charge like this during sex. But something about the way he'd taken charge earlier made me want to return the favor in spades. Him saying he was madly in love with me had made me want to fuck his brains out. "I fucking love you, Brayden Foster." I panted as I rode him harder.

"I love you so much," he breathed, never taking his eyes off mine.

A minute later, my hips slowed as I felt ripples of pleasure coming to the surface. I pressed my clit into him, and his breathing became erratic as he dug his fingers into my sides. That gave me permission to let go, so I bent my head back, releasing my orgasm. Within seconds, Brayden's body shook beneath me as he came harder than I'd experienced with him before, his yell echoing through the room. I tightened my muscles around him to receive every bit of the cum he'd released inside me. I loved feeling his warmth. I loved *everything* about this. About *us*. And I knew I couldn't go back. Never again. This situation was far from perfect, yet Brayden was perfect *for me*. That was the fact of the matter, regardless of right or wrong.

After we came down from our high, I lay next to him on the bed as we faced each other. "What got into you tonight—besides *me?*" he asked. "I have to say, I love this version of Alex." He caressed my cheek.

"What got into me tonight? I might ask you the same after what you pulled today."

He moved his thumb along my face. "I guess we *both* decided to give up the fight together, huh?"

"What does this mean?" I asked.

He leaned in to kiss my forehead. "It means we take it moment by moment and stop worrying about what anyone thinks, start accepting what's already in our hearts. Stop being fucking miserable because you think that's somehow the right thing. The right answer is *never* to lie to yourself, Alex."

I nodded, understanding that for the first time.

"You asked me what got into me... There's a bit more to the story."

I listened as Brayden recalled the fortune he'd come across at Ryan's gravesite. It did seem like a message from above. And I was grateful for the timing.

"I think he's sending me another message," Brayden said, looking up at the ceiling.

I straightened. "What?"

"He says I need to go for round two." He wriggled his brows and laughed.

"Glad to see Ryan has time to be concerned with such things from up there."

"Right?" Brayden pulled me toward him and nuzzled my neck. "He's so considerate."

We fell into a kiss, and I spoke over his lips. "Well, lucky for you, I don't think I can go another second without having you again."

"This time, I take the lead, okay?"

"Yes, please," I murmured.

Brayden flipped me around and pressed his body against my backside. The next thing I knew, his hand was between my legs. He massaged my clit before sliding his fingers inside of me. "I love feeling my cum inside of you."

I tightened my muscles. "Me too."

"There's gonna be more where that came from." He chuckled against me, sending a shiver down my spine. He cupped my breast as he kissed my back. I could feel his rock-hard cock at my butt crack and pushed my ass into him.

"You hinting at something, Miss Jones?"

I pushed again. "Not so subtly..."

"Ask, and you shall receive," he whispered against my neck.

"I want it."

"What do you want?"

"You to fuck me from behind."

He let out a low groan. Within seconds, I felt the burn of his cock entering me. He thrust in and out and gently bit my back as he fucked me. "You're so fucking perfect, Alex..."

I moved my hips to meet his thrusts, which grew harder and faster by the second, his balls slapping against me. There was nothing else like this—our bodies skin to skin, him inside me, his hot breath caressing my body, the noises he made. It was a symphony of pleasure I'd never experienced before him. Brayden Foster had officially ruined me for all others.

"Shit!" He groaned, his body shaking.

I felt the heat of his cum filling me, and I convulsed around him, experiencing an orgasm even more intense than the last. He moved in and out of me slowly until we'd both relaxed, and when he pulled out, I turned to face him, running my fingers through his messy hair.

"I couldn't hold it this time," he said. "I'm sorry."

"I was right there behind you. Every time with you has been more incredible than the last."

We finally dragged ourselves out of bed, and after we took a shower together, I put back on the black dress Brayden had bought me, sans underwear this time. But then we decided to order in rather than going to the restaurant where he'd made a reservation. I, for one, didn't feel like sharing Brayden with the world tonight. It felt too good being in our own little bubble. Unlike all of the other times we'd been together, somehow there was no guilt tonight. I couldn't explain it. Maybe it was hearing him declare his love for me, or finally realizing I was fighting a losing battle. I needed to receive Caitlin's acceptance of the situation as a gift. And finally seeing Brayden as mine made me almost feral.

After we finished our meal, I climbed atop Brayden, who was sitting in a chair across from me. I wrapped my arms around his neck. "I don't want to leave you this weekend."

He lowered his hands to my ass and squeezed. "I don't want to leave you *ever*."

"What are we going to do?" I asked. "I mean, we live hours away from each other."

He nodded. "Yeah. That's not going to work. I want you in my bed every night. I want coffee together every morning. I want to have dinner with you during the week and talk about our days.

We've wasted so much precious time, Alex." He paused. "I think I should move to Connecticut."

"You?" My eyes widened. "How?"

"I'll figure it out. You have the spa there. You can't leave. My job is more mobile."

"But you're a landlord—that's part of your job."

"The guys will attest to the fact that I am probably the least hands-on with the building stuff. As long as I'm financially in, they don't need me in the City every day. I'd still be close enough that I could drive down whenever I needed to."

"But won't you miss them?"

"Of course I will. But not as much as I'd miss you." He cradled my face. "You're my fucking queen, Alex. I don't want to be anywhere you're not."

That filled me with pride. While it brought immense relief to know Brayden would move to Connecticut for me, it also gave me a new reason to feel guilty. His friends were his family. But I vowed not to think about that right now. I'd been doing so well at freeing myself from guilt tonight, and I needed to enjoy the moment with my man.

My man.

It felt so damn good to finally say it.

CHAPTER 28

Alex

Damn it, *I made myself bleed.*

And here I'd thought my childhood nervous habit was long gone. It had been years since I'd bitten my nails. Then again, I couldn't remember the last time I was this nervous. I lifted my phone from the counter to check the time and bobbled it when it started to buzz. *Brayden.*

Just seeing his name on the screen slowed my pulse a little. Maybe I should've let him be here when I told my stepdaughter about us, like he'd offered. If I had, I might still have my favorite teapot, and my house wouldn't smell like charred metal. Which reminded me, I needed to light a candle. I swiped to answer my phone as I headed to the cabinet where I kept them.

"Hey."

"Freaking out?"

I smiled. "How did you know?"

He chuckled. "I know you, Alex."

"Well, so far today, I've had to go to the liquor store twice, I put the tea kettle on the stove without filling it first, and then I forgot I put it on at all while I went in the shower. Oh, and I also cooked a brisket for two hours without turning the oven on."

"You bought wine and had to go back to the store a second time? You drank what you bought on your first trip?"

"No, I brought two bottles of wine up to the counter at the liquor store, paid for them, and walked out without the bag. I didn't realize until I went to take the package out of the car after I'd pulled into my driveway."

Brayden laughed. "I wish you would've let me be there with you. I have a special injection that works wonders for calming nerves."

"I bet you do…"

"Seriously though, babe. Everything's going to be fine. And even if it isn't—which it absolutely will be—we're going to get through it together. We're a team now."

I sighed. It had been a long time since I'd had anyone to lean on. It was going to take some getting used to. But even when he wasn't physically standing by my side, I knew in my heart that Brayden was here for me, no matter what. I smiled. "Thank you."

"No thanks necessary. But I do need you to do something for me—before Caitlin arrives."

"What's that?"

"Go to the front door and grab the stuff that was just delivered."

"How do you know something was delivered?"

"I got a notification on my phone. I thought you might be freaking out tonight, and since I'm not there to comfort you, I mailed you some supplies."

I walked to the door with a different type of anxiousness. This kind made me smile. Out front was a large cardboard box. It had my name on it in Brayden's familiar slashy handwriting.

"What did you send me?" I brought the package inside and set it on the living room coffee table.

"Switch me to FaceTime so I can watch you open it."

"Okay." I hit a couple buttons, and Brayden's handsome face came on the screen. He had no shirt on, which went a long way toward distracting me. "Hi." I gave him a goofy smile.

"Hey, beautiful." He lifted his chin. "We probably don't have long before your company arrives, so why don't you open that up?"

"Alright, but you'll have to call me back later with no shirt on so I can properly ogle you."

He chuckled. "You got a deal."

I ripped open the box, lifted a sheet of bubble-wrap packing, and found a bunch of small items inside. On top was a package of cookies, but I'd never seen the brand before. I held them up. "Comfort cookies?"

"They're infused with CBD. I thought you might need to nibble one. It won't make you high or anything, but it should relax you a bit."

"Oh, that's a great idea. We just started doing CBD massages at the spa, and people seem to love it."

"Keep going."

Next I lifted a candle. The glass container was all black, except for the white label which had only one big word: *Calm*. "This is perfect timing. I was just about to light a candle to get rid of the smell of my charred teapot."

The packed box also had bath salts, chamomile tea, a scalp massager, and a stress ball. The last item at the bottom was in an unmarked red velvet box. I lifted it. "What pretty packaging."

"That one is my favorite. It might also be a gift for me."

My eyes widened as I opened the box to find a hot pink vibrator. I felt my cheeks heat as I slipped it out. I wasn't a vibrator virgin, by any means. There was one in my nightstand right now, though it was nowhere near as big as this thing.

"I wasn't sure if you had one," Brayden said. "But your face is never so relaxed as it is after you come. So maybe we could have a little video sexting later. I'll tell you all the things I'm going to do to you when I get there tomorrow while you use that on yourself."

"It's…big."

Brayden winked. "I was going for as life-like as possible so you can pretend I'm there with you."

I shivered. "Look what you did. I have goose bumps already."

"And you look a heck of a lot calmer than you did before you opened the box. So I guess mission accomplished, even though you haven't enjoyed any of the contents yet."

I took a deep breath and smiled. "I do feel a lot better. Thank you, Brayden. That was very thoughtful of you."

He laughed. "Some of them are *dirty* thoughts, but whatever it takes."

Then the doorbell interrupted our conversation. My eyes flared. "Oh God. Caitlin is here. I need to hide this stuff." I tossed the vibrator into the box, not even bothering to put it back into its pretty case, and looked around in a panic to find where I could hide it. Whatever calm had come over me quickly disappeared. "I gotta go. She's here! She's here!"

"Okay…give me two seconds first."

"What?"

"Look at me."

I looked into the phone.

"Close your eyes and take a deep breath."

I was pretty sure I could use everything inside the box all at once and I'd still feel stressed now that Caitlin was at my door. But Brayden meant well, so I did as he asked and closed my eyes. When they opened, he smiled.

"I love you, sweetheart. Everything is going to be fine."

"I'll call you later."

"Good luck."

My heart raced as I searched for a place to stash the box. Not wanting to keep Caitlin waiting, I stuck it on the top shelf of the broom closet at the back of the kitchen. No one ever went in there. I wiped my sweaty palms on my jeans as I headed to the door.

When I opened it, Caitlin held up a bottle of merlot. "Is it wine o'clock yet?"

I brought her into a hug. "It most definitely is."

But from the moment she stepped inside, an overwhelming awkwardness came over me. I prayed it was only in my head and Caitlin didn't feel it, too. I'd always been told I wore my feelings on my face, so I tried to keep busy so she wouldn't notice—opening the wine, checking dinner in the oven, setting the table—though the nervous energy radiated through me.

"So, what's new?" I asked.

My stepdaughter smiled funny, and I wondered if I was talking too fast, or maybe my pitch was too high. That happened when I was nervous.

She smiled. "Justin asked me to be exclusive with him."

"Oh! Wow. That's good, right?"

"It's really good. I like him a lot."

I hated to make her news about me, but I was thrilled about her new relationship for selfish reasons. "I'm so happy for you, Caitlin."

"Thank you. I want you to meet him. Do you have plans tomorrow night? Maybe the three of us can go out to dinner?"

"Umm…" Brayden was arriving tomorrow morning, but I didn't want her to think I wasn't excited to meet her new boyfriend, so I nodded and smiled. "Sure. I'd love that."

Caitlin sat on a stool on the opposite side of the counter and sipped her wine. "He asked me to go to a wedding with him in a few weeks. His sister is getting married."

"Does that mean you'll meet his entire family?"

She nodded. "I'm nervous, but I'm over the moon that he wants to introduce me already. I didn't get to the meet-the-family phase even after a few months with most of the guys I've dated. I asked Justin if his family had met a lot of his previous girlfriends, and he said only one. So it feels like a big step."

"That's wonderful. Tell me more. Does he have a big family?"

"Ginormous. He's one of six kids, and his dad is one of ten. He seems pretty close to his mom, which I like, but not *too* close like that weirdo Eric I went out with once. Remember that guy? He brought his mother with him the first time we met for drinks?" Caitlin set down her wine glass. "And then there was that guy Wes I went out with a few times, the one who looked like such a badass— tattoos all over and drove a motorcycle—but lived in his mother's basement and talked to her on the phone five times a day."

I laughed, grateful she was doing most of the talking. "Are Justin's parents still married?"

"No. They've been divorced since Justin was little. His dad is a dentist, too. Not an orthodontist, but a regular dentist. I actually met him already. Their offices are in the same building. It works out great because his dad refers a lot of business to Justin. But I have to say, his dad is pretty damn hot. As soon as I met him, I thought to myself—would it be weird to fix him up with Alex? Probably not now, but if I married Justin and you married James, then you would be my stepmother and my mother-in-law." She laughed. "I figured between that and the Brayden situation, we'd belong on one of those Jerry Springer daytime TV shows for sure."

Oh, God. Great. Just great.

I gulped half my glass of wine. Caitlin kept talking, but I got tangled up in my own thoughts. After a minute, she paused and looked at me funny. "Is everything okay, Alex?"

"Of course. Why wouldn't it be?"

She looked pointedly at the cutting board in front of me, where I was slicing a loaf of bread. "Because you usually *cook* the frozen garlic bread before you try to cut it."

I looked down. *No wonder it's so damn hard to slice.*

I shook my head and tried to laugh it off. But Caitlin was studying me now. It made me sweat, and I stood there like a deer in the headlights, unable to come up with anything to say—not a damn word. After a minute, she looked concerned, and I suddenly felt like a pot of boiling water whose lid was about to pop off. I couldn't contain the secret anymore.

"I slept with Brayden," I blurted. "I'm in love with him. And we want to give the relationship a try. I wanted to forget about him. I swear to God, I tried, Caitlin. But he's impossible to forget. I know he's way too young for me, and the entire situation is crazy, but he's only the second man I've ever loved, and I'm so afraid to lose love again. Losing your father nearly killed me, and I didn't think it would ever happen again, and I was okay with that until I met Brayden. But then…" Tears welled in my eyes. "Landon died, and Ryan is dead, and life is so short and…" I took a deep breath because I ran out of air. "And I don't want to go on Jerry Springer. I'm so damn terrified I'm going to lose you."

Caitlin rushed around the counter to my side, pulling me into a hug. "Oh my gosh. Who is Landon and who is Ryan? I'm so sorry they died. But you're never going to lose me, Alex. You're stuck with me forever."

A week of pent-up emotions bubbled to the surface, and I started to cry. I wasn't even sure what I was crying about. Guilt for loving someone other than Richard? Happiness that Caitlin said I won't lose her? Grief over Landon's death? Whatever the reason, I ugly cried in my daughter's arms—shoulder-shaking, snot-sniveling, hysterical ugly crying.

"Oh, Mom, don't be upset." She pulled back and looked at me, pointing to the tears streaming down her face. "You're making me cry. And you know how I get. My face is going to get all puffy and red, and I was going to surprise Justin with a booty call on the way home tonight." Caitlin laughed as she wiped her cheeks, and together we sniffled our bawling back under control. "What the hell are we crying about anyway? The fact that we're both in love and happy?"

I laughed through the last of my tears. "I have no damn idea."

After a few more minutes, we both finally calmed. Caitlin held my shoulders. "Are we good? Because I'm pretty sure you're burning something in the oven."

I swiped a rogue tear from my cheek. "I can't be. I forgot to turn it on earlier today, so dinner still has a while to go."

Yet sure enough, smoke billowed from the oven behind us. I grabbed a hand towel and fanned it away as I turned the knob and opened the door. Inside, sitting directly next to the beautiful, half-raw roast was a folded-up piece of paper, now charred brown. I pulled it out.

"What in the world is that?" Caitlin asked.

I closed my eyes. "It's my grocery list. I was looking all over for that this afternoon."

"You ready?" Brayden squeezed my hand. The next night, we were parked outside the restaurant where we were meeting Justin and Caitlin for a double date.

"Not really."

He cupped my cheeks and pulled me close. "Come here."

I thought he was going to give me some words of wisdom or a pep talk. But his mouth went to my ear. "Spread your legs. I brought the vibrator, just in case you freaked out. We have ten minutes before we have to go inside."

My jaw dropped open. "Are you joking?"

He took my hand and slipped it into his sports jacket. Sure enough, he had the vibrator in the inside pocket.

Brayden grinned and flipped the switch on. His jacket hummed to life.

"Are you out of your mind? We're about to have dinner with Caitlin."

"I know. That's why I brought it. I wouldn't have needed it for a quiet dinner with you and me. I can move the car around the corner if being in front of the restaurant freaks you out. Though the thought of secretly making you come right here while people are passing by turns me on like you wouldn't believe." He moved my hand from the inside of his vibrating pocket down to between his legs. The man had a full-blown hard-on.

So of course, that had to be the moment my daughter walked up. She bent and knocked on the car window, waving. *Oh. My. God. My hand is on his dick!* Now she was going to think I was the instigator of this mess. I growled at Brayden, who looked pretty damn amused, and yanked my hand away. "I'm going to kill you."

"You're going to have to survive dinner first."

If Caitlin noticed what had been going on in the car, she didn't show it. I had no choice but to force a big smile and open the door. Brayden took a minute to get out, and I suspected I knew why. I also noticed he stood partially behind me while Caitlin and I made the introductions. *Serves the jackass right.*

Surprisingly, the first few minutes weren't as awkward as I'd expected. Inside, our table wasn't ready yet, so we went to the bar for a drink. Brayden ordered some obscure liquor that I'd never heard of, and Justin said it was his favorite. That sent the two men into a long conversation, jumping from one subject to another like they were long-lost friends.

Caitlin and I stood to the side, watching. She sipped her wine and whispered, "If you guys wind up getting married, I hope you don't mind if I don't call him Dad. You know, because I used to call him *Daddy*."

My eyes practically popped from my head.

She grinned. "I'm kidding. Still too soon?"

"About a hundred years too soon, Caitlin Marie."

But as weird as it was, her off-the-wall comment turned out to be just the ice breaker I needed. Laughing about the lunacy of our situation allowed us to acknowledge it and tuck it away, rather than letting it loom over the evening.

The four of us spent the next two-and-a-half hours laughing and enjoying each other's company. Justin was a great guy, and once Brayden found out he'd invented a few gadgets for his orthodontics business, they pretty much forgot we were in the room. The evening couldn't have gone better. At least until we were saying goodbye out in front of the restaurant.

Caitlin and I hugged, promising to call tomorrow, but I knew we'd probably be texting from the car in five minutes. When she pulled back, one of her earrings caught on my sweater and fell to the floor. Always the gentleman, Brayden bent to pick it up. When he did, something slipped from his pocket. His *inside jacket pocket*. Worse, when the hot pink vibrator clanked to the ground, the damn thing *turned on*. The four of us stood in the middle of the sidewalk, staring down at an eight-inch vibrator *vibrating* on the concrete.

I shut my eyes. "Please tell me that didn't happen."

Justin chuckled. "What? That my girlfriend's mother's boyfriend who used to be my girlfriend's boyfriend just dropped a sex toy bigger than my junk on the ground?"

A smile bloomed on Brayden's face. "Justin, you are going to fit in perfectly with my friends."

CHAPTER 29

Alex

With the Ryan's House renovation over, Brayden and I now had our weekends back, so I spent an amazing couple of days in the City with him. On Friday we'd gone to the MET and had dinner in Chinatown. Then Saturday, since it rained, we'd had a cozy day and night in watching movies and making homemade pizzas.

Today, though, was about catching up with Brayden's friends before I had to go back to Connecticut on Monday morning. An emptiness always followed me around when I knew I had to leave Brayden soon. But I was excited for a surprise I had for him later this afternoon. The sun was shining today, and I felt optimistic about the future.

Our first stop was Holden and Lala's for Sunday brunch, and we'd just finished telling them the story of the infamous pink dildo.

Holden nearly choked on his coffee. "That sounds like something that would happen to me."

"Actually," Brayden corrected. "You'd plant a vibrator in someone's jacket just to mess with them. Then you'd watch to see how the hell they explained themselves."

"You're right. That's more my speed," Holden agreed. "You might've just given me an idea for Colby's next birthday gift."

Lala bounced baby Hope and turned to me. "So, when are you moving to the building?" She winked. "I know you haven't figured anything out yet. I'm just kidding." She shrugged. "But maybe secretly hoping?"

"I could get used to it around here." I smiled. "We've had such a fun weekend, and I certainly don't feel like going home."

Brayden wrapped his arm around me. "But alas, her entire career and business is in Connecticut. We can't take the spa with us. But I can do my job from anywhere and will just travel when I need to. So, looks like I'm gonna be a bit scarce around here for a while. I'll be spending most weeks up there with Alex once I move my stuff at the end of this week."

"You? Scarce?" Holden taunted. "What else is new? You're the most scarce one around here anyway." He faced me. "Alex, don't let him fool you. We don't need Brayden around these parts. Colby and I have everything under control since Owen flew the coop, too."

"We see Owen a lot, though," Lala said. "He's still in the City. Brayden will be a few hours away."

Brayden having to leave this place had always made me sad. While he had a good relationship with his father back in Philly, his true family was right here. Found family could be much more important than blood family. Just look at Caitlin and me.

I looked over at Brayden, who was playing peekaboo with Hope. He revealed his face with the most adorable expression. It melted my heart and made my ovaries explode all at once. Hope giggled and flashed him the cutest toothless smile.

"Look at the way she's looking at you," Lala said.

"Hope loves her favorite uncle," Brayden cooed. "Right, baby girl? You and I both know I'm your favorite. These other guys are all tied up with their own kids, but Uncle Brayden gives you all of his attention." Brayden lifted Hope out of her highchair and onto his lap. He blew raspberries as he bounced her. She erupted into little giggles again as she looked up at him.

I thought about her name. *Hope.*

I held on to hope by a thread when it came to having a baby of my own. Supposedly I'd ruled it out years ago, and I wasn't even sure it was possible, but more and more lately, I found myself thinking about it.

Longing washed over me as I watched Brayden with her. His gaze drifted to mine for a moment, and he narrowed his eyes as if he could sense something on my mind—almost like he could see right through me. I wished I hadn't made it so obvious. That wasn't my intent.

He returned his focus to Hope, but there was a new, unspoken tension in the air after that.

After we left Holden and Lala's, we stopped back over to Brayden's apartment to use the bathroom and freshen up before heading out again. But before I could get to the bathroom, Brayden wrapped his arms around me and gently backed me against the wall.

"What are you doing?" I chuckled.

He placed one hand on each side of my body, locking me in to kiss me passionately. He spoke over my lips. "I saw the way you were looking at me and Hope."

I swallowed. "Okay…"

"I feel like I know what you were thinking, but I want you to tell me if I'm wrong."

"What do you think I was thinking?"

"I guess it was more what you were feeling…"

Feeling exposed, I looked down at my feet. "It was a mixture of hope and fear." I sighed. "I worry I won't be able to give you one of your own, but I hope there might still be a chance."

"I've told you before, there are lots of ways to have kids."

I ran my fingers through his hair. "Yeah. But not with your beautiful eyes and face. I want that for you, a child of your own."

"What about *your* beautiful eyes and face? What do you want for *you*, Alex? Never mind me. Take me out of the equation. Is there any part of you that regrets not having a biological child? Because if the answer is no, you shouldn't feel pressured because of me."

"I'm afraid to let those feelings in."

"Don't be afraid," he whispered.

"There *is* a part of me that regrets it, yes," I said after a moment. "Very much so."

He nodded. "You know what I was thinking when I was looking at Hope?"

"What?"

"It wasn't that I wished I had a baby of my own. I was thinking how much I could see Ryan's face in hers." He smiled. "And it felt like a gift. I felt such gratitude for all I have in my life right now. There wasn't any part of me wishing for something else. Would it be a dream to share the experience of having a baby with you? To see your beautiful body growing with my baby in your belly? God, I want that so much it hurts. But even so…there's nothing I want more than to have you in my life and for you to be happy, whether we have a kid of our own or not." He placed his forehead against mine. "I'm a true believer that what's meant to happen will. What I won't accept is letting fear of an imagined future outcome steal our today."

I needed clarification. "Are you telling me you'll be fine if I can never give you a biological child of your own?"

"I am." He raised a brow. "Will you?"

I took a deep breath in and exhaled. "I think it was easier when I'd convinced myself I didn't want a baby. Back when Richard and I got married, he was adamant that he didn't want any more kids. He'd had a vasectomy before we met. That made it easier to accept the finality. I told myself my life was better off, that I had more independence and more time for Caitlin. And mostly I believed it. But the truth comes out intermittently—a feeling in my chest sometimes when I see a mother with her baby in the park or a woman walking hand in hand with her little one." I looked into his eyes. "It's regret. But it's one thing to regret something, and another to long for the unattainable. I've never longed for a baby more than I do now. Because of you. Because I'm in love with someone who also wants a baby someday, which makes me want it more. And I hate that I could be the one holding us back—not because I don't want one, but because my body can't make one." I shut my eyes and let out a long breath. "It felt good to let that out."

He pulled me close. "I'm so glad you did."

"We're not even engaged. I know it's premature to be thinking about this, but the truth is…" I stepped back to look at him. "I don't have a lot of time, Brayden. I'm panicking a little. I feel like every day that passes, I have less of a chance. When you get to a certain age, every day matters." I teared up.

"Oh, baby. I'm sorry. I didn't know this was weighing on you." He cradled my face. "I love you so much. And I'll do whatever it takes to make you feel better. What do you need from me?"

I wiped my eyes and sniffled. "I need you to turn back time."

"I would never do that if it meant not ending up exactly where we are now." He smiled. "Look, I can't turn back time, but I sure as hell *can* avoid wasting a second of the time we have. I don't ever want you to have regrets. Why don't we throw caution to the wind and see what happens?"

My eyes widened. "Start trying to have a baby? We don't even live together yet."

"I'm suggesting we have lots of sex—which we do anyway—and not do anything to prevent it. There are no guarantees, but there *is* a lot of power in belief. Your body listens to your mind. If we believe it will happen for us, I think it will. Instead of pushing the thoughts away, let's let them in. Let yourself imagine us with a baby. Believe it. And I'll do the same."

Believe it.

Believe was like the opposite of hope. Hope was wishing for something. Belief was *knowing*. Could I do that? Would it hurt even more if I convinced myself it could happen and it didn't? I had to try. I narrowed my eyes. "Would you be ready if by some chance I got pregnant?"

"I'd be as ready tomorrow as I would be next year."

"You promise you're not just saying that…"

"I've never lied to you, Alex." His eyes were sincere. "I promise."

I exhaled. "This is crazy."

"Well, even if I manage to knock you up, we won't be able to say that's the craziest thing to ever happen to us. That ship's sailed."

Later that afternoon, I'd told Brayden I wanted to see the West Village, but I actually had a very specific destination in mind. When we arrived, I stopped in front of the building. "There's a place I want to show you," I told him.

"This is my city. I'm supposed to be showing *you* around."

Almost as soon as he'd said it, Owen appeared, walking toward us. Brayden's face lit up in surprise. "Hey, man. What are you doing in this neck of the woods?" he asked.

"Alex asked me to come."

Brayden's eyes filled with suspicion. "Did she now?"

Just then a car pulled up, and none other than Wells exited the vehicle.

Brayden's brows knitted. "What the hell are you doing here?"

"I missed your pretty face."

"Besides that…"

Wells put his hands on his hips and turned to me. "Did you tell him yet?"

Brayden looked back and forth between Wells and me. "Tell me what?"

Owen took out a set of keys and led the way to the building. "Let's step inside, shall we?"

"What is this place?" Brayden asked.

"It's a space that's for lease," I finally said.

"Yeah, I kind of got that."

"Wells and I have been talking about taking over one of the medi-spas here in the City for some time," I began.

"Alex never wanted to bite the bullet until recently," Wells added. "Any reason you can think of that she might've had a change of heart?"

"You're thinking of opening a business here?" Brayden asked, shock on his face. "What about the Connecticut spa?"

"Wells and I have decided to sell it and use the money toward this acquisition," I explained. "We'll be taking over all of the New York spa's existing services and staff and adding some of our own in this new location. It's going to be a win-win for their clients, and a win-win for me because I'll get to be in the City with you full time." I could see the information hitting him in waves.

"Holy shit. You're *moving* here? I can't believe you've been keeping this from me."

"Well, I wanted to surprise you. I hope it's a good surprise?"

"Um…yes! You've given me everything I could ever ask for. No wonder you've been wishy-washy about me moving my stuff to Connecticut, telling me to take my time. Here I was thinking you might've been having doubts about me invading your space."

I grinned. "Not at all. Instead, I'll be invading yours. I know you didn't want to move. You were doing it for me. And I so appreciate that. But it will be a good change for me to be here. Living with you in the house Richard and I built never quite felt right. It's time for me to move to a new chapter in my life."

Brayden shook his head. "I can't believe this."

Wells smacked Brayden on the back. "Believe it, loverboy."

"Let's look around," Owen said, beaming.

After we toured the space, we sat down with Owen, who ran specs for commercial properties that had been recently leased in this area. Since there were several other interested parties, we wanted to move fast, so we ended the afternoon by signing a preliminary agreement to lease the space.

Later that evening, Brayden, Wells, and I met Colby and Billie for dinner to celebrate.

"I'm so happy for you guys," Billie said. "Here I thought we were gonna be losing Brayden, but we're gaining Alex instead."

I looked at Billie and Colby across the table. "I can't thank you enough for being so welcoming to me."

Colby poured some of the celebratory champagne Brayden had ordered for the table. "Thank you for making my buddy so happy."

"Thank you for making *my girl* feel at home," Wells added. "Any apartments open in the building for me, by the way?"

Colby scratched his chin. "Nothing at the moment, but we can put you first on the list."

"I'd appreciate that." Wells grinned.

"Are you moving into Brayden's apartment, or are you guys thinking of getting a different place?" Billie asked.

I turned to Brayden. "His apartment is big enough for the two of us. It just needs a little tender loving care, maybe some art on the wall."

"If you look up *bachelor pad* in the dictionary, I'm pretty sure Brayden's apartment comes up," Colby teased.

Brayden shrugged. "Hey, at least I gave her a blank slate to work with, right?"

I brushed a piece of his hair off his forehead. "You're so thoughtful."

"Correction," Wells said. "You gave *me* a blank slate to work with, Brayden." He turned to me. "Kitten, we need to rectify this fast. *I* can't wait to decorate."

As dinner began to wind down, I leaned over to Billie. "I was thinking of taking you up on your offer to ink me, if that's something you have time for."

"I'll *make* time for you. You have no idea how exciting it is for me to give someone their first tattoo. You know what you want?"

"I do, actually. It's simple, and you'll probably think it's boring, but I have to start somewhere."

"What is it?" Brayden asked.

"You'll have to wait and find out," I told him.

Billie slapped her cloth napkin down on the table. "Well, hopefully not too long. Let's go over to the shop after dinner."

I stilled. "Tonight?"

"Why? You gonna change your mind or something?"

"No. I just figured I'd have to book an appointment well in advance."

Billie shook her head. "I have a six-month wait. There's no booking for friends. It'll be fun. Like a little nightcap."

"Any chance your hot, tatted, very gay employee might be there?" Wells asked. "The guy with the name that sounds like *dick* Brayden has been telling me about?"

So wrapped up in my own stuff lately, I'd nearly forgotten Wells had broken up with his boyfriend and was now on the hunt again.

"I can definitely call Deek and ask if he'd like to come downstairs and join us," Billie said. "He lives right in our building."

Once we'd finished, the five of us headed straight from dinner to Billie's tattoo shop.

Deek was indeed available and was waiting for us when we got there. I'd seen him once in the past, and he was everything I remembered: hugely tall, buff, and inked from top to bottom.

Wells's eyes lit up like I'd never seen before. "So, this is the famous Deek."

Deek held out his big hand. "Well, well, *Wells*. Nice to finally meet you. I've heard all good things from Brayden."

"Same."

Did my friend just blush? I smiled at the prospect of something happening with them. How fitting for my best friend to end up with one of Brayden's friends. It might've been a pipe dream, but it was fun to think about. And then before I knew it, Wells and Deek had taken off without even saying goodbye. I guess the night was just starting for them. I had to laugh.

Billie and I went to one of the workstations, and I described what I wanted softly.

"You sure that's it?" she asked.

"If you don't mind, yes."

Brayden gazed over at me from the other side of the shop while Billie went to work, inking a single word in beautiful script on the inside of my wrist: *Believe*

CHAPTER 30

Brayden

Two months later

"I love this song." Alex turned, watching a sea of couples sway to the music. "Do you want to dance?"

I sucked back the rest of my gin and tonic and tossed my napkin onto the table before standing and offering my hand. "Sure."

She smiled, and the fact that I wasn't in the mood to dance became a distant memory. Hand in hand, we stepped onto the dance floor. I pulled her close, wrapping my arm around her back and letting my hand settle on her bare skin.

"You can dance!" she said after a minute.

"You sound surprised. And here I thought I was showing off my good rhythm in the bedroom."

She laughed. "I have no complaints in that department, but you haven't asked me to dance all evening, so I thought maybe dancing wasn't your thing."

"Sorry. I guess I've been preoccupied." As soon as I said it, I realized it was a dumb thing to say. She was going to dive right into that. "The attorney who's helping me submit for that new patent I told you about sent me a bunch of questions right before we left tonight," I explained. Not a lie, but also not the issue.

"Oh. I didn't realize."

"It's not a big deal. Sometimes I just get lost in my thoughts, I guess."

"You're allowed." She pushed up to brush her lips against mine. "As long as you get lost in *me* once in a while, too."

I leaned my forehead against hers. "There's nothing I like better, sweetheart."

Alex settled her head against my chest. She fit so damn perfectly. It's hard to believe I'd once thought the idea of spending a lifetime with one woman was insane. These days I didn't like to spend more than a couple of hours without her. When she was gone for a few days, it felt like part of me was missing.

I glanced around the room, my eyes finding the happy bride and groom. Owen must've sensed someone watching, because his head lifted, and he raised his glass with an approving nod and smile.

And bachelor number three bites the dust. Who would've thought this day would come? My three best friends were all happily married, all of them with kids, and I was head-over-heels in love. I nodded back at my friend, and his attention returned to his bride.

Alex and I stayed on the dance floor for two more songs. Just as we were swaying past the DJ, he stepped out and covered the top of the microphone with his hand. "Hey, Brayden?"

"What's up?"

"Just giving you a heads up that I'll be calling you for your speech soon."

"Oh. Okay. Sounds good."

A few minutes later, the music changed to a new pop song, so Alex and I headed back to our seats. I stared off, again lost in thought.

"Are you nervous about your speech?" she whispered, squeezing my hand.

"Who me?" I leaned back in my chair, trying to seem casual. "Nah."

Alex lifted our joined hands. "Oh good. Then maybe you can loosen your grip? You're cutting off my circulation."

I smiled, thinking she was busting my chops, but when I looked down, her fingers were turning white. "*Oh shit.* Sorry."

Holden leaned over, a giant grin on his face. Of course, he had to overhear and couldn't give me a pass. "He's scared shitless because he knows his speech is going to suck compared to the one I gave at Colby's wedding. That's why *I* was picked as best man first—everyone knows I put on a good show."

I shook my head. "Dude, first off, you were the best man at Colby's wedding because we picked out of a hat and you *happened* to pick the scrap of paper that said *Best Man* instead of *Douche Bag*. And your toast consisted of a five-minute explanation of the words *yin* and *yang*, which you had to look up before writing that dumb speech."

Colby leaned across the table. "If we're talking about best-man speeches, mine was a hell of a lot better than Holden's."

I chuckled. "If I remember correctly, all you did was remind everyone that the groom was a dumbass and the bride should've married someone more intelligent."

Colby smirked at Holden. "The truth can be ugly, my friend."

The DJ cut the music, interrupting our debate. When he lifted the mic and pointed toward our table, I thought I might throw up the beef Wellington I'd eaten a little while ago.

"Ladies and gentlemen, please give a warm welcome to our best man, Mr. Brayden Foster, who is going to come up and say a few words about our lovely bride and groom."

Alex kissed my cheek. "Good luck."

I stood and walked to the middle of the dance floor to a round of applause. *Damn, there isn't even a podium to hide behind.* It was just me and the mic, swinging in the wind.

I cleared my throat. "Hello, everyone. For those of you I haven't met, I'm Brayden Foster, Owen's best friend."

"*I object!*" Holden shouted from our table.

I chuckled and pointed. "You'll have to excuse our friend Holden. He's not the sharpest knife in the drawer, so whenever he's wearing a suit and someone speaks into a microphone, he assumes he's in court—arrested for a barroom brawl or indecent exposure *again*." I waved my hand and spoke slowly in the direction of our table. "This is a wedding, Catalano. We'll explain the difference later."

Everyone laughed. That helped me relax a little.

"But seriously, folks, I'm thrilled to be up here tonight to celebrate Owen and Devyn's marriage. I'd also like to point out that Owen actually *picked me* for this special honor of being his best man, and my name was *not* merely selected out of a grab bag." I looked over at Owen and Devyn, both of whom were smiling bright.

Since I hadn't taken my speech from my pocket yet, I figured it was okay to go *off*-speech. I slipped the mic out of the holder, leaned my elbow in its place on top of the stand, and pointed to the bride and groom. "Do you guys see that smile? That's all Devyn's doing. Before my buddy met his beautiful bride, he was a grumpy workaholic. He worked eighty hours a week, and I couldn't have told you for sure if he had teeth anymore. But now he never stops smiling. It almost makes me think something's wrong with him. You didn't hit your head recently, did you, buddy?"

Owen laughed and shook his head.

"Alright, good. Well, I guess I can't blame him for smiling all the time, because the dude seriously married *up*." I bowed at the bride before continuing. "Devyn, you look absolutely beautiful tonight. Welcome to the family."

She mouthed *thank you*.

"In case you all weren't aware, Devyn is a casting agent. She's found actors for several parts that have gone on to be nominated for Academy Awards. Yet somehow her little brother's video of Colby trying to save a blow-up doll has gotten more views than any of her actors' movies."

The room broke out in boos and hisses.

I shook my head. "Oh, come on now, I'm an equal opportunity toaster-roaster."

Colby wagged his finger in warning, but he was still smiling. It was all in good fun.

"All jokes aside, Devyn is amazing. Not only is she beautiful and smart, but she also runs her own business, is raising a baby, and pitches in to take care of her brother and sister. She's as caring and compassionate as anyone I've ever met. So she really deserved an equally wonderful husband. Thank God Owen got her to say yes before she found one."

Owen flipped me the bird, still laughing. It wouldn't be one of the guys' weddings without someone giving the finger. That made me feel like I'd done my job, and it was time for my planned speech. So I reached into my suit jacket and took out an index card with my notes and a small bag of fortune cookies. Holding the bag up, I shook the plastic so it crinkled into the microphone.

"Even though I'm the official best man today, I'm just one of a five-man team of brothers. Owen, Holden, Colby, and I have been friends since we were kids. Our fifth brother, Ryan, passed away almost a decade ago. Recently, I went to visit him, and I found these sitting on his grave—fortune cookies." I held up the bag a second time. "Ryan didn't ask much of us in the twenty years we were all friends, but he left us very specific instructions when it came to visiting him after he was gone: '*Don't come to my grave empty handed. Bring me something to eat.*' The guy liked to chow down. Anyway, last time I was there, I found a bag just like this that his sister, Lala, had left behind. At the time, I'd been struggling to figure out how to proceed with something important to me, so I talked to Ryan about it. I asked him for a sign on what to do. No lightning struck and no rainbow appeared out of the blue, but before I left, I opened one of the fortune cookies, and the message inside inspired me to take a chance in my life. And I'm happy to report, things worked out pretty great. Not to be too hokey, but it felt like Ryan helped manifest my destiny. I thought it was pretty cool, so I asked my buddies to each write out their wish for Owen and Devyn to see if we can't manifest good things for them, too."

I walked over to the table where my crew were all seated and set a hand on Colby's shoulder. "Now, I haven't read the wishes they wrote yet, and I'm not stupid enough to blindly say what these bozos wrote out loud—especially not Holden's. So I'm going to have them read their own wishes."

I held the bag out for Colby first. He grabbed a cookie and snapped it open, pulling out the little slip of paper.

"What are you manifesting for the bride and groom?" I tilted the microphone toward his mouth.

"May you never go to bed angry and wake up with a smile when you look at your wife every morning."

The room broke out in a round of *awws*.

I moved the mic back to my mouth. "Their baby is with the sitter tonight. He just wants to get laid."

Everyone laughed, and I walked around the table to Holden. "Alright, Mr. Catalano, what does yours say?"

Holden grabbed a cookie, snapped it in half, and hung his head. "I forgot what I wrote until just now. And I also thought these were supposed to be funny, not sappy."

"*Uh-oh*. What does your fortune for the happy couple say, Catalano?"

Holden grinned. "Every exit is an entrance to a new experience."

The ballroom exploded in a roar of laughter. Devyn cracked up so hard, she had to wipe tears from her face. I gave it a minute for the room to settle down before slipping the last fortune cookie from the bag. My nerves from earlier were suddenly back with a vengeance. I took a deep breath and stole a glance over at Owen. He and his bride were the only ones in on what I had up my sleeve. Owen winked and nodded.

I stepped over to Alex and extended the last fortune cookie to her. "I don't have my glasses," I said. "Would you do me a favor and read this one for me?"

"Umm…you don't wear glasses, but sure."

I held my breath while she cracked the fortune cookie open and slipped out the tiny piece of paper. "I wish the bride and groom a lifetime of the happiness I'll have today." Alex looked up, her adorable nose wrinkled.

"Turn it over…" I circled my finger around. "There's more on the back."

"Oh."

"If you say yes…" Alex looked up, still a little confused.

"Read it again," I said. "The whole thing as one."

She turned the slip of paper back over and read without stopping this time. "I wish the bride and groom a lifetime of the happiness I'll have today, if you say yes…"

She still didn't seem to get it—until she looked up and found me down on one knee.

My hands shook as I opened the red velvet box. "Alex, will you marry me?"

EPILOGUE

Brayden

A Year and a Half Later

Holden buttered a bagel. "Seriously? This caviar probably cost more than my Tama drum set. Who the hell knew dentists made so much money?"

"Who knew caviar was on the menu for breakfast?" Colby spread some of the black stuff on a piece of toast.

"Well, apparently, not only does Justin come from a family of dentists and orthodontists, but his father owns this chain of dental practices," I said.

Owen nodded. "So, yeah, they can afford the caviar."

Colby, Holden, Owen, and I sat poolside, enjoying the brunch laid out before us. My crew and I had invaded the Hamptons's home of James Cartwright, father of Justin Cartwright, Caitlin's now-husband. Caitlin and Justin had gotten married about six months after they met and were now expecting their first baby, a girl due in three months.

We were all in Bridgehampton for their baby shower, which was a full-weekend event. Since Caitlin didn't have a ton of family on her side, Justin's dad had asked her to invite lots of friends. There was a guest house on the property with four bedrooms, which was big enough to house our entire crew. Justin's mother and sisters would be hosting the baby shower later today under a massive tent in the backyard, and we'd all be there.

Looking over at the white tent across the lawn, it reminded me of my wedding to Alex last summer. We'd chosen a venue back in Connecticut near the water—definitely the best night of my life, even if Owen threw one too many age-gap jokes at me in his speech. I'd wanted to punch him and hug him all at once that day.

This weekend here in the Hamptons was nothing short of a miracle, because for the first time in a long time, it was grown-ups only. Lala's, Colby's, and Owen's parents were all back in the City, staying at the building and looking after the little ones so us adults could have some fun. I couldn't remember the last time we'd all hung out together with none of the kids around. Alex and I would've given anything to have to find someone to watch our kid, but alas, a baby hadn't been in the cards thus far. Still, Alex was thrilled for Caitlin, and so excited about her baby. We'd joked a lot about the fact that I was going to be a stepgrandfather. That just added to the craziness of our history.

But even with the joy of knowing Caitlin would bring a new life into this world, some underlying sadness had been eating at me, particularly this weekend. And while I wanted to comfort Alex, surrounded by all the baby stuff today, I hesitated to bring up the subject at all. She wouldn't want to take away from the happiness of this occasion. She wouldn't want to admit that Caitlin's pregnancy was a reminder that we hadn't conceived despite trying for two years, with medical intervention added for the past six months. I chose to continue believing it would happen, but with every month it didn't, believing got a bit harder. I'd read that Halle Berry had a baby at forty-seven, and I hung on to that fact tightly. While I could accept a world where Alex and I didn't have a biological child, I couldn't accept my wife blaming herself. I wanted her to be happy.

"Hey, Foster!" Colby interrupted my thoughts. "Come hang with us in the pool."

While I'd been sitting on this chaise lounge, the guys had migrated into the water. Colby was on a float, while Holden and Owen tossed a foam football back and forth.

I shook myself out of my thoughts and hopped in the pool to join them. It was just us guys for now. Billie, Lala, and Devyn had gone to a blow-dry bar to get their hair done for the baby shower later.

"Did they say what time they were getting back?" Colby asked.

"No," Holden answered. "But my wife is getting her crazy-ass curls blown out, so it might take all day. I told her she'd better leave a massive tip."

I chuckled. Lala did have a wild mane of hair.

Alex was spending the morning helping Justin's mother get ready for the shower. Even though Justin's parents were divorced, they apparently got along for the sake of the kids, and his dad was here for the co-ed event as well. I was certain there would be endless beverages, which was reason enough for my friends to make the trip. We were never ones to turn down free food and drinks.

Colby floated past me. "Look at us, all oldish and married and living it up in the Hamptons. Who woulda thunk it?"

Holden swam over. "You think these rich bastards would mind if I pissed in their pool?"

Owen chimed in, "If I know you, you already did."

"Damn." Holden splashed him. "Busted."

I looked up at the main house to find my beautiful wife looking down and waving at me from the window. The sun caught her blond hair, and she wore all white. She looked like an angel. It reminded me of seeing her walk down the aisle in her wedding dress. Wells had given her away, of course.

Alex disappeared from the window almost as fast as she'd appeared. *Damn.* I hadn't seen her all morning, and that little glimpse made me realize how much I'd missed her. But I knew she was busy with the shower stuff.

About a half-hour later, the ladies returned from their blow-dry date. I had to cover my mouth to keep from laughing, because while Devyn and Billie were both rocking totally smooth hair, poor Lala's hair was one big frizzball.

Lala sighed. "Apparently, I hadn't accounted for the humidity today."

"I swear it looked halfway normal when we left." Devyn laughed.

"Don't worry," Billie said. "I'll fix it, Lala. We'll give you an updo."

Holden swam over and climbed out of the pool. "Hold up. Who electrocuted my wife?"

Are baby showers always this freaking boring?

I'd promised Alex I'd watch as Caitlin opened all of her gifts, but it seemed never-ending.

How many freaking onesies does a baby need? And I swore she'd gotten enough diapers to last until the baby was three. But like the proud *granddad* I was, I sat patiently, counting the minutes until I could have Alex all to myself. We'd planned to take an evening walk on the beach, just the two of us.

My wife sat next to Caitlin with a notepad, writing down every single gift and who it was from. I was so damn proud of her for enduring this with a smile on her face. Alex looked up at me at one point, and I blew her a kiss. She winked, and all felt right in the world.

But I'd nearly zoned out again when I heard someone call my name.

I looked up. "Huh?"

Caitlin held up a wrapped gift. "This one is for you, Brayden."

I pointed to my chest. "For me?"

I stood and approached. Caitlin looked giddy as she handed me the present.

As I unwrapped the pastel paper, I started to laugh, ready for something with a funny joke about becoming a grandpa. We'd laughed about that constantly lately.

Inside the box was a mini Philadelphia Eagles cap, for a baby—a sweet ode to Ryan I was sure Alex was behind. She knew all about Ryan loving the Eagles.

"There's a card inside," she said.

I pulled it out. "You didn't have to do that, Caitlin. Thank you." Then I read the note. And I read it again. I had to read it at least five times to understand. My hands shook as I looked up at Alex. Her eyes were glistening as she nodded.

I looked over at the guys and noticed Holden crying, too.

What the hell?

They knew. All the wives were also wiping their eyes. No one had read the note, yet they *all* freaking knew.

This baby shower might have been planned, but this was the surprise of a lifetime. Officially the happiest moment of my life. I couldn't get to Alex fast enough, lifting her up and spinning her around—spinning *them* around.

I looked down at the note again, making sure the words were still there and this wasn't a dream.

My unborn niece might call you Gramps. B
ut I'm the lucky little miracle who'll get to call you Daddy.
Love, The One You Always Believed In

ACKNOWLEDGEMENTS

Thank you to all of the amazing bloggers, bookstagrammers and BookTokers who helped introduce everyone to *The Rules of Dating series*. Your excitement is contagious, and we are grateful for every post, video, share and review!

To our squad: Julie, Luna and Cheri – Writing can be a lonely profession sometimes, but you are always being there to brighten our day.

To Jessica –Thank you for making all the men of this series shine!

To Elaine – An amazing editor, proofer, and formatter. You do so much for us, and we are grateful to also call you a dear friend!

To Julia – Thank you for your amazing attention to details. Your eagle eyes make our manuscripts squeaky clean.

To our agent, Kimberly Brower – Thank you for helping to get our books into the hands of readers internationally. We are so excited to see this series in bookstores next year!

To Kylie and Jo at Give Me Books Promotions – We appreciate all that you do to promote our books and keep us organized!

To Sommer – Thank you for bringing this series to life on all four covers!

To Brooke – Thank you everything you do for us in the background!

Last but not least, to our readers – We've said it before but we could say it a million times and it still wouldn't be enough: Without you, there would be no us. Thank you for always showing up. We love and appreciate you!

Much love,
Vi and Penelope

OTHER BOOKS BY
Vi Keeland & Penelope Ward

The Rules of Dating
The Rules of Dating My Best Friend's Sister
The Rules of Dating My One-Night Stand
Well Played
Not Pretending Anymore
Happily Letter After
My Favorite Souvenir
Dirty Letters
Hate Notes
Rebel Heir
Rebel Heart
Cocky Bastard
Stuck-Up Suit
Playboy Pilot
Mister Moneybags
British Bedmate
Park Avenue Player

OTHER BOOKS FROM VI KEELAND

The Unraveling
What Happens at the Lake
Something Unexpected
The Game
The Boss Project

OTHER BOOKS FROM PENELOPE WARD

Vi Keeland is a #1 *New York Times*, #1 *Wall Street Journal*, and *USA Today* Bestselling author. With millions of books sold, her titles are currently translated in twenty-seven languages and have appeared on bestseller lists in the US, Germany, Brazil, Bulgaria, and Hungary. Three of her short stories have been turned into films by Passionflix, and two of her books are currently optioned for movies. She resides in New York with her husband and their three children where she is living out her own happily ever after with the boy she met at age six.

Connect with Vi Keeland

Facebook Fan Group:
https://www.facebook.com/groups/ViKeelandFanGroup/)
Facebook: https://www.facebook.com/pages/Author-
Vi-Keeland/435952616513958
TikTok: https://www.tiktok.com/@vikeeland
Website: http://www.vikeeland.com
Twitter: https://twitter.com/ViKeeland
Instagram: http://instagram.com/Vi_Keeland/

Penelope Ward is a *New York Times*, *USA Today*, and #1 *Wall Street Journal* Bestselling author. With millions of books sold, she's a 21-time New York Times bestseller. Her novels are published in over a dozen languages and can be found in bookstores around the world. Having grown up in Boston with five older brothers, she spent most of her twenties as a television news anchor, before switching to a more family-friendly career. She is the proud mother of a beautiful girl with autism and her amazing brother. Penelope and her family reside in Rhode Island.

Connect with Penelope Ward
Facebook Private Fan Group:
https://www.facebook.com/groups/PenelopesPeeps/
Facebook: https://www.facebook.com/penelopewardauthor
TikTok: https://www.tiktok.com/@penelopewardofficial
Website: http://www.penelopewardauthor.com
Twitter: https://twitter.com/PenelopeAuthor
Instagram: http://instagram.com/PenelopeWardAuthor/

Made in the USA
Las Vegas, NV
15 September 2024